Changeling Press. LLC

ChangelingPress.com

The Accidental Fairy Tale
A Women's Urban Fantasy Romance
Crymsyn Hart

The Accidental Fairy Tale
A Women's Urban Fantasy Romance
Crymsyn Hart

ISBN: 978-1-60521-880-9

Publisher:
Changeling Press LLC
315 N. Centre St.
Martinsburg, WV 25404
ChangelingPress.com

Printed in the U.S.A.

Editor: Jean Cooper
Cover Artist: Karen Fox

The individual stories in this anthology have been previously released in E-Book format.

Table of Contents

Falling for Love (The Accidental Fairy Tale 1)
A Women's Urban Fantasy Romance
Crymsyn Hart

All Jasmine wanted was a quiet vacation. What she got turned into so much more than she could have ever imagined -- her own fairy tale. Micha Hook saves her from death by pushing her into the pages of his magic book. Jasmine finds herself in a land she never thought existed -- the Land of Oz.

However, in this magical kingdom, the Wicked Witch has been replaced. Books write themselves, and the magic is disappearing. While reuniting the old crew, Jasmine has to find out what's happening in Oz before the magic is gone. All the while, she finds a handsome prince or two.

Chapter One

Jasmine stared up at the dark sky. The breeze pulled the remaining heat of the day toward the mountains and away from her campsite. It tugged at the staked lines she had pounded into the hard ground, trying to claim the shelter for itself. Even if the gust caught it, she wouldn't blame the wind. This vacation had been planned for months. A whole week off was a dream because she didn't have a backup at work. Jasmine needed time away from all the clients who called her for answers when she didn't have them. The stress of it weighed on her.

In the middle of nowhere, silence greeted her, and she loved it. Half an hour from the nearest town, no lights polluted the view of the night sky. The illumination from her campfire relaxed her. *I really have to do this more often.* Jasmine let out a contented sigh and watched the vast expanse. Her gaze followed the three stars of Orion's belt. Her grandmother had taught her about finding the shapes in the stars like the Big Dipper or Cassiopeia. Before she could locate another shape, a star broke the line of Orion's belt. It sparked, seeming to bounce off the neighboring stars, before it divided into four separate trails. Each took a different path.

Her grandmother's words filtered into her mind about making a wish upon a falling star. Jasmine closed her eyes and thought about what she wanted. Something to shake up her life a little. Maybe an adventure. Nothing too wild. Maybe a handsome man. The night greeted her when she opened her eyes -- the falling stars had already burnt out on the horizon. Jasmine felt a bit disappointed. *Probably a satellite breaking up as it hit the atmosphere. Let's be realistic. The world doesn't revolve around fantastical events or strange creatures offering people three wishes.*

Jasmine pushed her thoughts away as the haze of sleep settled over her. She studied the stars to see if another would plummet. When none shattered, she banked the fire and slipped into the tent to sleep the night away.

The next morning the stillness of the desert greeted her. Jasmine rubbed her eyes and pulled on her jeans. Her stomach growled. She'd left her food in the car. She went outside. Pieces of her camp chair were scattered around the campsite. The stones from her fire pit were knocked across the campsite as though someone had swept them aside. The seat of her chair lay near the tent. She picked the fabric up and examined the tears in it. It looked as though an animal had invaded her spot. But her tent remained untouched and nothing had woken her up. *What the hell happened?*

Jasmine's hands shook as she cleaned up the mess before heading to her car. Her spot should have been safe. Nothing at the site looked like an animal had been there. Nonetheless, she'd camped on a distant part of her friend Landis's land. Landis had left her the key to the house in case she wanted to get away from the elements. At the moment, she didn't feel comfortable staying in her tent.

Jasmine grabbed her bag. She patted her pockets and felt the box of matches she'd shoved in there the night before and her keys underneath them. She went to open the car door when a flapping sound made her stop. The back quarter-panel on the driver's side swayed in the breeze. *What in the holy hell?* The metal over the tire was flayed like a half-peeled orange. Long gouges clawed the top of her trunk. Jasmine pressed her fingers into the grooves. Each was three times as big as hers. *Good thing I bought the insurance.*

She glanced around for whatever had done this and prayed it hadn't stuck around. A Gordian knot twisted in her stomach. She quickly took the tent down and threw everything from the site into the back of the car. *Why didn't it touch the tent?* Her keys jangled in her shaking hand. *I'm not waiting around to see if something comes back. What does it want? What is the rental company going to say?* Jasmine turned her phone on, but it didn't pick up a signal. *This is what I get for wanting to be completely alone.* Jasmine got into the car and drove to town, praying the creature was long gone.

Half an hour later, she arrived in the thriving metropolis of Shifting, Arizona, a booming town of a thousand people. She parked in front of a strip of stores and grabbed her phone. Fifteen voicemails popped up on her phone. The last five didn't show the callback number. "What's going on?"

The first message when she tapped the app. "Hi, Ms. Thorne, there's been a grievous mistake with your rental. We need you to return the vehicle as soon as you can. Please call us immediately."

"Mistake? What kind of mistake?" Jasmine listened to another nine messages, each from a more frantic salesperson. *Is the engine going to fall out? What's wrong with this jalopy?*

The remainder of the messages were from a man she didn't know. "Ahh… hello. This is a bit awkward. The rental company leased out my personal auto. Apparently, it looks exactly the same as the one you rented, except for a little bumper sticker showing it's a rental. Someone wasn't paying attention. I can't imagine how inconvenient this is for you, but I really need my car. If you could please give me a call at…"

The call dropped out before she could make out his number. All his messages cut off at the same point.

Poor guy. I have his car. Someone was sleeping on the job. The best thing to do is call the rental company since I can't get his number. Maybe there's something in here. She reached inside the glove compartment and located the registration under a pile of napkins. Sure enough, a Micha Hook owned the auto.

"Hey!" Someone banged on the passenger window. Jasmine nearly jumped out of her skin at the sudden intrusion. A man cupped his hands together and peered in through the glass. "Can you roll down the window?"

She hesitated but brought it down enough she could see him clearly. The man looked to be a castoff from a body-building convention. His white smile against his fake orange tan made her squint. His square face and dark beady eyes clashed with the expensive suit he wore. After the morning she'd had, his appearance didn't seem out of the ordinary even though it should. The whole ordeal with the attack and her being in a stolen car did not happen in her daily routine. *If an animal came looking for food, then it should've nosed around the tent because I had chips inside with me. Maybe it was Bigfoot. They have sharp claws, right? Or maybe it was a werewolf. Who am I kidding? Maybe when I wished upon a star it conjured up some invisible creature who ransacked my camp site.*

The man knocked on the roof this time, jarring her from her thoughts. She gritted her teeth and addressed him. "Can I help you?"

"You're driving my car." He tried the door handle to open it.

"You're Micha Hook?" she asked.

"Sure am."

"How did you find me?"

"Lojack. I had the company turn on the GPS. See!" He flashed his cell phone screen with a map and a red dot where the car was supposed to be. "Took me a little bit because you were off the grid for a while."

Something about him turned her stomach. As he smiled, the corners of his mouth curled a little too far into his cheeks. Jasmine's intuition screamed for her to start the car and get as far away from him as possible. Her fingers brushed the unlock button. His beady eyes grew bigger and darker. The voice of reason in her head quieted, but she couldn't break his gaze. Something about his eyes held her. They moved on his face traveling from the center of his head to the sides and back again. She blinked and the effect had vanished. When she looked again, his nose and mouth seemed more pronounced, like a rounded muzzle. His lips were pulled back in a grimace. Jasmine shook her head and his appearance returned to normal.

"Sure," she heard herself say.

What the hell am I doing? Jasmine didn't want him in the vehicle because his creep factor was off the charts, but she hit the unlock button anyway. He opened the door and began to climb into the car. The door bounced back and hit him. The man slid to the ground. A bright flash of light snapped her out of her trance. The stench of burning hair made her scrunch up her nose. She rubbed her eyes until the little flashbulbs in her vision faded. A strange man picked up the one who'd tried to get into her car and threw him into the empty parking spot next to hers. Jasmine leaned over the passenger seat to close the door. She couldn't quite grab the handle quickly enough before the mysterious man slid into the passenger seat and slammed the door.

"What the fuck, dude? Who the hell are you, and why are you in my car?"

"Drive. We have to get moving to lose him. Not your car." He gazed at her from behind dark-framed glasses. His blue eyes held her gaze until she lost her train of thought. Jasmine heard what he said, but it didn't sink in.

"Excuse me!"

He smashed the heel of his hand against the dashboard. "Damn it, woman, listen! Unless you want to be hunted to the ends of the Tales and back again, drive until I tell you where to stop. We have to get to sacred ground to throw them off the scent."

Jasmine gripped the wheel, trying to stop her hands from shaking. The man spoke and gestured for her to drive. Her brain scrambled to catch up and piece together what happened. Her stomach fluttered. She caught movement out of the corner of her eye. The man on the ground stood up and drew something black out from under his coat. *Holy Jesus. He has a gun. What've I gotten involved in?* Another goon in a suit sprinted toward them. Bile crept up her throat as she struggled to keep her nerves in check. *I'm getting carjacked.*

"Drive. Didn't you hear me?" he shouted.

His loud command snapped her out of the haze. *I can do this. I have to stay alive. They always say to cooperate with the bad guys. Do anything to keep breathing.* Her hands hurt from holding onto the wheel. She looked over at the man and tried to keep her voice even with her stomach doing somersaults. "Yes. I heard you. I'll do whatever you want. Please don't kill me."

The man scoffed as he dug into his jeans' pocket. She braced herself for him brandishing another gun, so he could shoot at the men coming toward them. Instead, he pulled out something small and silver -- the size of a pen -- with a pointed end. "I'm not going to kill you and I really hate to do this," he muttered.

She waited for the sharp jab of the knife. Instead, he wrote in mid-air with the penknife. The letters burned silver for a split second as he scrawled out a long sentence in cursive that she couldn't read. Once he dotted his period, the faint scent of burning ozone filled the car and extinguished in a burst of heat. Jasmine tried to process the impossible. *No way could he write, and have the writing burn into the air itself.* Warmth settled on her face like a gauzy blindfold and whited out her sight.

* * *

Jasmine found herself leaning on the driver's side door outside the car. Her view included wooden tombstones and white, angled crosses marking off burial plots. Broken wrought-iron fence sections ringed a forgotten cemetery. About to fall behind the distant mountains, the sun blazed low on the horizon. It had been morning when she arrived in the town. *How did I get here?* Dread crept up into her throat as she tried to recall what had occurred after the stranger wrote in the air with his penknife. Her thoughts remained blank. Her tongue felt thick and her throat dry. Her stomach tumbled around. *He drugged me. That's the only explanation. What did he make me do? Did he kill the other two men in broad daylight in the middle of a busy street?* Her stomach turned and the contents came back up.

"Here." The man held out a bottle of water to her.

"I don't think so. You're going to drug me again."

"I didn't drug you. The seal hasn't been broken

on the cap. I'm deeply sorry for what happened back there. If I hadn't written in the scene changes, her goons would've gotten it."

Jasmine snatched the water bottle from him and scrutinized it for puncture marks. The sides weren't wet from any leaks, and the cap remained attached to the plastic ring around the neck. She opened it and tested a small sip. It didn't taste different than any other water. It slaked her thirst and got the vomit tang from her mouth. After she downed half of the bottle, the coolness gave her the ability to think again.

Jasmine examined her kidnapper more closely. Dark, hay-blond hair stuck out at angles behind his ears. He wore a red T-shirt over his wiry frame, ratty blue jeans, and a scuffed black pair of Doc Martens with frayed laces. His jeans hugged his calves and thighs. From her angle she couldn't see his ass, but if the front was any indication, then she figured his back half would be even better to look at. He leaned against the trunk and didn't seem to notice the talon marks or the flapping panel.

"How did we get here? Why did you attack that man in my car? Why are we in the middle of a graveyard? Did you kill someone? Are you planning on murdering me? Is that why you brought me here?" She hoped to see the keys dangling from the ignition, but no such luck. Jasmine slid her hands down her sides and patted her hips, feeling for the keys.

"Looking for these?" He held up the keys for her to see.

"Shit," she muttered.

Jasmine tried not to let anxiety get the better of her. The landscape showed nothing more than flat land with a few scattered cacti reaching toward the sky. Her kidnapper held the keys to her escape, so she had to play nice.

"I know you have questions about how you got here and why you can't remember anything after my scene change."

"Damn straight I do." She tried to act self-possessed rather than like the quivering mess she felt inside. Her kidnapper took off his glasses and wiped them on his shirt. Without them he looked more approachable. "Who are you?"

"Micha Hook. I left you several messages."

The car guy. "Is this really your car?"

"Yes. I took my vehicle to the dealership for an oil change. Some stupid tech got the car confused with a rental of the same make and model. As soon as they realized their mistake, they tried to contact you, but you were unreachable. I raised Cain because I knew whoever had the car would be in great danger."

"Are you hiding drugs in the car? I didn't see a body or the remnants of one. Maybe some money in a side panel? Running away from a cartel?"

"Something more valuable than any of those. It's a cartel of sorts."

"Fucking great! Now I got a mob boss and his goons after me. What's more precious than money or drugs? Did you steal some jewels?"

"If only it were that simple. I can always rewrite this scene if I show you. You'll have no memory of it." He paced, talking to himself with his head down. "I don't want to mess you up any more than I have. It has strange effects on those who see it. I --"

She put her hands up, not sure what he was rambling on about. *He's gone off the deep end.* Hook retraced his steps and gestured with his hands before running them through his hair, making it even wilder. Watching him made her dizzy, but she did get a good look at his tight ass. Jasmine bit her lip and felt her heart flutter at the sight before she stepped in front of him. Micha kept mumbling and bumped into her.

"What's with you?" Hell, the longer she was around him, the longer she wondered if he *was* capable of kidnapping her. *Maybe the thug gassed me when he stuck his head into the window. All the stuff with Micha getting into the car and writing with a magic pen has to be a hallucination.*

His eyes flashed green for a split second when he looked up. "Sorry. I've never shown it to anyone. It has a profound effect on those who see it. I don't know how it will change you."

Talking in circles with him tired her out. If Jasmine hadn't been out in the middle of nowhere, she would get the hell out of there. "Show me, already. After all this, I kinda deserve to know what *it* is."

He flashed her a half-crooked smile that made him look cuter. The last of the sun glinted off his glasses. "You're right."

Anticipation hung in the air. Jasmine held her breath while Micha rooted around in the trunk. He came back out with his precious cargo clasped protectively against his chest. She chuckled and threw her hands up. "Your mob boss is after a book?"

"It's more than just a *book*," he whispered. His expression fell as though she'd killed his favorite kitten. Tattered greenish-yellow velveteen covered a book the size of a dictionary. "It's more than a book." His voice dropped. Micha patted the cover lovingly. "You don't want to hurt her feelings. She can get a bit temperamental. I think that's how it all went wrong in the first place, but it… Well, never mind."

"Her? Why do you… It's just a ragtag book that's seen better days." She ran her fingers through her hair and tried to figure out how she had gotten into such a messed-up situation. "Forget it. At least tell me it's a Shakespearian play no one has published. An undiscovered Mark Twain manuscript. Fuck, even a first edition of the Bible written by the son of God himself for it to be worth all the trouble you've gone through for it."

Micha petted the cover. "You should apologize for insulting her."

"I'm not apologizing to a book. When did it become a her?" Jasmine reached out to take the volume, but Micha stepped back. "This is ridiculous. Give me the darn thing."

Jasmine went after him and grabbed the volume. The smooth cover slid under her fingers. Warmth glided over the fingertips as she yanked it away and nearly pulled him back. However, he wrestled it back from her. Micha grunted as he jerked it away. He lost his footing and stumbled backward. The book tumbled from his hands and landed a few feet away. Jasmine fell on top of Micha, knocking the wind out of her. They locked eyes for a few precious seconds. The guy might have been a little off, but he was something to look at. *It's his eyes. I've always been a sucker for the eyes.* The green faded back to their vibrant blue. A blast of heat singed her arm until she cried out.

"Get off me." Micha pushed her away.

She landed a few inches from the book. The ground shook and cracks appeared underneath it, spreading into the graveyard. An emerald glow emanated from the tome and slipped into the fissures. Each widened as another small tremor hit. The earth rolled under Jasmine's feet. The green radiance highlighted the white crosses of the cemetery. The atmosphere turned eerie as Jasmine tried to understand what was happening.

"Shit. Now you've done it. Once she uses her powers, they can home in on her. I brought you here so we could rest, and she could reset. Even if I rewrite the scene and erase your memory again, it won't matter this time."

The pages of the volume rustled back and forth. Each time the book reached its end and started over again, the green illumination transformed to a burnt gold. Heat radiated off the pages and warmed her face. Another tremor hit them, causing a small fissure to open underneath her. Jasmine rolled out of the way, but closer to the book. She blinked at what she saw on the pages. Words ripped themselves off the page and floated above the volume. They glowed like the writing she thought she'd seen Micha do with his pen. An earsplitting screech came from the sky. The noise chilled her to the marrow of her bones. Jasmine looked up and saw several black shapes splayed against the bright half-moon like wayward bats trying to find a home. She tore her gaze from them and went back to the book. The writing resettled back on the parchment and became regular text. She tried to read it, but couldn't understand the language. Next to the page was a picture of a village at night. A light shone in a window at the top of a bell tower, but she couldn't make out the rest of the buildings. A shadow blacked out the window as though someone walked across it and cast their shadow. No book could show movement in it. Jasmine reached over to touch the book to make sure all this was real. Micha jumped between her and the hardback. His eyes burned green.

"They're coming. Neither of us is safe now."

"What about the book? It… How is it doing that?"

"Don't worry about her right now. We have to get away. I know of another place we can escape to."

"Does this have to do with the cartel you were talking about?"

"Yes. They'll eat you alive if they get you."

The loud cry came again. It sounded like a screech owl mixed with a dying seal. "What was that?"

"Her gangsters. They'll tear your heart out and suck on your eyeballs for a snack. I've seen them do it. They show no mercy. All they want is the book and anyone associated with it. I can't fight off all four of them. I got lucky with the last one because I surprised him." Micha offered her his hand. "Come with me. It's the only way you'll be safe."

She wasn't about to be beaten up or killed over an old book. "Where are we going to go?" Jasmine headed toward the car.

A streak of purple raced across the sky toward the vehicle. A great whoosh of heat passed over her. The loud boom made her ears ring and her heart race. Micha tackled her to the ground. His weight on top of her made her squirm to get out from underneath him. Micha grabbed her wrists and held her down. Another blast hit next to them. The burning of the explosion passed over her exposed skin and singed the hairs on her arms. The earth moved again, and another fault appeared. The golden glow jumped from the crack and zapped her hand. Jasmine cried out as it crept up her arm. The illumination sank into her skin and disappeared. Micha got up. He held out his hand to her. Jasmine took it as he helped her up.

"Are you okay?" Micha asked her.

His mouth moved, making words, but her ears rang too much for her to hear them. Nothing remained of the car except four black blobs of rubber that used to be the tires. Jasmine couldn't stop shaking. Tears burned her eyes and slid down her cheeks. Her hand shook when she went to wipe them away. Jasmine noticed her fingernails had a strange golden sheen. Micha shook her shoulders. The ringing in her ears faded as another shriek made her tremble.

"Hey, we gotta get outta here. Are you okay?"

Jasmine nodded and wiped her nose. A streak of blood came away with it. "No. Not really. Was that a rocket launcher?"

"I'll explain later. You ready to go?"

"Yeah, but if they're in a helicopter we can't outrun them. We're toast if they have more rockets. What're we going to do?"

"You're going to have to trust me. Come on." Micha grabbed her hand and pulled her toward the book which hovered an inch off the ground.

What the hell is a book going to do for us when we're trying to escape the mob? The picture in the book changed. The light no longer lingered in the bell tower, but it bobbed between buildings. *It's moving again. How is that possible? Books can't float off the ground either. Pictures can't move.*

"They're almost here. We have to go through the portal. It'll give us some time and throw them off our scent. Come on, Jasmine."

Before she could wrap her head around how Micha planned their escape, his hands hit her back. The world tilted. Jasmine tried to catch herself before she went nose first onto the ground. She expected to hit the hard dirt, but the book came close to her nose. Except she didn't hit the earth or the pages. She kept falling. Cold air sliced through her flesh until it chilled her to the bone. Jasmine somersaulted in the air like being thrown out of an airplane without a parachute. The wind shrieked around her. She tried to find something to grab a hold of, but she kept on dropping and screamed to rival the wind.

Chapter Two

Jasmine landed on something with a bit of a bounce, but it still knocked the wind out of her. Small pinpoints of pain pressed along her body. She felt like she'd settled on top of a cement truck after the fall she endured. Miraculously, she was alive. Her brain hadn't caught up to how she had fallen for such a long way when she should have hit the dry desert floor. Once she could breathe, Jasmine glanced around. She'd landed in a thick carpet of ropey vines with small prickly burrs which stuck to her body and clothes.

She moved her fingers and toes and found nothing broken except her sense of where she was. Jasmine got up and picked a few of the burrs off. She expected to hear the sound of a helicopter or another screech like the ones in the graveyard, but an eerie silence penetrated the night. A few moments later, she heard a thud, and what sounded like Micha muttering to himself. A half-moon dangled above her. Vines clung to buildings and blanketed the street. Cobblestones peeked through the large plants. *This can't be real.* Jasmine touched one of the vines creeping up a fence next to her. The waxy texture of the leaves felt real. A few feet more to the left and she would have been speared on the wrought-iron point. The pain from the sticky burrs she pulled from her flesh felt real.

"Where the hell am I?" Jasmine followed the sound of running water to the town square where she discovered a clogged fountain. The plant-engulfed ghost town gave her the creeps. Every building crumbled under the plant life. A light splash drew her attention back to the cascade. A statue of a small child holding a lollipop over its shoulder stood at the top with spurts of water coming from it. One of the creepers slithered over the carving, embracing it in a tighter grip. White water lilies twice the size of her hands combined floated in the fountain. Their intoxicating scent made her sway closer to the fountain. Jasmine reached for a flower, but Micha seized her wrist.

"I wouldn't do that if I were you. They look harmless, but they'll take your fingers off and continue to munch on your hand."

"That's impossible. Flowers don't eat people." Jasmine looked over at Micha.

"These do. Ever heard of a Venus Flytrap? This is like that but on a larger scale. Think man-eating plant." Micha grabbed a stick from the debris at the base of the fountain and stuck the end into the mouth of the flower. The petals snapped around it. He tried to pull the branch away, but the flower growled.

"Did that just snarl?"

"It did. Things here are not always what they seem. Come on, we have to get to shelter before we rouse them. Best to be as quiet as you can. They're sleeping, and I don't want to wake them. Actually, I don't want to awaken her." Micha adjusted a bag -- large enough to hold a book -- he had slung over his shoulder.

"Hey, where did your glasses go?"

He touched his face and shrugged. "Must've lost them in the fall. They weren't important anyway. Just a way to blend in with the rest of your lot. We have bigger fish to fry than finding my glasses. We shouldn't be here. Why did she bring us back?" Micha stroked the top of the bag as if to open it.

"Where did you get that bag? You didn't have it before. Where are we anyway? Shouldn't we still be in the graveyard? Who shouldn't we wake up?" Her voice rose from the panic that bloomed in her chest. None of this made any sense.

Micha put a finger to his lips to shush her. She started to protest, but a light pierced the darkness of the village. She squinted until she made out the outline of a man walking toward them carrying a lantern. Jasmine didn't know if she should run toward him and away from Micha, but her intuition told her Micha was the safer bet. He could be an axe murderer. Not that Micha wasn't, but he *had* saved her from the cartel that blew up the car. The man wore a dark blue suit smeared with dirt and patched in several places, along with a bowler hat.

"You shouldn't be out here at this time of night." He held the lantern up close to his face. His beard glinted crimson in the candlelight. He reminded Jasmine of an overgrown leprechaun.

"Hi, Fergus. How are things?" Micha asked.

The man's face paled even in the wan light. "You were warned not to come back."

"Didn't have a choice. The monkeys are after us. Do a guy a solid and give us a safe place to stay for the night. No one will ever know. We go way back."

Fergus rubbed his beard and grunted. "I'm the last of the Munchkins. She keeps me around as a reminder to anyone who comes through here as to what she'll do. You can stay the night unless you wake her up." Fergus gestured toward an ivy-covered steeple. "Come quietly."

Something slid across the bottom of her jeans. Jasmine shifted her weight and stepped closer to Micha. She went over the events of the day in her mind. The morning started off normally except for the ransacked campsite. *Why are they after the book? How did we get here? Why can't I remember anything after him writing with his pen?* There was no logical answer on how she'd fallen and landed in a bed of vines when the cemetery was nothing but markers and dry land. Jasmine shook her leg as something brushed her ankle. When she looked down, vines twisted around their feet like a nest of snakes. She pulled her foot up, but they tightened their grip around her ankle.

"Ahh… guys. Someone want to help me get out of these?" She tugged on Micha's shirt.

"Witches be damned." Fergus pointed behind them. He nearly dropped the lantern. A small squeak came out of his mouth. "S-she's awake."

She followed his finger to the top of a church from the shape of the building. Atop the spire, an enormous orange eye with a slitted pupil stared down at them like a god passing judgment. A mass of twisted tentacles rotated around the tower, unfurling like a massing plant octopus.

"I can see that." Micha drew out his silver pen. The creepers wound up to her knees. He clicked the pen. A spark filled the night but sputtered and died. He wrote in mid-air, but no words came out the way they had before. Micha shook it and tried again.

"What's the matter? Is your magic wand broken?" she joked, trying not to give in to her skulking fear as the burrs serrated her jeans and dug into her flesh. Jasmine locked her gaze to the thing crawling down the church.

"No. It's not. It needs time to… recharge. I've used it a few times already today. The harder the scene is to edit, the more magic it uses. It's not a wand. It's a pen. Fergus, give me the lantern."

Fergus drew the lamp back. "Don't think so. You're the smart one. Figure out how to get yourself out of this mess. This light is the only thing that's kept me safe. Only one person can kill her and you sent him away because of your stupid ego." Fergus turned to leave, but then spun back. "I'd wish you luck, but you don't need any, Oh Mighty One." Fergus abandoned them to their fate with the plant monster.

"You certainly pissed him off. What was that about? You want to tell me how we're going to get free of this plant octopus thing?" Jasmine asked him as she tried to pull her other foot free.

"Shut up and let me think," he snapped at her.

The plantapus crawled down the church. In the gleam of the moonlight, the white points of the barbs on the slithering vines resembled teeth. The tendrils twisted up to her waist and tugged on her to make her lose her balance. Every time Jasmine tried to move they tightened their painful grip.

"Think fast because we're going to be dinner. What about the book of yours?"

"Shush. I'm thinking. Something's wrong here." He pressed his fists to his temples.

Jasmine tried to keep it together. *I'm about to be eaten alive by a giant, one-eyed plant creature with teeth on its tendrils covering an entire village. What the fuck is going on? It's all some drug-induced dream. But if this were a dream, I wouldn't be feeling the pain of being crushed by a monster.* The beast skittered toward them. "If you're going to think of something, it'd better be now."

Hundreds of tentacles undulated as the plantapus shifted its great weight and inched toward them. Jasmine held in a scream as the vine's teeth dug into her stomach and shoulder. That's when she noticed the green glow around Micha's fingers. Micha grabbed a handful of his own blond hair and yanked. He winced as he tugged. Before she could say anything, the green glow wrapped around the tendrils, turning them into long strands of hay.

"How did you --?"

"Fire. Do you have anything to light this with? Damn it, woman. She's afraid of fire. Hurry up or we're going to be dinner," Micha shouted at her.

Matches. I have matches. Jasmine shoved her hand into her pocket, shredding her skin on the teeth of the vines. She prayed they hadn't fallen out in her great descent. Her fingers brushed the flattened box. Jasmine pulled out a match and fumbled to strike it against the surface on the box. The monster slunk closer. The eye burned orange like an overripe pumpkin glaring at her. The rancid odor of its foul breath nearly knocked her over. Its circular rows of teeth had bits of bones stuck between them.

"Now would be a good time to light the match."

She tried to stop her fingers from shaking. The match head broke off. She fished out a second one. It tumbled from her fingers. She got a third one out and upon striking, the head sputtered to life.

"Give me the match."

"Give me the straw." Jasmine gestured to him, not wanting the chance of the flame going out if she moved too quickly.

Micha handed it over. She yanked an arm free and screamed from the barbs. She lit the hay. It whooshed to life and burned her fingers. Jasmine ignored the pain. The vines next to her shoulder shrieked. Jasmine waved the flames around the vines on her legs until they recoiled. With each pass, they retreated farther.

"Quick, before it goes out." Micha handed her another bundle to ignite.

She moved the second clump around Micha until the creepers released him. They were freed before the straw burned out. The courtyard became visible again. It was filled with scattered sticks and other debris. Micha grabbed a branch, tore his shirt, and wrapped a strip around the limb. He plucked a few more hairs from his head that turned into straw and added it to the makeshift torch.

"Fire can only keep you safe for so long. You never should've returned." Sharp whispers echoed all around them in overlapping voices.

He motioned for Jasmine to get behind him. She didn't need any encouragement. The monster kept its distance. Some vines encroached, but when Micha shoved the torch at them, they retreated. The flowers gnashed their petals at them as they crept slowly toward the edge of the village and away from the maze of vines connected to the plantapus.

"I didn't have a choice," he muttered.

Dark laughter consumed the night. Jasmine yearned to give in to the old fight-or-flight instinct and run as far away as possible. Instinct told her if she ran into the shadows, something darker and much more dangerous waited in this alien world. The safest place remained with Micha. The torch sputtered whenever he waved it. They had to get out of the village before the plantapus decided to charge them when the torch went out.

Jasmine gripped his arm. "We should get out of here while we still can." Layers upon layers of questions circled her mind until they threatened to drown her. Once they were out of danger, she would get her answers from Micha.

"I agree. Come on." He took her hand and pulled her after him. Even with his fierce grip, something about it made her feel secure. The laughter of the flowers followed as they ran into the darkness away from the village with only the small torch to light the way.

Once they reached a safe distance, Jasmine broke away from Micha and bent over, taking in the air after the run. Her lungs burned from the escape. The cool darkness offered comfort because the plant monster remained far behind in the Munchkin village. Her stomach unknotted when she knew they were free. *I swear I'm going to go back to the gym and work on my cardio. After sitting in an office all day, I need to get out more.* She looked up once she had gotten her breath. The moon hung above them in the midnight sky. Enormous trees blocked the way on one side. Branches thicker than her arms held enormous fruit shaped like apples. The skins of the fruit gleamed in the moonlight. Stars winked at her, but she didn't recognize the constellations they formed. Her stomach growled. Her dry throat ached for some water. At least she could satisfy her hunger with the fruit. Jasmine reached to pick one.

Micha caught her hand before she could complete her motion. "I wouldn't do that if I were you."

I don't know how much more I can take. What is this, Snow White's forest? "Are they poisoned?" she half joked.

"Yes. The whole orchard and the forest beyond it, too. If you pick one, you'll wake the trees. Word travels fast here. The trees might've already heard the shrieking from Munchkinville. Even the wind talks here. I know a safe place a little way up the road where we can rest. Once we get there, I can also get us some food."

"Will you start being straight with me? All this is a bit much to process. A people-eating plant? Poisoned apples? What's next?"

"Yes. I'll answer your questions. What comes next? Let's not think about it. I'll happily walk this road without her finding us."

"Great. Let's go." His answer reassured her and also made the mystery surrounding him deepen. At this point, Jasmine concluded she wasn't dreaming. The events happening to her were real. She should have died from the fall, but somehow she had survived. What facts she knew was that someone was after Micha because he had this book. The person who was after it would kill for it. Now her fate entwined with his.

She had no choice but to trust him to remain alive. Jasmine forged ahead of Micha, nearly tripping over a few loose bricks. Micha caught her. His fingers slid over an exposed bit of her stomach. The sudden feeling made her heart drop. His touch brought a flash of heat through her. Jasmine tugged on her shirt and shot him a glance. Micha locked his gaze with hers and she felt a pull toward him. Even with the risk of life and limb, Jasmine couldn't deny the attraction building between them.

Time seemed to stop as she took in a breath. Being this close to him and actually stopping without her life being in danger allowed her to get a whiff of the man next to her. He smelled like fresh hay dusted with morning rain mixed with his manly scent. His chest heaved along with hers as he tried to catch his breath. Jasmine almost wanted to feel his hands on her again, but then she remembered how he had gotten her into this mess. The torch popped and she jumped as the sparks fluttered into the air.

Micha took his hand away and put space between them. "Right. The road's seen better days. It's gotten worse since the last time I was here. Come on, the house isn't too far ahead."

Jasmine picked her way over the boulevard to keep up the fast pace Micha set. Bricks jutted from the earth. Grass grew between the paving stones, in some places reaching to her knees. Small trees sprouted in the middle of the lane while roots snaked underneath them and raised them up. Every other step she stubbed one toe or another. Pain shot up her foot. Jasmine silently cursed everything that happened. She stumbled again and grabbed onto Micha's waist. The movement unbalanced him. They both toppled into the tall grass on the side of the road. The torch skittered across the lane out of his hand. His body felt good against hers. It had been a while since she'd been with anyone. The warmth and hardness of his body pressed into her. Their lips were inches from one another. He slid his arms along her sides. She squirmed underneath him.

"Is this some part of your plan?" Micha asked her. His eyes flashed green.

"What are you talking about? You're the one who got me into this whole mess. I just wanted to go on vacation, and then you called and…"

Micha cut her off when his mouth met hers. Her surprise didn't stop her from returning the kiss. The taste of his lips inflamed her desire for him. She tried to fight it, but his tongue pushed into her mouth. She set her hands on his hips, pulling him tighter against her. The bulge pressing against her stomach told her how turned on she made him. Her heart slammed into her chest and she could barely think beyond his fingers running through her hair. All the world seemed to fall away and nothing else mattered except the sparks firing between them. She could almost put all the high strangeness that occurred to her today aside for a taste of Micha. What strange man had she fallen in with? What spell had he cast over her? Never had she let a strange man kiss her the way he had.

He broke the kiss and stared down at her. His eyes remained clouded with desire until they burned green instead of blue. He shook his head and rolled off her. Micha stood up and put some space between them. Jasmine stared up at the sky. Lightheaded and out of breath, she needed something to make sense. This crazy man had knocked her head around. She could barely think, let alone curse him any longer for getting her into this situation. The cool night air helped to bring her back to herself. She touched her lips and craved another kiss, but she needed answers more. It took her a moment, but she finally stood up. Micha remained with his back to her, staring into the night. The torch flickered, but somehow it remained lit.

"What's going on here?" Jasmine touched his shoulder.

"Nothing," he muttered and jerked away from her.

"Your lips and your hard-on would say otherwise."

"Forget it. We have to get moving again. We're almost at the safe house. Come on." Micha picked up the torched again and went ahead of her.

What the fuck? The warmth of his body lingered as she hurried to catch up to him. Her legs felt leaden. She tried to push his behavior from her mind, but it crept in. She needed answers not only about his behavior, but about what she had gotten herself into. Silence grew between them once more. She concentrated on not tripping and on keeping up until Micha stopped outside a half caved in relic of a building.

"You sure it's safe to go in there? It looks ready to fall down." A curtain of ivy cascaded over the roof of the house.

He went around to the side of the structure and swept back the vines for Jasmine to enter. "It won't. You're safe here. This place is like the graveyard in your world. It's sacred ground. At least it used to be. We should be protected for the night."

He went around the room lighting a few smaller lamps and then threw the torch outside into the dirt. Furniture remained scattered in the house. Ivy hung through a hole in the roof. A tattered sofa with a broken leg leaned against the wall. A beaten-up chair rested next to a three-legged coffee table pushed against it. Micha sat on the couch and motioned for her to join him. Jasmine fell into the chair across from him. A puff of dust went up around her and stung her eyes. Jasmine coughed and tried to wave away the cloud. Her legs thanked her as the exhaustion of the day descended over her. She laid her head back against the chair. So much had happened in a few hours, and she needed to know what was going on.

"You said something about food and answers." Her stomach rumbled and her heart felt like it had been pulled out of her chest. Her emotions hadn't settled down after his kiss. It seemed clear to her Micha had some interest in her, but she couldn't read him.

"Can't you give a guy a minute to catch his breath? Damn, woman!"

"Don't 'damn' me, mister. I'm the one you dropped here so you could escape the cartel and keep the book away from whoever was after it. You kissed me. I'm not talking about a peck on the cheek. You planted one on me and kept on going."

"You wouldn't be in this mess if they hadn't mixed up the --" Micha raked his fingers over his face and through his hair. "It's late and we're hungry. It doesn't matter how you got here. The kiss was in the heat of the moment, okay? We've escaped a couple of deathly scenarios. I needed an outlet, and you happened to be there. It meant nothing. Forget about it."

"Forget about it," she whispered. "Fine." She turned away so he wouldn't see her disappointment. She wiped her eyes and glanced back at him.

He pulled out his magic pen and clicked it. A bright flash and a sharp thwack made her wince. Words remained suspended in the air as Micha wrote. He came to the end of the sentence and dotted the period like trying to pierce the fabric of night. The scent of burnt ozone made her sneeze. Jasmine tried to make out what it said, but Micha's handwriting was worse than a doctor's. A weight landed on her lap. Jasmine jumped from the sudden shock of things coming out of nowhere. A knapsack and a bottle of water lay on her knees. Micha had the same. She opened her bag and pulled out a plastic container with a Greek salad with chicken, a piece of chocolate cake, and the utensils to eat it. The scent of greasy, cooked meat filled the house along with the odor of onions.

"How did this get here? You didn't run down to the local deli and have them make you a salad or grill a burger."

Micha chuckled between bites of his burger. "It's magic. I wrote it so the bag will provide you with whatever you need, at least food- and drink-wise. Maybe other things, too. Magic in Oz can be a little fickle."

Jasmine nearly dropped her feta cheese. "Oz. As

in the Wizard and the Wicked Witch of the West?"

Micha stared at her with an unimpressed expression like he'd explained this a handful of times before and the whole conversation annoyed him. "The very same, but don't believe everything you've read. This place is nothing like the book and the movie is pure fantasy."

It all sounded farfetched. She had grown up on the movie with the heroine wearing red shoes that got her home in the end. The book was one of her favorites as a child, and she still read it from time to time. Jasmine prided herself on being rational. The guys in the office depended on her to keep them straight. She handled million-dollar accounts. Any little deviation from the norm and peoples' businesses could be screwed up.

How can we be in Oz? How can that pen be magical? It's not every day I get attacked by a plant monster. Or be kissed by a handsome stranger. He said it was in the heat of the moment. It didn't feel that way.

Her mind spun at the idea of multiple realities and magical books existing. Someone kissing her in the middle of the night. She couldn't help but admit she wanted to feel those lips again. Jasmine hung her head in her hands to focus on something besides his lips and the feel of his body along hers. One breath in. One breath out. That was normal. That made sense. Her pulse thundered in her ears.

"Hey." His light touch made her jump.

Jasmine looked up into Micha's eyes and saw genuine concern. His warm smile didn't show anything of the asshole who snapped at her earlier. Instead, she found herself lost in his gaze. He slid his thumb along her cheek. The gentle caress made her hold her breath. Was he going to kiss her again? She bit her lip and waited. His thumb crept a little lower along her jaw. His breath warmed her face. Jasmine couldn't take it. She brushed her mouth along his to see his reaction. Instead of pulling away, Micha returned the light kiss.

"Jasmine, we shouldn't pursue this thing burning between us." Micha laid his hands on top of hers. His skin felt rough. His blue eyes flashed green. Emerald light zipped down his arms and over hers, making the hair stand up on her arms.

"Believe me, I would normally say the same, but you can't deny something is literally sparking between us."

"Whether it is or not, now is not the time. We need to focus on getting to safety after this. You need to accept the fact of where you are and how we got here."

Jasmine nodded. "We're in Oz. Y-you're some kind of magician. You pushed me into the pages of a book which is a gateway between worlds. What if I can't ignore it?" She trailed her fingers over his skin, watching the green energy play over their flesh. It was almost like touching a plasma ball and the electricity arched where her fingertips touched him.

"You should. It doesn't mean anything. All this is a lot to take in. It's confused you a bit. In your reality you have stories from books and movies. Those tales don't tell the whole truth about the worlds they describe."

"This is so weird." Jasmine kept on moving her fingers and watching the energy trails and how they played over his skin and hers.

"Did you hear what I said?" Micha pulled away.

"I heard you. Ignore whatever dynamic is going on between us, and books and movies are something more than what they present themselves to be." He had given her some answers, but it left her confused and in need of some air. Putting space between them felt right so she wouldn't be tempted to kiss him again or run her fingers over his arm.

"Excuse me." Jasmine took her dinner and walked outside. She speared a piece of chicken and chewed it. The meat tasted like normal chicken. Her stomach turned. She shoved the container back into the knapsack and examined the landscape. The house sat in the center of a perfect circle of barren land. No grass grew in the hundred-foot space. Beyond it lay the road and the apple trees in the poisoned orchard they'd passed. The remnants of the torch lay nearby. She saw that what she'd thought was a stick was actually a bone, a femur. Jasmine lost her lunch. Once she regained her cool, it hit her.

Oz was real, and she had gotten a one-way ticket with no way back to reality.

Chapter Three

"Hey." Jasmine opened her eyes to Micha's concerned gaze. "Are you okay?"

"Yeah. Fine. Seeing the leg bone outside kinda put me over the edge after everything you've told me. I don't even remember passing out."

"I brought you inside and put you on the couch. You were out for the night. I let you sleep as much as I could, but we have to get moving. I hate to push you, but by now word's gotten out I'm back. There will be… people after me. After us."

"Because of the book?"

"Because of the book. It's the key to many other realms. It… well… she… can do other things, too."

Jasmine sat up. Her throat burned from thirst and she could taste the acrid tang of last night's dinner. She pushed her hair off her face and stood up. "Any where I can freshen up before we leave?"

"Off the kitchen where we came in. For whatever reason, the plumbing still works. Go ahead."

"Sounds like you've stayed here a few times before." She retrieved the bag he had conjured for her and took it into the bathroom. The room rested on a slant. The ceiling sagged so she had to duck in places. Plants grew through the window and along the floor, but the sink and the toilet were free of debris. Jasmine jumped at the mirror and realized it was only her reflection staring back at her and not some evil monster. The door creaked open even after she shut it. She rested her bag against it to keep it closed before taking another look in the mirror. Dirt and leaves caked her brown hair. Scratches from the plantapus etched her face. Dark circles were drawn under her chocolate brown eyes.

She studied her reflection. Was there something wrong with her so Micha wouldn't be interested? Sure, her full figure put off a few men, but she'd had plenty of relationships. *I'm kidding myself. I barely know him and yet I can't stop thinking about how he kissed me. How he felt against me. Micha told me to forget it so that's what I'm going to do. He's right. Just a gut reaction for being thrown into the upheaval his life is. Must have been the shock.*

Jasmine turned the faucet on, splashed some cold water on her face, and wiped a little bit of the grime away. She even found the toilet worked.

"Ahh… are you almost ready? Not to hurry you at all, but we should get going."

She rolled her eyes. "In a minute."

"Sorry."

Jasmine finished up and eyed her clothes. They were tattered and spattered with blood. She needed something else to put on. Jasmine grasped the side of the bag and the zipper opened. She reached in and pulled out the chocolate cake, but the salad had vanished. Under the cake she found a pair of jeans and another shirt, one of the plaid button-down shirts she wore when she wanted to escape the world. Micha did say the bag could bring her food, but she didn't realize it could also bring her clothes. *It's a magic bag. What else can it give me? Maybe it could become a doorway and get me home. Maybe it can open up his mind and let me see what is going on inside it.* She glanced at it and decided against trying to step inside. Instead, Jasmine changed. The jeans fit, but the shirt was big. It was comfortable and smelled a little bit like fresh straw. She tore a piece off her old shirt and tied her hair back with it. Jasmine took one last look in the mirror and felt a little more human. She stuffed the cake back into the bag and left the bathroom. *Never know when a chocolate craving will hit.*

Micha had also changed into some cleaner clothes. He was dressed in darker blue jeans and a green T-shirt. Jasmine couldn't help but notice how those pants hugged his ass. She shook her head. *Not the time to think about his ass. Need to follow along with whatever he has planned so I can get home. Playing nice is more important than jumping his bones.*

"I see you also got new clothes."

"Yeah. Seems like your bag is more than a fast-food restaurant."

"Like I said, the magic in Oz is a bit fickle even at the best of times. We have a long way to go before nightfall. We need to put as much distance between us and Munchkinville as we can. This isn't the place I left. Oz has gotten darker. The air feels less somehow. It's difficult for me to conjure things. I don't know what's happened. Come on."

The blue sky had a purplish tint to it. The air tasted sweeter than it had the night before, almost like it did at home after it rained. The house sat in a perfect circle of brown earth and dead grass. Emerald green ivy covered the entire building. The apple trees looked like trees on steroids with fruit the size of grapefruits. Her stomach growled, but she had the chocolate cake from earlier and munched on that as they walked. "You said last night the trees were asleep. Are they awake now? I can't tell."

"I'm sure they are. They're good listeners. Some used to be my friends, but I don't know how many have turned and sided with her. She can be very persuasive." Micha pointed out a few of the spaces in the tree line where only jagged stumps remained.

"Who is this *she* you're referring to?"

He glanced around as though afraid someone

was watching. "I'd rather not get into it now. Maybe when we're in a safe space I'll tell you the details."

Jasmine stopped and crossed her arms over her chest. "Maybe? I don't think so. Look, Micha, you told me last night you were going to answer my questions, so I'll know what's going on. I've gone along with you this far and…" Jasmine drew a breath to control her emotions. The rage built up and if she didn't get some clarity, she would lose her shit. "…been nearly eaten by a plant monster that devoured a village. Then you tell me we're in fucking Oz. Then you pretty much rebuff me. Unless this *she* is the Wicked Witch of the West or even Cinderella, I'd like to know who --"

He covered her mouth with his hand. "Enough already with the shouting. If the trees weren't awake before, they are now."

Jasmine wanted to bite his fingers. *Let them wake up. It's not like they can pull up out of the dirt and attack us.* A loud groan and a crack sounded next to them. She froze and waited to see the trees surrounding them. They all remained rooted in the ground. A great whoosh of wind came out of nowhere, tearing leaves from the branches and ripping the hair tie from her hair. The massive maelstrom forced them apart. Jasmine backed up a couple of steps. A roar like a freight train deafened her. Micha yelled something to her, but she couldn't hear him. He clutched her shoulder and pointed at something raging toward them. She followed his finger over to the orchard. A large funnel cloud barreled toward them, picking up debris as it got closer. The shape of the cloud seemed to have a face in it. The definition was hard to tell, but she could see eyes leering at them. A mouth pulled back into a sneer. It rounded into scream and a piercing shriek from the wind made Jasmine wince.

Micha jerked her after him, but she couldn't move as the tornado came at them. Jasmine tore her gaze from the spinning dust cloud and saw Micha running away. Her fear broke, and she could move. She secured her bag and raced after him, trying not to trip over the bricks. In the daylight, she realized they were yellow. That hadn't occurred to her until now. Jasmine tried to keep up with Micha as she dodged some flying rubble. She was sure death would claim them in the guise of a fast-spinning wind funnel. A large clod of dirt came flying at her. Jasmine dashed out of the way and tripped over an upturned brick. She went down on her knee. Pain rode up her leg, and wind tore the groan from her throat.

Micha tried to help her up, but she shook her head and pointed to her knee. It hurt to put weight on it. He made a face and yelled something. Jasmine glanced backward and saw the funnel cloud sucking up the trees coming toward them. The sky remained clear. The cyclone had a life of its own, appearing out of nowhere.

Micha hauled her up and wrapped his arm around her waist. He helped her over to the side of the yellow brick road. With each step, pain jabbed her leg. Micha pulled out his pen. He drew a large rectangle in the air and wrote furiously. The letters glowed. Halfway through the paragraph the letters stopped shimmering. He shook the pen, scowled, and began once more. The script changed color from golden to green. Micha finished and the writing disappeared.

The tornado's winds pulled at Jasmine as it drew closer, ready to suck her up. The edge of the spinning winds latched onto the house and yanked it off the ground. Jasmine half expected the Wicked Witch to fly down on her broomstick and curse her. Leaves and wreckage obscured her view of Micha. It seemed he wasn't having any luck with the spell he was casting. A ribbon of green fought its way through the winds to her. Jasmine tried to get away from it, but the strip wrapped around her knee and tied itself in a tight knot. Her knee snapped, and her leg jerked. It hurt like hell, but then pain disappeared. Jasmine wanted to question it, but it made her leg feel better. Her need to survive overwhelmed her, and her instincts insisted that she had to move. The tornado whirled closer. Jasmine got up. Her knee could now support her weight without any pain. She braced herself against the wind and went through the debris to find Micha. He lay crumpled on the ground in front of a doorway that hung in mid-air. The pen still remained clutched in his hand. On the other side was a great hall filled with mirrors. She didn't know where it led, but it was better than where they were.

"Come along, dearie. Do help me get Micha on this side of the door before you both get sucked up." An arm came through the opening, and then a head appeared. Both were attached to a man. He tried to get to Micha but couldn't reach him.

Jasmine could barely keep herself anchored without being blown away. Terror bubbled up in her chest. This was her only way to safely. Seeing Micha sprawled out on the ground hurt her heart. He might have blamed their attraction on the heat of the moment. However, as she looked at him, she couldn't turn off her emotions. She'd thought she could and had sworn to herself she wouldn't let him in but found it impossible to avoid. Besides all the conflicting feelings, he was her way home. He had to stay safe. She grabbed Micha's shirt and tried to lift him. It took all her strength to haul him up. Jasmine made sure to grab the pen and shoved it into the bag around his shoulder along with the book. The bag kept hitting her hip as she got Micha the last few feet to the doorway. The man caught Micha's arms and heaved him through to the other side. Jasmine got to that edge of the doorway and looked down. The man stood on a ladder with Micha over his shoulder.

Here goes nothing. She swung her leg through and stared back at the orchard in time to see the twister yanking up a group of trees. As her foot hit the ladder, the cyclone rushed toward her. In the sidewall of dust and debris circling the funnel a more defined face formed. The eyes widened and the mouth snickered into a scream. The wind whooshed at her. The force unbalanced her. Jasmine toppled backward off the ladder and the opening closed. As she fell, Jasmine could see her end. She would hit her head on the marble floor and lights out. Instead, strong arms caught her and set her down safely on her feet.

Chapter Four

"I wasn't sure you were going to make it there for a second," the man told her.

"I wasn't sure I would, either." Jasmine looked around the room. Cracked mirrors showed her distorted reflection twenty times over. Blank spaces where mirrors used to be caught her attention. Some had cloths tacked over them. Gold and green veins threaded through the white marble floor. Puddles of water pooled in low spots. Micha lay on the floor. The other man picked him up again. A drop of water hit her nose. She glanced up. Large gaping holes in the roof allowed her to see the sky above. Something shimmered over the holes like a thin skin. It rippled over the openings as a cool breeze swept through the room. More water splashed down on her face.

"Come on, sweetie pie. You can marvel at the wonders of Oz later. We have to get this fellow here some rest. What he did was no small feat considering the current state of things here."

The sound of high heels echoed off the marble floor. She expected the man to have on some hard-soled shoes. When she looked down, the man wore four-inch chucky heels, showing off his pink-painted toenails through fishnet stockings. He wore a pink leather miniskirt with a studded black leather belt and garters holding up the fishnets. His pink jacket reminded her of a tuxedo with long tails in the back. She didn't care what he wore. He'd saved her bacon. Jasmine shook her head and raced to catch up. As they dashed through deserted hallways, Jasmine saw the disarray of the building they were in. Great doors hung off their hinges. Dried leaves and animal bones littered the corridors. They went up a flight of stairs and passed through a swinging door. A sting of energy hit the center of her forehead and made her sneeze. They moved into another part of the building: a plush bedroom with a green-and-gold color scheme. Jasmine looked behind her and the door became a wall. Their host laid Micha on the bed and smoothed the blond hair from his face. A line of pink energy moved down Micha's forehead and hit his nose.

"Is he going to be okay?" Jasmine asked.

The man looked up. His black curls bounced as he flashed her a frown and tapped a hot pink-painted fingernail against the stubble on his chin. He sized her up. Jasmine dropped her gaze and fidgeted with the straps of her backpack.

"What's your name, princess?"

"I'm not a --"

"Really? You didn't give a rat's ass about what Micha was dealing with. I'll give you being a little befuddled because this whole magic stuff is new to you, but you never thought what Micha was doing was draining him to make sure you were cared for. He drew the doorway and then used the rest of his energy to heal you."

She held up her hands to stop him. "Whoa! You don't know anything about me. Yes, magic and this whole thing is a little off-putting, but we landed in the middle of a fucking plant monster nest. We had to get out of there. It wasn't my fault a cyclone with a face on it came out of nowhere. He pushed me through that damn book! Nothing can happen to Micha because without him, I'm stuck in this storybook hellhole with you. Whoever you are. And I can't…" Jasmine felt the wetness on her face. She wiped away her tears and felt the lump of emotion in her throat. She had escaped death again. The words stuck at seeing Micha passed out on the bed. He looked so helpless and part of her wanted to comfort him. However, she remained silent, not sure what else to say to the man who rescued them.

"I'm the one offering you sanctuary. Don't you forget that, girlie. I'll send some food up for the both of you. You're staying here for a little while. Keep an eye on my boy, will you? If he dies, it's on you."

"What am I supposed to do?"

"Why don't you read him a story? Sometimes words are the strongest balm to lead someone back to themselves or bring people together. I'm damned sure he could use it right now. He's been gone a long time. I barely recognized him. Be thankful he's still alive. If not, your ass would've been sucked up and tossed to the Outerlands." He stopped and looked her up and down. "You might need some balm, too. Something's going on between you two." He took her chin and turned her head from side to side. "Hmm... could be, but we'll have to see how it goes."

"H-how what goes?" she forced out.

Her host flashed her a smile and then popped out of the room -- there and then gone.

Jasmine spied a door, but it led into a bathroom. She splashed some water on her face and stared into the mirror. Her reflection hadn't changed even though her world had. She never thought of being stuck on herself the way their host made it seem. *Wouldn't that be normal for anyone who gets thrown into another world? If our host knows so much about me, then he's been observing me somehow.* She tried to see if there were any cameras. *Maybe some magic looking glass or a crystal ball? Did the Wicked Witch of the West use a crystal ball? Or maybe it was a mirror? God, it's been a long time since I read the book.*

Jasmine hung her head and thought about their

host's instructions to care for Micha. She owed Micha for saving her ass a couple of times over now. She wet a towel and perched on the edge of the bed. Guilt overwhelmed her at seeing him hurt. It seemed he was sleeping, but he was further away, wandering in a world she couldn't enter. Jasmine wiped the dirt from his pale flesh. He was handsomer than she let herself think. His expression remained lax even as she washed the grime away.

"What am I going to do with you? You got me here. I know you were trying to save me. I'm sorry for being a bitch. I'm scared. You brought me to a place that shouldn't exist." She pushed a lock of his hair back into place. Her recollection of the feel of his lips along hers made her quiver. Never feeling them again made her cringe. She needed to do anything to get him to come around again. *What's wrong with me? I don't know him, and I don't believe in love at first sight, but damn.*

She shivered at the rush of desire inflaming her when she thought about him. "Mr. High Heels told me to read you a book. I don't see any books in here so…" Jasmine turned her gaze to the bag holding the magic book still slung around his shoulder. She hesitated about touching it. *I don't want to get sucked into its pages and thrown into yet another story.* Jasmine took her bag first and rooted around inside. It contained more wrapped food, water, and another pair of jeans. *Micha did say it'd give me what I needed. Food and clothing are essential.* Jasmine flung the bag into the chair and finished cleaning the dirt and grunge from his face. Micha remained unconscious throughout her care.

She needed him to wake up. He was her lifeline in this world. Without him, she was screwed. The bag around his shoulder remained her only option. Her skin prickled at the thought of touching the velveteen cover again. Reading it was her only solution. Maybe it would answer some of her questions or provide insight about what she felt for Micha. She drew the volume out. It didn't weigh what she thought it would based on its size. The tome felt familiar, as if her fingers knew where to embrace it. She set the book on her lap. Her hands trembled at the thought of opening it. *This is silly. It's a book. It works for Micha because he's the sorcerer.* Jasmine drummed her fingers on the cover, but her gaze hadn't left Micha's pale face.

"I never did thank you for saving me. Mr. High Heels was right. I was an ass. What did you expect? You rushed into my world and told me all this crazy stuff about drug cartels being after a book. How could I believe you? Magic doesn't exist in my world. Day to day I'm surrounded by paperwork."

Her life was kinda boring. She didn't even have a goldfish. A few house plants, but they were already dying. Work consumed her life. Her friends weren't really close because they were all married and had children. They invited her out, but she always felt like a third wheel. Now she found herself in a kid's book where things moved beyond the fairy tale.

"I hope this book won't eat me. Maybe I don't have to read this since we're in a fairy story. What if…" She brushed her lips along Micha's hoping he might wake like some sleeping prince or maybe turn into a frog. The light caress of her mouth along his made her lips tingle. She wanted to do so much more with him. The image of them entwined flowed through her thoughts, but so far he didn't want that to happen. How could she ignore the lure she felt toward him even if she didn't understand it? It had become an itch under her skin she couldn't scratch. Besides, she didn't want Micha's death on her. At least that was what Mr.

High Heels said.

She owed Micha to try to help him, whether or not he acted upon their mutual attraction.

Jasmine opened the book. She waited for the pages to start flipping on their own or for it to float out of her hands. It remained docile. The tome started like any other book with a first chapter. She thumbed a few pages ahead. It read like any other novel. Some pages had pictures and others had ornately drawn borders. The text was typed so it was easily read.

Here goes nothing.

"Once upon a time --" *How original!* She rolled her eyes. "-- there was an ordinary girl who lived in an ordinary world. Growing up she lived a humdrum life with few friends and migrated to an insipid job. The world passed by and she found herself caught in a paper prison. Everywhere she moved, the bars cut her, but she never saw the wounds until it was too late. One day, she escaped and experienced true freedom. The question was, what *would* she do with that freedom?

"With this hard-earned autonomy, this ordinary girl embraced the night. Little did she know an evil plot had been hatched. She was about to find herself in the middle of a great war between an evil sorceress and the handsome prince."

Jasmine flipped to the next page. A picture sat above the text. Bright stars lay scattered in the dark sky. The silhouette of a sleeping woman inside the tent against far-off mountains was centered in the image. Outside the tent a figure of a man trailed his fingers along the side of a car. Her mouth dropped. *What in the holy hell? How is it possible it's showing me my campsite and what happened to my rental?*

Micha moaned, and his eyelids fluttered. A green sheen glimmered over the book. Her fingers tingled. A shimmer of emerald zipped across her hands. It burned her palms and made her nails appear golden. She tried to pull away, but the book wouldn't release her. The letters took on the same shine. Her heart hiccupped. Jasmine tried to stay calm and kept on reading.

"The evil monkey tried to retrieve the precious item his mistress desired, but a protection spell shielded the book and the one whose possession it was in. It burned him to dust before the girl awoke. Upon seeing the damage to her campsite, she raced into town hoping to solve the mystery of the strange phone calls she'd received. She tussled with the second evil minion until the prince saved her. The prince tried to tell the girl she was in danger, but her stubbornness forced him to bespell her.

"The prince was bone weary from traveling to keep the magical book out of the hands of the evil enchantress. He rested for a day, maybe two. If he stopped for too long, then the evil sorceress's goons could find him. Having the girl under his spell only complicated things. His power wasn't infinite, and his magical weapon had to recharge. It was dangerous for him to deplete his magic, but the girl didn't know that. Something within him said he had to keep her safe. Even if he didn't understand why."

Jasmine stopped reading and looked up at Micha. *He wanted to keep me safe. Shit.* The emotion caught in her throat. The energy from the book crackled around her hands. Micha moaned again, and Jasmine touched his hand. Some of the color returned to his cheeks. *Seems like Mr. High Heels was right. Reading to Micha is making him better.* His breathing deepened. Jasmine squeezed his hand and he returned the gesture. *Please be okay.* She kept on reading.

"The prince informed the ordinary girl about the danger they were in, but she didn't believe him. Magic didn't exist for her. They couldn't wait any longer. The sorceress's minions found them once more. The prince barely convinced the girl she had to go with him in order to save her life. Because she'd interacted with the spell book, its magic rubbed off on her. It made her a little less ordinary, even if she didn't know it. The book scoured its pages for the right scene for them to escape to. To save her, the prince threw her at the book, and she fell into its pages. Together, they plunged into the scene, crossing realms, and a new adventure began for the prince and his ordinary girl."

Jasmine ran her fingers over the smooth page. Greenish energy surged up her arm once more. She shivered at the sudden rush and studied the passage. It reflected her journey so far with Micha. It gave her some insight into what he'd endured. He cared enough to keep her safe even though she was a total stranger. He could have left her to the goons.

"Even as the prince struggled with escaping Munchkinville, something about the girl intrigued him. Her fire lit up something within his heart he thought he would never have again. She pressed his buttons. All his years of loneliness faded when he tasted her lips. Within her, he saw a glimmer of hope. Even she felt the spark growing between them. However, the prince couldn't hang his hopes on the ordinary girl. She would eventually let him down. The prince stowed away his emotions. When it was evident the evil sorceress had found them, he used all the magic in his pen and everything he had within him to rewrite the story and create a doorway. With the last of his strength, he conjured a ribbon to save the girl and heal her. Even with the tornado barreling down, he couldn't see her get blown away."

The writing stopped in the middle of the page. If the book told the truth, then he did have some kind of feelings for her. Micha ignored them because he didn't want to be hurt again. Wet blobs landed on the pages and were absorbed into paper. She wiped her eyes, and flipped through the book. The remaining pages in the volume were blank. Micha groaned. She patted his hand. More energy flowed from her hands and up his. Faint crackles of green zigged and zagged over his body. Jasmine's eyes drooped. The book weighed a thousand pounds in her arms, for no reason. She stifled a yawn. It felt like all the energy had been sucked out of her. She heaved the spell book between them and shoved a pillow over it in case anyone came in. Jasmine stretched out next to Micha and rested her head beside his.

Chapter Five

Jasmine opened her eyes to an empty bed. The covers were pulled up to her chest. She slipped her hand under the pillow and around the bed, but the book had vanished. A shot of panic hit her when she didn't see Micha or find the book. *Please don't be dead or gone invisible. I wouldn't put anything past this place.* She got up slowly as haze drifted from the open bathroom door. Inside, she nearly tripped over a pile of discarded clothes. The splashing of the water drew her attention to the shower. Steam caressed Micha's body as he ran his fingers over his face to clear the water away. Jasmine's throat went dry. He seemed a god bathing in the waters of a sacred waterfall. The bathroom smelled of citrus, and she couldn't bring her gaze away from his toned body. The definition of his muscles and his tight ass made her heart seize up.

"Are you going to ogle me or are you going to join me?"

She jumped, not sure she heard him correctly. "Are you sure? You told me --"

His blue gaze met hers. "I know what I said. But it's what we both want. I need you, Jasmine, as much as you need me."

She bit her lip, not able to break away from his gaze. Her desire for him took hold. His words rang true. The yearning she had for him burned in her chest. It didn't matter that she barely knew him. The attraction between them overrode her senses. She stripped off her clothes and slipped under the warm water. The shower cascaded over her, and she took a moment to enjoy the water before she felt a hand slide down her arm.

Micha had a strange look on his face. She glanced

over at his hand. The same green sheen danced along their flesh. The water seemed to enhance the energy playing between them. She could even feel it pulsing over her. Micha trailed his hand down her arm and held up his palms. She mirrored him and the sparks danced between their hands. The lights dimmed in the room until she could only see the light playing between them. As the steam wound around, it gave the room an eerie feeling.

He brought one of her hands to his mouth and kissed the back of it. Jasmine's eyes fluttered as it felt like she could sense his lips all over her body in a light caress. "What's going on?" she moaned.

"I woke up and you were on my mind." Micha released her hand and pressed his body against hers. The water pooled in the spaces where their bodies met. The green glow grew stronger. Looking into his eyes, she didn't see the blue anymore. They had gone completely emerald and drew her into them.

"You didn't move in the bed and I kept thinking..."

Micha claimed her lips. She ran her fingers down his back and clutched his ass. His cock pressed into her thigh. Her toes curled at the sudden heat searing her from his kiss. His tongue thrust into her mouth. Jasmine could feel herself slipping away and falling under his power. Nothing else mattered except soothing the ache building within her. She returned the kiss and let all the strange things that happened to them so far flow through her mind. Being alone with him while the strange energy played over their skin -- all of it seemed worth it to soothe the yearning within her.

She took Micha's hand, brought it to her breast, and gripped it. Passion ignited within her and Jasmine gave herself over to it. She broke the kiss and Micha squeezed her nipple until she cried out. The sudden pain made her groan and squeeze her legs together. Jasmine grasped his cock and moved her hand along his shaft.

"What do you think you're doing?"

"Making sure I get a piece of what I want before you change your mind again," she told him.

"Do you like what you're holding?"

She pumped her hand along his dick until he quaked under the warm water. "The question is, do you like how it feels?"

Micha thumbed her nipple again until it ached. "Do you?"

She massaged his shaft a few times until he squirmed. "We can keep going around and around with this conversation, with this strange energy passing over us, or you can fuck me and kill this yearning inside me. Whatever this thing is between us, we have to resolve it before it drives both of us crazy."

"I agree. I want you, Jasmine. More than I've wanted anyone in a long time, or thought I could let myself… feel for someone. If this is… never mind. I'm going to make you scream. Turn around. Put your hands on the wall."

Jasmine caressed his dick one last time and did what he asked, not sure what he was going to do to her. Micha's hand ran over the back of her thighs and pushed her legs apart. He cupped her ass and spread her legs wider. She felt his fingers slip into her depths. Micha teased a moan from her lips, and she backed into him. Jasmine splayed her fingers against the tile and glanced behind her, seeing him through the spray of the water.

His other hand reached around her and found

her hard clit. Micha rubbed her throbbing bud until small tremors ran along her nerves. Her body ached with the hunger of wanting to be fucked. It had been such a long time since she'd truly let herself give in to the pleasure of the act with another. Micha bit along the line of her shoulder. He pumped his fingers into her pussy faster while keeping a gentle pressure on her buried clit. Her nerve endings came alive.

"God, what are you waiting for? I'm ready for you," Jasmine moaned.

Micha didn't waste any time. He pulled her toward him a little and plunged his cock deep into her. Once he was inside of her, he grabbed hold of her hips and pulled her against him, controlling their rhythm. She curled her fingers against the tile and let Micha take her over the edge into an orgasm. Jasmine backed into him, struggling to keep up with their combined rhythm. The power joining them together raced through her body. For every thrust, it felt like her pleasure doubled and then rebounded inside of her. It felt so damn good, she could barely catch her breath.

"Yes, Micha. Fuck me."

"Here it comes. God, Jasmine." His nails dug into her hips.

He plunged into her one last time so she came at the same time as he did. The moment she came, she felt a rush of energy flash through her and a tinge of green lit up the shower stall. His head rested against her shoulder, and hers hung down with the water flowing over her back. The water was still warm while she tried to catch her breath. Micha's arm wrapped around her waist. He hugged her closer and kissed her nape.

"That was something," she told him. Jasmine noticed the energy around them had faded out.

He chuckled. "Yeah, it was."

"I think we should get washed up and figure out where to go from here."

Micha separated from her while she focused on washing her hair and getting the grime off from the day before. When she was done, she handed the cloth to Micha and brushed his chest with her fingers before stepping out of the shower. She wrapped a towel around her body, which still hummed where Micha had touched her, and left the bathroom.

Jasmine replayed the scene in her mind and wondered what the next step was. What would he say when he found out she'd read to him from the book? Had Mr. High Heels known what would happen to her? Had the book? Jasmine shook her head while she dried off and checked out her magic bag to see if she could find some clean clothes -- which she did.

She sat on the bed to put her socks on. Micha came out of the bathroom into the bedroom with a towel wrapped around his waist while he towel-dried his hair. Her mind focused on him and she forgot all about her socks. He caught her looking at him and smiled. Her heart stopped after what they had shared in the shower. Whatever happened after she read the book seemed to have worked and he'd recovered. His expression eased as he threw the towel he'd used on his hair back into the bathroom.

"You were dead to the world earlier. I figured if you hadn't woken by the time I had gotten out of the shower, I would've woken you up then and enticed you."

"How would have you enticed me?" Jasmine asked.

He sauntered over and brushed his lips over hers. The tip of his tongue pushed her mouth open. The sweetness of his citrus shampoo added a tang to his lips. He wound his fingers through her hair and deepened the kiss. The other hand slid over her side and cupped her breast. Her nipple hardened at the light caress as he moved his lips from her jaw and nipped her ear. Jasmine moaned. Micha slid his fingers under her shirt and caressed her stomach.

"Something like this," he whispered. He undid a button on her shirt and placed his lips on her flesh while he undid the button on her jeans. "Do you want me to stop?" He pulled the zipper down. His fingers slipped under her panties until they found her clit. She moaned and sucked on the side of her cheek. She watched as he tugged down her jeans and panties. He knelt at the foot of the bed and ran his hands over the insides of her thighs and spread her legs farther. The top of his head came up and he had a devilish smile on his face.

"Tell me now or I'm just going to leave you like this."

Her heart beat thumped along her ribcage as her head felt light from the anticipation of what he would do to her. "Don't stop."

Micha slid his fingers along her wet slit before he pushed them inside of her. He kissed her clit and then swirled his tongue over it. Jasmine whimpered when he moved his fingers inside her, pushing her closer to the edge. He worked her clit with his tongue. Jasmine clawed the blankets and pushed her hips into him. She needed him to go faster. The pleasure building within her came to a crest, but Micha left her wanting. He moved his fingers a little deeper within her.

"Please, Micha."

"That's what I'd hoped to hear as I drew you from your dreams. I love how my name rolls off your tongue," he crooned. "I imagined what it'd sound like and how you'd taste."

"Even when you wanted to tell me to fuck off?" She laughed, trying to fight the bliss rising in her.

"More so. Whatever it is about you, Jasmine, you make me yearn again. You give me hope that all this might end."

Jasmine didn't know what he meant, but it flew from her mind when his tongue flicked over her clit. She shut her eyes shut and bit her lip. Flashes of light filled the darkness as she lost her grip on reality. He pumped his fingers into her as his tongue worked her faster. Jasmine could already feel herself falling under his spell again. She heard someone screaming but couldn't connect it with her body. Green and golden light danced behind her eyes until it exploded in fireworks. She opened her eyes as the relief flooded her, but Micha wasn't done with her.

"What are you doing now?" she asked, trying to catch her breath.

"Trying something." Micha lifted his hand and ran it over her stomach. The green light phenomena they'd shared between them in the shower returned. He dragged his hand over her body and settled it below her navel. "Do you feel that?"

A small buzz electrified her. The more he glided his fingers slightly above her flesh, the more the yearning built within her. He rotated the energy in a slow circle. It felt as though he was inside her, moving at a slow pace. The bliss of it zinged along her entire body. Jasmine reached for him, not able to answer. She grabbed his shoulder and pulled him down to her lips. His hand rested on her tummy and caressed it. Jasmine groaned into his mouth as she came one more time, and it felt like her mind blanked out. Micha broke the kiss. She collapsed back onto the bed until her body stopped humming.

"Yes, I felt that." She sat up once she could. "What the hell did you do?"

"Something I didn't think I could do. You seem to be a wonder."

"You've kept saying that, but I'm not sure I really understand what I have to do with all this." Jasmine stood up and redressed.

"It is a bit of a mystery, as is the enigma of why I woke up here. I used all my energy writing the door into the scene so we could escape the tornado and to conjure the ribbon to heal your knee." Micha grabbed his bag and searched inside.

"I couldn't wake you up after you did whatever you did to get us here. Then our host locked us in."

"Glen wouldn't do that. See." He tried the door handle. It opened easily.

"That door wasn't there last night. I'm just telling you what happened since you asked." Jasmine ran her fingers over the bed. A moment of panic hit her. She lifted up the pillows and her heart dropped. It had disappeared. "Shit! Where's the book? I left it between us before I fell asleep."

Micha's grin dropped, and his eyes sparked jade. The attraction growing between them seemed to falter as he went cold. Jasmine could feel him retreat. The skin on his face rolled for a moment. His complexion took on a darker brown shade. His pursed lips almost appeared fake, as though he wore a mask. His hands shook and his voice came out in a frigid whisper. "Why did you touch the book? It won't open up and send you back home. She belongs to me." He glanced at the bag on the chair and snatched it up. "Never touch it again. Do you understand?"

She winced at the harsh comments. Whatever

blooming feelings were between them, they were suddenly chopped to pieces. He reminded her they were strangers. She was only along for the ride. His words stung her heart more than they should. Jasmine glanced away and composed herself as her anger crept back in. She took in a breath and faced him again. "Hey, I get it. You fuck me and twist me around your little finger. I thought you were dead. Mr. High -- Sorry. *Glen* told me I should read to you because if anything happened to you, then I was screwed. So I did." She recalled Micha lying lifeless on the bed. It was not an experience she wanted to go through again. Even if he was being an ass, she couldn't turn off her feelings. "Whatever this is… you make me want to be here for you. I don't give a shit about the book. Then I remember this powerful sorcerer who only loves his book and happens to be a dick."

"The only reason you're worried about me is because without me, you're trapped here."

"Maybe I'm trapped here, but it's not the whole --"

He shook his head and slung the bag over his shoulder. "That's what I thought. All you care about is yourself. This pull between us is… it doesn't matter. Trust me, if I could, I'd put you right back where I found you. Now I'm stuck with you."

Jasmine's mouth dropped, but she quickly closed it again. Each of his words struck like a slap in the face. They were true to an extent. She did need him to get home, but she hadn't even thought of touching the book until Glen told her to read to Micha. Jasmine wanted to ask Micha about the green energy passing between their hands while she read to him. It extended to how it played between them in the shower. It remained clear something more was going on between them he didn't want to acknowledge. He had thrown his walls back up and returned to being an asshole. Jasmine walked into the bathroom to get some distance between them. Steam fogged up the mirror. She tried to wipe it away, but it didn't fade. *What is going on? He says he was waiting for me to wake up. Wow, he showed me what he was going to do if I was still asleep. What is he hiding?* She placed her hand on the glass and sighed at the frustration Micha brought her. Her palm tingled. A green glow encompassed her hand and a sheen spread over the mirror. The haze receded, leaving the glass clear. The prickly feeling in her hands left her staring at her palms. They appeared normal, as did her reflection. *Must be left over from the shower. Nothing to worry about.*

Jasmine pushed the hair from her eyes and gathered her wits. *I'm not going to let him get to me.* When she rejoined Micha, she found him with a tray of food set on the table and two bowls. Her stomach growled. He barely noticed her when she sat across from him. A porridge of some sort with dried fruit, blueberry muffins, and tea became breakfast. A soft knock came on the door, and then it opened. She expected it to be Mr. High Heels, but a man held another tray in the doorway while he waited to be invited in. Long, shaggy brown hair framed his face and fell down his back. Big brown eyes gazed at them. His expression reminded her of a lost puppy. His face turned bright red as he came inside.

"H-hey, Sc -- Micha. B-been a while," the man stammered as he put down the tray.

Jasmine looked between him and Micha. The scowl on Micha's face told her whatever the other man nearly called him was not something she was supposed to hear. Jasmine stood up and stuck her hand out.

"I'm Jasmine. What's your name?" she asked.

"L-leon."

"It's nice to meet you, Leon."

"Don't pay any attention to her, Leon. She's just here until she can get home," Micha explained.

Jasmine forced a smile as Leon slipped his hand into hers. His eyes lit up and a small smile turned up his lips. "Micha seems to think I'm out to get his book." Jasmine squeezed his hand.

Leon returned it. He only broke the gaze when Micha coughed. A splash of color crept up his neck when he looked away. Jasmine caught a strange vibe between the two men. "I'll leave you two alone. I need to get some air."

She exited the room and found herself in a large ballroom or maybe a throne room. Jasmine turned around fast enough to see the door close behind her and vanish. Magic was starting to get on her nerves. A red carpet like a stripe of blood slashed the green floor in two. At the very end stood a large golden throne. Glen relaxed on the ornate chair. His legs dangled over the arm showing off his pink high heels with white fishnets. The fabric of his hot pink dress draped over the seat. Jasmine squared her shoulders. *I have to roll with it. I'm not in my world so I have to play by other rules until I can get home. If I ever get home.*

A silver tiara nested in the center of his dark curls. He didn't bother to look up at her while he filed his nails. "I was wondering when you'd get here."

She huffed and crossed her arms over her chest. "Considering you locked us in the room last night, and then made me look like a fool with Micha, I'm sure you're happy with yourself."

He looked up from examining his nails. "I

needed to be sure he was safe and see if the book would respond to you. She doesn't like many people. If you weren't meant to help Micha, then she wouldn't have let you. I think the book showed you it had protected you at your demolished camp. Besides, it seems like you and Micha were getting along well enough."

"You *have* been watching me."

"Well… not *you* exactly, but the book. I get a tingle when she gets frisky." The bracelets on his wrist jangled when he wiggled his fingers.

"Great. Your tingle made it so Micha thinks I'm after the book."

"Aren't you?"

"I don't know what the hell is going on. Sure, I want to get home, but there's more to it now. He says one thing and then he does another. Something's going on between us."

"Don't mind what's going on with Micha. It's been a long time since he's been here. His emotions are all in a tizzy, I'm sure. You need the book to get back home. Give him some time."

Jasmine threw up her hands. "I don't have a choice but to rely on him. Time to shred my heart and… Fuck it. I don't know. I'm sticking with Micha because I don't have a clue about where I really am or if this is some dream gone wrong."

Glen scrutinized his nails again. Something about the way he sat reminded her of someone. "Not a dream. Stop trying to convince yourself it is one. I can't answer for Micha and how he's treating you. Micha's been hurt and his only companion has been the book. She can take on a life of her own. I want to know, what happened while you read aloud last night?"

"I guess some of its magic rubbed off on me so I

could transmit it to Micha. In the story, the book said it protected me from the creature who destroyed my camp." Jasmine glanced down at her hands. Her palms itched again. She thought about touching Micha last night and how the energy transferred to him. He'd looked so peaceful lying there. She half smiled when she remembered kissing him, but he hadn't stirred. Her stomach churned when her mind wandered back to their shower scene. None of it made any sense. Jasmine pushed the thought of him being cute out of her mind. All that mattered was returning home.

"I could send you back home."

Great. Now Glen's reading my *mind.* "Then why don't you? It'll make my life easier and solve my problems." Jasmine looked at her hands. A hint of the greenish gold remained in her nails. She rubbed them against her jeans to see if it would wipe off.

Glen stood up and clicked his high heels together. Jasmine waited for something to occur. Another tornado to spin her around. Maybe a doorway appearing out of nowhere. Nothing happened. "I tried. Something else is keeping you here."

"Your shoes are pink. Aren't they supposed to be silver? In the book, Dorothy got them from The Witch of the North."

"That'd be my sister."

"Then who are you?"

"If you know the book so well, then you tell me."

Jasmine rolled her eyes as she tried to remember anything she could about the novel she enjoyed as a child. The story contained four witches. "Well, Dorothy killed two of the witches, so you have to be Glinda the Good Witch who rules over the south."

"Ta-da!"

"But you're not... how could you be?"

"Not the woman you were expecting? Yeah... Frank kinda embellished a few things when he wrote the series. Those things got spun out and caught up in the Hollywood hype, but we don't talk about the movie here." He shivered in disgust. "It would've been difficult for your world to understand who I truly am. I'm Glen-da, the Good Witch of the South. I know I'm not exactly what the book describes. I keep what I can of the Emerald City afloat, but Oz is dying. The magic here is slowly being sucked out of the land. I followed what was left of the magic from the southern lands and came here. This city is the last stronghold of Oz. I wish my pink heels were the real silver slippers, but those were lost a long time ago."

Everything is different from what's in the books. That's what Micha said. Why am I here? Does the book have plans for me? Can it write its own story? Is it writing this thing between me and Micha? I know it's not in my imagination. There's a spark, but he's turning his back on it. Why? Her fingers tingled again when she thought about Micha. Green energy resurfaced and tinted her nails. Jasmine held up her hands to Glen-da. "What is this? What did the book do to me?"

"It gave you a gift. It gave one to another girl it brought here as well. Although something went wrong with her in the end."

"You mean Dorothy?"

Glen winked at her as the echo of the door opening bounced around the room. "Glen, what's the deal?" Micha called out.

"The deal is, my friend, I wanted to chat with your lady friend without you around. She's the reason you're up and walking right now. Didn't she tell you?"

"I recall seeing you coming into the ballroom with a ladder before I blacked out," Micha replied. He glanced at Jasmine, but already the wall had thickened around him. She was as good as a piece of furniture to him.

Glen-da met Micha in the middle of the room and put his hands on Micha's chest. Leon remained behind him with his gaze locked on Micha, following him as he moved around the room. Jasmine tried to put two and two together. She thought of the trio who accompanied Dorothy. The Scarecrow, the Cowardly Lion, and the Tin Man. Leon had to be the Cowardly Lion. Although, she couldn't figure out which one Micha was supposed to be. He didn't have an axe, but he wasn't made of straw. Then again, she could have it all wrong.

"I rescued your asses, but if it wasn't for Jasmine, you wouldn't be standing before me. The words in your story all but ran out until the book wove you into Jasmine's tale. Ever think she might have a reason to do that?" Glen raised an eyebrow and his lips turned up in a secretive smile.

Micha's eyes widened as though he didn't believe what Glen-da told him. "The book wouldn't tell her story."

"Really?" Glen's eyebrow lifted. "Have you consulted the book lately? She has a mind of her own. You share a spark with Jasmine, don't you, Micha? You're ignoring it. If she's here and your stories are intertwined, then you have to know what it means."

"Can we not talk about this right now?" Micha glared at Jasmine.

Glen-da shook his head. "Not right yet. You still owe Jasmine thanks for saving your life."

"Is this true?" Micha turned to her.

"I tried to tell you, but you didn't want to listen." Jasmine resisted the urge to stick her tongue out at him. "Last night you were the color of death warmed over and barely breathing. Then I started reading from the book. This energy of some kind radiated from the pages into my hands. When I touched you, it went into your skin. It was similar to what happened between us in the shower."

"I think you owe her an explanation. I'll give you two a little bit of time." Glen-da wiggled his fingers at them and then clicked his heels together three times.

"Glen, don't do this. You son --" Micha shouted at Glen-da, but his voice was lost in the whoosh of wind that swept through the throne room.

Jasmine felt it lift her up and spin her around. When it stopped, she found herself with a field of red flowers on either side of her standing on the yellow brick road that ran through them. However, this road was perfect and it hadn't been ravaged by time. She glanced up and saw a glass dome above them. Cracks spider-webbed along the glass, but something with a sheen glistened in the light over the dome -- the same thing she'd seen covering the holes in the roof when she first arrived.

The perfume of the flowers made her a little light-headed and she sneezed. She glanced around and saw Micha standing in the field of flowers. He ran his fingers over their large petals. The blossoms were the size of dinner plates and stood three feet tall. She walked over to him, but he didn't seem to acknowledge her. His eyes misted over and he seemed to be staring beyond. "This is all that's left of the land I knew. Glen's been trying to preserve it, but she keeps draining the magic from this place. I could feel it when I came back here, but I was too busy trying to keep our asses alive. She's turned into the very thing she defeated. She's not the person I knew."

Jasmine wasn't exactly sure who the *she* he talked about was, but she had an idea. His expression remained stoic and sad. The wall he had around his emotions seemed to crumble as he stared at the flowers. "You're talking about Dorothy, right? It sounds like you cared for her." *Whatever happened between him and Dorothy must've really messed him up. Is she the reason why he won't let me in, or is there another reason?*

He blinked and his eyes focused back on her. "Dorothy didn't see me as a bag of straw whose singular purpose was to scare away crows in a field. She made me understand love. I never did a very good job of it either. The man who stuffed me didn't realize the magic of Oz infused itself within me and brought me to life after a while." Micha stopped and touched Jasmine's cheek. The softness of his flesh showed nothing of the creature he was supposed to be. She sighed with the gentle caress. It brought her some peace of mind, even if it was for just a moment. His statement also answered her question as to which character he was: the Scarecrow.

"Why did Glen-da put us here?" Jasmine asked.

"Isn't it obvious? He wants us to get along. He wants me to open up to you and spill my heart out. Tell you why you're so important being here. Knowing him, he won't let us go until he's satisfied with the outcome. He can be an ass."

"Why don't you tell me, then? Or at least reveal why you keep denying this connection between us because it's driving me nuts. I can't figure out if you're going to be a dick or if you're going to turn around and kiss me. You're giving me whiplash and ripping my heart out all at the same time. Look, I'm not one who believes in the love at first sight bullshit, but whatever this pull is between us is maddening. All I want to do is touch you and pacify this burn inside me." Jasmine felt her cheeks sear at admitting to him what had been tramping through her mind. However, it was true. She couldn't keep doing the back and forth with him because it was wearing her out trying to keep up. The pull between them might not have been love, but something drew her to him. The longer she was around him, the more her feelings deepened. It all revolved around the book. Maybe the book was to blame and planted the seed for their relationship. Maybe she was more aware of Micha because he saved her. Whatever the reason, she couldn't deny the attraction. Their sexual encounter earlier had soothed the ache, but being with him now had stirred it again.

Micha let out a long breath and gazed at her. She could see a longing in his eyes. He brushed his knuckles along her cheek. Then the wall came back up suddenly, but he didn't become as cold as he had before. Instead, something seemed to resolve within him. His thumb ran over her bottom lip. A sharp sting made her jump like she had been zapped again. She touched his hand and again the green energy flowed between their two palms.

"Why won't you tell me what this means? Why am I here? Glen-da tried to click his magic heels together and send me home, but he couldn't. He said something was keeping me here. Is it the book?"

"If you can't go home, then yes, something beyond Glen-da's magic is keeping you here. The book has written you into the story. She has plans for you."

"Can a book do that? Write its own story?" Jasmine asked. "Is it creating this thing between us? Last night when I read from those pages, the magic or its power moved from the words and into my hands.

When I touched you, the energy went into you, but I can still feel it. I can see the sheen of it in my nails and it kept going farther up my arm. What is it doing to me?"

Micha took her hand. The energy between them dissipated as he examined her fingers. "The book... she can't write the future by herself. She can influence it here and there. It's like my pen. I can change a scene. The more I edit it, the more magic it uses. That's one reason I ran out of magic. Whatever power she gave you to revive me, it's lingering in you. I don't know the reason why. I'm sorry about before. When you said you read from the book, I overreacted. I've been protecting her for so long now. The threat of someone taking her has been branded into my psyche."

"I understand why you would get defensive. The way you reacted was like a slap in the face after what we shared. Look, I don't go sleeping with every guy who pushes me into a book." Jasmine tried to ease the tension between them.

He chuckled. "Well, if it makes you feel better, I don't go around pleasuring those who steal my car."

"I did not steal your car. That's on the rental company and --"

Micha pulled her into his arms and kissed her before she could finish her sentence. Jasmine couldn't recall what she was going to say because the urge to be with him flared up once more. She wrapped her arms around his neck and pressed her body along his. Being so close and kissing him eased stirrings within her. Whatever walls around his heart, she could almost feel them falling down. He kissed a path along her jaw until he nibbled her ear. His hands worked down and covered her ass. Micha squeezed one of the cheeks. Jasmine moaned and tugged on his shirt. He broke away.

"No. Not here. I don't need Glen-da watching us and getting his jollies off."

Jasmine hung her head and tried to catch her breath. "Okay. Does this mean you're not going to be a cold-hearted ass to me now?"

He lifted her chin so she could see his deep green eyes. "You might have to remind me now and again. I've been stuck in my ways for many years. I might slip up."

"You never did tell me why the book's written me into this story of yours. Why me?"

Before Micha could answer, the poppies clacked together as a light breeze came through. A light chill wrapped around her and settled in her middle. It tickled her chest, but she couldn't stop it as it speared her. It spun her around in its grip. She could still see Micha, but the breeze pulled her away even when she tried to stay.

Chapter Six

Jasmine found herself in another room. The windows were boarded up, allowing a little bit of light to peep through. Dust floated in the streams of sunlight. She made out a bed and a dresser. Jasmine pulled at one of the boards covering the window to get more light. It took a couple of tugs before it came off. Once she did, she could see the walls were a faded blue, but in places where the light hadn't touched it had once been vibrant. She glanced around but didn't see a door. As she took in the lay of the room, she tripped. Jasmine took a tumble and got back up to see what she had fallen over.

An oval-shaped pillow the size of something a small dog or a large cat would sleep on. She picked it up to examine it and saw a crude name tag stitched into the bed. "Toto." *So Dorothy really did have a dog*. Jasmine tossed the dog bed onto the larger bed and took another look at the room to see if she could find more clues about the girl who once lived there. A mural next to the window of Dorothy, the Scarecrow, Tin Man, and the Cowardly Lion caught her eye. They walked down the yellow brick road. The house that crunched the Wicked Witch remained in the background with the apple trees along the other side. In Dorothy's hand was clutched a large green book. The same one Jasmine had read from the night before.

In another mural on the other side of the window, Dorothy no longer happily skipped down the yellow brick road. Instead, she held the open book with an evil smile on her face. The three who used to be her friends were being held by what looked like large apes with wings. Something happened to turn Dorothy into an evil witch.

Jasmine heard a click and a crack of light appeared in the wall. She walked over and found a door had been opened for her. She slipped out of the room and found herself in a rundown hallway with pictures lining the walls. They were all water damaged and ruined. Some were so torn she couldn't make out who they were, but there were dozens as she walked down the long passageway. It had no doors, but the corridor had leaves piled along it and puddles of water. She couldn't make out any doors and it seemed like she walked half a mile until she came to a turn in the passage.

When she did turn, she found herself in a room that actually looked lived in. The smell of wood filled the space. She tried to find the door she came in from, but found it had disappeared, leaving her alone in the room. A carving of a fierce lion caught in mid-roar with its claws extended as though it were going to pounce on someone drew her attention. Its detail made it seem real as it were going to jump off its pedestal. Light from a fireplace flickered off the carving. Something snapped behind her. She spun around, not sure what she would find, and discovered a man staring at her from the shadows.

"Who's there?"

"It's Leon. This is my room." He stayed in the shadows.

"Sorry. I didn't mean to invade your space. I was walking down a hallway and when I turned a corner, I ended up here. I don't know how."

"It was probably the book. She wants you here for some reason."

"You sure it wasn't Glen-da? He put me and Micha together to work out some stuff."

Leon moved in the shadows as though he stalked

her. It made Jasmine watch him to make sure he wouldn't spring on her. Her heart sped up a bit as a little fear knotted her stomach. He seemed much different in his own space than the meek man she met earlier. She assumed he was the Cowardly Lion, but she didn't know for sure.

"Did you work out the stuff you needed to?" Leon threw another log onto the fire. The flames shot up into the chimney. Ash flitted into the room.

Jasmine backed up toward the table to keep space between them. "I think so. Why do you ask?"

"Micha and I are friends. I haven't seen him in a long time. If you're here with him, then it means something."

"What does it mean? Micha didn't tell me. He's been really secretive about the book."

Leon shrugged. "I'm sure he has a good reason for not telling you. What kind of perfume are you wearing?"

She was nearly taken aback by his question at the sudden change of subject. "I'm not. Maybe you're smelling the shampoo or the soap I used."

He stepped out of the shadows so she could see the golden highlights in his hair and the deep tan of his skin. The light of the fire played along the angles of his cheeks and made his lips look fuller than they had before. Jasmine shook her head and tried to focus her thoughts back on Micha. Leon walked behind her and trailed his fingers over her shoulder and down her arm. Jasmine shivered a moment.

"Amazing," Leon murmured.

"What is?" His fingers came over her palm. Golden energy played between the two of them, the same way it did with her and Micha.

"Something I think we all have to be sure about.

Maybe that's why she sent you here, so I could be sure. So we could truly know."

A haze of confusion flowed over her. The same kind of weird attraction she had for Micha, she could feel it starting with Leon. She didn't know if she could handle it. How could it be possible? Then she recalled what Micha said about nothing being what it seemed here. "You guys really have to stop being so cryptic."

"It's more about making sure what we hope is true." Leon lifted her chin and turned her head this way and that. His honey brown eyes held hers while he looked her over. Jasmine tried to understand why she had this sudden allure to the man before her.

"Which is what?"

Leon shook his head. "I'm sure all will be revealed when it needs to be." He traced her lips. Jasmine let out a small sigh at his touch. He leaned in and brushed his mouth along hers to get a taste of her. It really wasn't a kiss and yet Jasmine yearned for more.

"Why is this happening?" Jasmine asked.

"I think it's time you go. Micha will be looking for you." Leon separated from her and went to open the door. She turned and looked at him wanting to feel his lips one more time. Their gazes met. He took her hand and the same spark jumped between them. He brought it to his lips and brushed the back of it. Jasmine shivered with sudden pleasure. Leon released her and she stepped out of the room. She turned back around to say something else to him but found the room was already gone. Jasmine found herself in the throne room where Glen-da had been before. This time no one was there.

Wind whistled through the room. She looked up and saw the holes in the roof and the same shimmery shield that covered the whole city. The setting sun made the sheen over the city look like a rainbow had been cast over it. She wondered what the city had been like before all the destruction. What had it been like in the days when Dorothy and her other companions had thrived in the city? Jasmine ran her fingers over the arm of the throne and stared at the threadbare red carpet. She sank down into the chair and felt the weight of exhaustion fall over her.

Jasmine leaned back in the oversized chair and tried to gather her thoughts from all that happened to her today. *Micha said the magic was draining out of Oz. Where is it going?* It must have taken magic to teleport her around the city. If the book had done that, would it also be losing magic? Jasmine felt a stab in her temple. The more she tried to figure how magic worked it made her brain hurt. *Suddenly I'm an expert on magic?* She chuckled and leaned back in the throne.

"You look like you belong there," a voice boomed from the other end of the room.

Jasmine jumped up and saw Glen-da walking toward her. "Sorry, I ended up here and…"

"No need to be sorry, dear. Sit. Sit. I was just coming to get you for dinner anyway."

Glen-da pushed her gently back into the seat. The room spun. Before she knew it, the scene changed. She found herself sitting at a table with Micha across from her, Leon next to him, and Glen-da at the head of the table. The table set before them had a small feast laid out on it. The aromas on the room made her mouth water. The seat next to her was empty, but a place setting was there.

"Are you expecting someone else to come?" Jasmine asked.

"No one has sat there for a long time," Leon

whispered.

"Was it for the Tin Man?"

"Let's not talk about him," Micha growled.

"Yes, we shouldn't bring up all the badness. Tonight, we're celebrating," Glen-da told them. Jasmine saw the pain flash across his face. Whatever the subject was, it seemed none of them wanted to get into it. Something happened between them involving the Tin Man. She didn't want to push the buttons.

"What are we celebrating?" Jasmine asked as Leon reached for a bowl of mashed potatoes.

"Micha is home where he's supposed to be and we have… Well, we have you as a needed friend. Let's have a toast to a new friend." Glen-da raised his glass to her. "To our new friend who has brought a bit of magic back into Oz." Glen-da smiled.

The others raised their glasses and then they drank. Jasmine could taste the citrus, but the drink packed a punch as the cinnamon in it sat on the back of her tongue. She set it down and focused on her food. As she ate the first few bites, she noticed Micha and Leon looking over at her. She could feel their stares. While she kept on eating, silence bloomed in the air. Something was growing between all of them. She didn't know what it was, but she could feel it. Even as they ate, she couldn't help but wonder when the other shoe would fall.

Jasmine cleared her throat. "Can one of you tell me how I ended up in Dorothy's old room?"

Leon dropped his fork and a look of fright crossed his face. Micha's neck grew red as the veins pulsed in his temples. Glen-da forced a smile. "It wasn't me. After I spun you out to be with Micha, I sank into a bath and then to see about this feast. I had a lovely time among the bubbles."

"It was the book," Micha chimed in. "She must've been having fun with you."

"After being there, it sent me into Leon's room, too." Jasmine glanced at Leon and saw him blush and look away again. It appeared he was back to the same shy character she'd met earlier in the day.

"She must've wanted you to meet Leon," Glenda said.

"Yeah, and that's all fine, but what is it that you're not telling me? I'm a bit tired of not knowing what's going on. I've accepted I was thrown into Oz and magic exists. I accept Dorothy went evil and wants to get this magic book back. I don't like being kept in the dark. Micha, you've never answered my questions fully. You all keep saying I'm special. What the hell does that mean? Does it have anything to do with the sparks that fly with me and Micha and also with Leon?"

Micha glanced at Leon. "You feel something for her?" His tone held astonishment and anger.

The other man kept his gaze focused on his empty plate. He shrugged. Leon muttered something she couldn't hear, but his cheeks turned red. Micha's gaze met hers. Jasmine didn't look away, but she could see he was trying to figure out how much he should say. His eyes kept going back from blue to green. Glenda went over to Leon and whispered something in his ear. He glanced between him and Jasmine and nodded. Glen-da guided the other man out of the room, leaving her alone with Micha.

"Why don't we go for a walk?" Micha suggested to her.

"Are you going to talk to me this time?"

He offered her his hand to help her stand from her chair. Jasmine gritted her teeth, not sure she would get the answers she needed. However, the urge to touch him got the better of her. The slight zing that rushed up her arm made her shiver. She couldn't deny the connection between them. Jasmine didn't comment as they walked out of the room. Instead of the hallway, they ended up in another room. Micha growled.

"Enough with the scene cuts," Micha said to the thin air.

"Not happy your book is calling the shots? What is this place?" Jasmine looked around the new room they had entered. It reminded her of a cathedral with high ceilings. Everything had a tint of green to it. Moonlight streamed through the intact windows. The air stirred as they walked. She could feel something like a force or a presence in the room with them. She couldn't quite figure out what it was, but this place seemed special in a way she couldn't describe.

"No, I'm not fond of her taking control and editing. She's doing quick cuts to get us to this place. It uses magic that she shouldn't be using, but she's an enigma unto herself. I don't control her, but I have to protect her. If Dorothy gets ahold of the book, then those left in Oz will face an even worse life than they already do."

"Is that why you brought me back here?" Jasmine leaned against one of the pillars.

Micha leaned against another pillar across from her and slid down to the floor. Something in his face seemed so tired. His eyes returned back to green. He drew designs in the dust on the floor before he looked up at her. All she could think about was someone so lost he didn't know his next step. Or maybe he'd had enough and wanted to take a break. Whatever it was, she felt for him. She couldn't imagine what Micha had been through in all the years of running and finally being able to come home, but it wasn't the home he knew any longer. Or maybe he was the one who had changed too much. He threw a pebble across the room.

"This place used to be where the Wizard held court. I remember coming in here and asking him for a brain, thinking I would have something the humans had. He gave me a brain made of bran, pins, and needles. When he left, he turned over leadership of Oz to me. I wanted nothing of it and, well… the book says one thing. But I let Glen-da run it. Dorothy, Leon, and the Tin Man wanted to go on a few adventures. So off we popped.

"No, I didn't bring you back here to save Oz. I brought you back here to keep you from her goons -- the flying monkeys -- and to get us away so we could save the book. I never knew she would write you into our story. I never realized I'd be drawn into yours. You were a surprise. There have been others in the past, but none of them have been right." He looked up and gazed at her with a look of pure longing. It broke her heart.

"I appreciate you saving my life. I did thank you before, but you were knocked out. Micha, I don't know why your book thinks I'm special or why I have this strange attraction to you and Leon, but I am grateful you're alive." Jasmine sat down next to him and threaded her fingers through his. She rested her head on his shoulder and took in the scent that reminded her of fresh straw.

"You're welcome. I've grown quite fond of you, too."

Jasmine giggled. "Wow, I'm glad to hear that after this morning. I was wondering if there might be something more."

He turned and their gaze met. For the first time it

felt their connection was mutual. Micha took in a breath and she could hear him swallow. The space between them fell away. It didn't matter she'd only known him for a short time. It didn't matter they were from different worlds or that magic brought them together. They were meant to be together. He inched toward her until their lips brushed. His fingers grazed her jaw and cupped her cheek. The small contact made her sigh. She returned the kiss with a slight pressure as though it were their first kiss. In many ways it was.

His eyes glinted in the moonlight spilling in from the windows. Micha ran his hand along the line of her collarbone. His touch intoxicated her. The more he caressed her, the more she yearned for him. Every muscle in her body tensed. Every nerve came alive. She yearned to feel his skin against hers. He let his fingers trail over the swell of her breasts.

Jasmine moaned as her tongue touched his lips. She tugged at his shirt and placed her hands on his chiseled abs. His flesh was warm beneath her palms. A smile caressed her lips while her tongue trailed up the center of his chest, over his heart, tasting the saltiness of his skin. She licked a path to one of his nipples and the sensitive skin between her teeth. Micha groaned when she bit down. Her free hand pinched the other nipple. Micha lifted her chin, bringing his mouth to hers and kissed her with a hunger she hadn't felt in him earlier. It seemed he wanted to claim her for his own.

Finally, he released her lips. "You taste ravishing."

She bit her lip and ran her hand along the bulge pressed against his pants. Then she found the button and undid it. He squirmed and pulled away. "Are you sure you want to do this here? We can go back to our room where there's a bed."

She shook her head. "Here. Now. While you're not being a dick."

Micha chuckled. "I may end up being a dick later. I'll have to take another shower."

"Fine by me. I can wash your back."

"Tell me what you want to do to me?"

Jasmine rubbed his cock a little. "I want to taste you. I want to wrap my tongue around your cock and see if you like it."

He rewarded her with a smile and shimmied his pants down for her. She pulled off his shoes, socks, and then his pants. He yanked his shirt off and tossed it onto the floor. Seeing him completely naked only stirred her desire. Without waiting, she wrapped her mouth around his cock and ran her tongue the length of it. He tasted like musk and a little bit of salt.

"Jasmine, for the love of --"

She looked up at him as her mouth slid up and down his cock with her tongue twirling around the soft and sensitive head. She trailed her teeth up his length. Micha shivered in pleasure. Her other hand slid down and rubbed his balls until he groaned. He threaded his fingers in her hair and tugged to get her attention. Jasmine pulled away from his dick and glanced up.

"Did I hurt you?" she asked.

"No. I just want to fuck you now," Micha demanded.

Jasmine laughed and stood up so she could undress. She watched Micha's eyes on her as she took off each piece of clothing. He nearly drooled. It made her feel all the more desirable. She undid her bra until her breasts were free. Kneeling, she kissed him lightly along the ridge of his shoulder, nipping as she went along. He shivered at her light touch. She raked her nails down his abdomen and felt him jump.

"Stop teasing me."

"Why? You put me through hell. It's fair I get a little revenge." She bit the tip of his ear.

Micha grabbed one of her arms and pulled her down on top of him. He kissed her hard and used his other to grab her ass. "I'm not in for revenge. I will do what I want with you."

Jasmine broke his hold. "You don't control me." She stepped back, not sure what had gotten into him. Everything had been going well.

Micha picked her up and settled her on the floor, using his knee to separate her legs as he leaned in close. "Forgive me, Jasmine." He kissed the side of her cheek. "We're both still learning one another and have each been through a lot." He kissed down her neck, along her stomach, until he came to her clit. His tongue caressed the small bud and Jasmine let out a long moan.

Her muscles clenched. She was brought to the edge with the slow and determined strokes of his tongue. Jasmine felt his tongue work her lower depths as he laved her in long strokes. Her fists balled into the clothes under her as her back arched. Moans escaped her lips as she lost herself to his manipulations. Her eyes closed as she tried to stay focused and she didn't completely abandon herself to Micha. With each flick of his tongue, ecstasy overrode her brain. Her muscles tensed, bringing her closer to coming.

Micha stopped and flashed her a devilish smile. Jasmine groaned as he left her hanging. "Get over here." She kissed him, tasting herself on his lips. She placed one finger under his chin and beckoned him back up to her. He didn't need any more encouragement. His fingers touched the swell of her breast, and then he brought his mouth down to the hard and sensitive nipple. Jasmine grabbed onto Micha's shoulder, drawing a sharp breath in through her teeth. She draped her leg over his as her free hand reached down and cupped his balls, squeezing them lightly.

"Ahh, God, Jasmine. I want you so bad," he whispered. His tongue flicked over her other nipple while her hand ran the length of his shaft. Micha stopped the torture on her breasts and licked his way up to the hollow at the base of her throat. Jasmine didn't say anything as he guided her hand away from his cock and slid into her depths.

"Yes."

Micha pulled himself out of her slowly and then plunged back in. As he did, Jasmine closed her eyes, relaxing into their rhythm. His lips plotted a course along her jaw and then found hers in another kiss. His fingers entwined with hers and they began to dance. Their tempo increased and her back was coming off the floor at each thrust as he entered into her moist depths, rubbing against her clit and making her moan in ecstasy. She was so close to coming. So was Micha. His whole body was rigid. He was on the brink, but he was holding back.

"I want you. Oh, please. Do it now," Jasmine moaned into his ear.

Micha closed his eyes, drove into her, and finally, miraculously, let go. It felt like stars had detonated in her mind. She buried her head against his chest and screamed. Micha held her in his arms as his lips trailed over the top of her shoulder. Her body still quivered from their lovemaking.

"What happens now?" she whispered. "Dorothy will come for the book, won't she?"

Micha nibbled a spot behind her ear, which made her squirm and sent shivers through her. "Yes, she'll come. I don't know when. We do what I've always done. Keep the book away from her no matter what."

Chapter Seven

"Can I ask you something?" Micha kissed her shoulder.

Back in their bedroom, Jasmine sighed, feeling the satisfaction of having no more tension between them. They seemed to have worked it out the night before in the deserted room they'd ended up in. His hands slid over her sides as he kissed her neck and cupped her breasts. "If you start this, then we're not getting out of bed. I thought you said Glen-da wanted to talk to you about a few things."

After their tryst the night before, they'd ended up back in their bedroom for another bout of lovemaking. Jasmine woke up after the best night's sleep she'd ever had. It felt as though she had awakened with a new outlook on life, and she could understand her part in the new story.

"Hmm… I might be okay with that, but a little later. I need to ask you something important."

She turned to him and saw the earnest expression. "You're not going to ask me to marry you, are you?"

Micha's expression paled. "I-I… what… no!"

"I'm kidding. What did you want to ask me?"

"You said last night you had the same attraction to me as you did to Leon. Is that true?"

Jasmine bit her lip. She had brought it up and couldn't deny it. When she was put in the room with Leon, something sparked the same way it had when she and Micha touched at times. "Yes. I can't tell you why. Does it bother you?"

He trailed his finger over the back of her hand. Jasmine shivered from the sudden pulse of energy that passed between them. "No. It doesn't bother me. I actually have a confession to make about Leon. We had a relationship before I left. He stayed behind. My feelings for him haven't changed."

"Are you asking my permission to continue this relationship with him?"

"I'm asking if you mind if I pick back up where I left off. I still love him. Seeing him reminded me how much I missed him. However, I haven't figured how you fit into the mix."

Jasmine leaned back and met his lips. "I wouldn't stand between you and him."

"It doesn't bother you I might want to be with him?"

"I'm sure we can work something out."

Micha returned the kiss. "Thank you."

Jasmine wondered how the two had gotten involved in the first place, but she wasn't going to pry. There were too many other things that were more important. She felt the stirrings of an attraction to Leon, but she wasn't about to start something with him. Someone knocked on the door. She got up to answer it and found Leon outside. He glanced up at her quickly and his cheeks turned red.

"Hi Jas-smine, is Micha here?"

"Come on in, Leon," he called.

Leon stepped into the room and she couldn't help but watch his gaze dart between her and Micha as though he couldn't make up his mind which of them to address. However, she could feel the pull between her and him and Micha and Leon. She pushed it aside and grabbed her clothes and got dressed. She noticed the bag sitting in the chair with the book. It would eventually draw Dorothy's goons back to it. Whatever Micha's role was, she was now in the mix. Jasmine tried to recall what it was like being in her world, but it all seemed like some fever dream.

"Glen-da wanted you in the throne room. He's seen something in his looking glass. You'd better come as quick as you can." Leon looked at Micha with a longing that hit Jasmine's heart.

"I'm going to look for Glen. You guys need some space." Jasmine retrieved her knapsack as an afterthought. Her stomach growled as she headed out of the room. Once she crossed the threshold, a sting hit the middle of her chest. In a blink she found herself in the throne room with Glen-da bent over, peering into a large, flat mirror. The glass floated three feet in the air. It was long enough to be coffee table. Glen-da glanced up and his dire expression told her all she needed to know.

"They're coming for the book, aren't they?" Jasmine peeked into the glass but saw a blank surface.

"Yes."

"How long do we have?"

"I'm not sure. Where are the other two?"

"I gave them some time together. It seemed like they needed it."

"They do need a little bit of time to catch up. Does it bother you?" Glen-da waved his hand over the glass and flicked his curls out of his face. "They've been separated for a long time."

"It should bother me, but somehow it doesn't. I'm still getting used to all this." Jasmine peered at the looking glass. "Can you see the future in this thing?"

"No, it allows me to see all over Oz and other places, too. It's how I knew Micha was coming. I got a rush of energy when the book showed back up. I checked in with my glass. I've always kept a lookout for her. Sometimes it lets me see into the other realms where the book goes."

She nodded. It all sounded understandable. A bit of fear bloomed in her gut at the thought of the goons coming to get them. After they blew up the car, she wanted to make sure they were safe and she didn't know what Micha had planned. "Guess it comes in handy. How did you end up being a witch -- or is it a warlock?"

Glen-da flashed her a large smile and flicked his hair behind his shoulder. His bracelets jangled as he did. "It's witch, and you'll have to wait for my origin story another time. Your men are here."

Her body went cold at the comment. "They're not *my* men!"

Glen-da winked at her. "Nice of you to join us, gentlemen. Micha, take a look into the looking glass."

Micha adjusted the bag around his shoulder, and he gazed into the mirror. He clenched his fists. Before he could say anything, a great boom shook the room. A crack formed in the ceiling, raining plaster down around them. The floor rolled before it split into several different cracks. Jasmine caught herself on the arm of the throne before another ripple rocked the floor. "Was that an earthquake?"

Glen-da's face paled. "Worse. They're here. They looked farther away in the looking glass. I can only defend the city for so long now she's come for you. My magic's dwindling. I keep up what I can of the Emerald City. Dorothy keeps sucking it all up. I can't protect you and the city."

Micha nodded. "I understand. Thank you for putting us up for as long as you have." He pulled out the book and looked at Jasmine. "If she gets the book, then no realm will be safe. If you come along, it's a crapshoot on what story we'll end up in. I want you to come with me. I won't deny it. This time, I'm not going to push you into the pages. You have to make the choice."

Her throat went dry. Her stomach flipped at the thought of where they could end up. Micha told it straight so she would know the consequences this time. Even if she decided to stay with Glen-da, would the book find a way for her to reunite with Micha? They had formed a bond, and she wanted to figure out where it would lead. The room shook again. Another fissure opened in the roof. Glen-da waved his hand. The looking glass flipped on end, positioned higher in the air so they could all see the events outside. A broom hovered in the sky with someone sitting on it. Jasmine couldn't make out any features, just the person dressed all in black with a pointed hat.

"Is that the Wicked Witch of the East? I thought Dorothy smooshed her with the house?" Several other black shapes flew around the woman. A bolt of crimson energy shot from the figure on the broom. Leon tackled her as the bolt landed where she had been standing, leaving a charred piece of marble. He stood and helped her up. "Thanks, Leon."

"It's no problem." He blushed.

"It's a big deal. You saved me." Jasmine kissed him on the cheek. His neck got as red as the bolt of energy that came at them.

"Guys, it's now or never. I can't hold up the shields much longer," Glen-da warned them. His face beaded with perspiration, leaving trails of blue eyeliner along his cheeks. He clenched his fists together. The roof was blackened in some places. Some parts had collapsed from relentless battering. The thinness of the shield around the palace shimmered in places as though the wind blew on the protective bubble. Jasmine didn't want to be the cause of the whole place coming down.

"No. I'm coming with you," she told Micha.

The book lay on the floor. Golden energy grew brighter each time the pages flipped back and forth until they settled. The picture it landed on showed a dark landscape with a foreboding fortress in the background. A chill swept through the room. Jasmine didn't like the looks of where they were going.

"Any chance you can pick another place?" she asked.

"Doesn't work that way. Come on." Micha held out his hand to her.

Before she could take it, Leon stepped forward. "I'm going, too."

"You sure, old friend? I suspect wherever we're going your roar won't do anything against what we find there," Micha said to him.

"Don't think it matters. You know how she is. The book has a reason for the places she chooses. See." Leon pointed to the volume. The picture changed and showed three figures heading up to the castle door.

"Looks like she took the reins and decided to write the scene the way she wanted," Glen-da commented. "Go on. I got this for now."

"Thank you." Jasmine took Micha's hand. She offered the other to Leon. The bashful man took it. Once they were all connected, something zinged through her. She glanced at both their clasped hands and saw the faint illumination of the green energy fading along her skin. Then her stomach dropped. It felt as though she were becoming transparent. A whoosh of air took hold of her and then she fell.

For now, they were safe, and a new adventure awaited.

Bitten for Love (The Accidental Fairy Tale 2)
A Women's Urban Fantasy Romance
Crymsyn Hart

Jasmine thought falling into a magic book and landing in Oz with the Scarecrow, Micha, and Leon the Cowardly Lion was odd. However, getting sent to Dracula's castle where she finds herself and her two men falling prey to the undead counts even stranger. There they discover an unlikely ally who will help them save Micha from Dracula's clutches.

Even as they venture deeper into the count's castle, her feelings for both Leon and Micha deepen. Magic is growing within her thanks to the strange book which tells their story. Even with saving Micha's very soul, the one most important thing they have to remember is keeping the book away from the evil Dorothy at all cost.

Chapter One

Jasmine landed on top of both Micha and Leon, a much softer arrival than she had when she entered Oz. The plant monster remained in Munchkinville. She and Micha had gotten away after he pushed her through his magic book. She rolled off the men quickly and double-checked to make sure everything worked. Micha wiped the grime from his jeans and shoved the book back into the bag slung across his shoulder. It was his most precious possession and the reason they were on the run. They couldn't let the tome fall into the wrong hands.

Jasmine went over to him, but tripped and planted her hands directly onto Leon's chest. A zing went through her when she touched Leon. She blushed and caught the slight flash of green energy connecting them. Leon gave her a small smile as he stepped away. The bags Micha had conjured for her and for himself landed next to them. She put her pack on her back and handed Micha's knapsack to him.

"Thanks. How did these get here? I left them in the room," Micha asked.

"Your guess is as good as mine. You're the one with the magic book that has a mind of its own and a wand," Jasmine replied. She plucked a few small pieces of dirt from her shirt.

"It's not a wand. It's a pen," Micha commented through gritted teeth.

She held up her hands in surrender. "Sorry. You wave the pen around and light comes out of the end. My mistake if I thought it was a wand." Jasmine tried to joke away her fear of where they had landed. "Has your *pen* recharged yet so you can write us out of danger?"

"Afraid I won't be able to handle what's coming next?" Micha snapped.

She sighed. "No. That's not what I meant. Good grief. Somewhere in all this, things have gotten all tangled up. I want to know if you're okay." Jasmine touched his shoulder. The image of him being lifeless and barely breathing hung in her mind. Micha was her way home, back to the real world, and if he died Jasmine would be stuck in Oz. "You were whiter than a sheet the other night. Now you're jumping through magic books once more. I wanted to be sure you were okay. Using your magic pen won't drain the life out of you again, will it?"

Micha's firm expression faltered, and his lips turned up into a smile. The same one she first saw when he asked her if she was okay after they took shelter in Dorothy's house -- the one she'd dropped on the Wicked Witch of the East. He touched her hand and brushed his lips across hers. Her insides lit up and her stomach flip-flopped when she thought how she felt about him. "I'll be okay. Everything's changed in Oz. I had to channel my energy into the pen to get us to Glen-da's. I used the last of what I had to heal your knee. I didn't thank you for saving me, did I?"

"No, but how about saying we're even? You saved me. I saved you. You finally figured out I'm not going to steal the book from you."

"You still need to get home. You might decide to take it from me while I'm not looking."

Jasmine crossed her arms over her chest and rolled her eyes. "After what's happened between us, do you really think I'd leave you high and dry?"

Micha ran his hand over the bag containing the book. "I've seen stranger things happen. She might have woven you into our story, but you're a wild card no matter what's happened between us."

"I thought we'd be over this, or you'd be over the idea I'm going to screw you after our con --"

"Uh… guys… can you fight later?" Leon asked.

"We're not fighting," they both replied. Jasmine glanced at Micha and laughed. The whole conversation sounded ridiculous.

"Micha, I'm not going to run away with the book. I promise. I want to know what she's doing to me and what role I play with you two." Jasmine poked him and tried to feel more confident in what she said. Truthfully, the idea scared her to death to think she played any kind of role in the messed-up story she found herself in, getting thrown into a magic book Micha was trying to keep away from Dorothy Gale from Kansas. All Jasmine knew was that Micha and Leon had been friends. Somehow, Dorothy took the place of the witch she killed. After Dorothy found Jasmine and Micha in Oz, they had to flee from the Emerald City. Micha used the book for her and Leon to escape to the new world they arrived in.

Where is here? Jasmine wondered. The air felt gritty along her skin. She caught the undertone of death on the breeze and the smell turned her stomach. Deep down, she was scared. Night surrounded them. Being stranded in another strange reality, where the rules were probably different from those in the universe she left, made it all the weirder. The worst was their journey was being handled by a book that had a mind of its own.

"We need to get going unless you want to be in the middle of that." Leon pointed to a dark cloud in the distance coming straight for them. The slight bit of fright in his voice made her look to where he pointed.

A massive black swarm barreled toward them.

Their flapping wings sounded like a thousand pigeons taking off. As the swarm got closer, Jasmine could see what Leon had warned them about. Bats the size of vultures formed into a cloud about to engulf them. Behind them, Jasmine saw the sky lightening. Leon bolted up the hill toward the castle they had seen in the book before they jumped through it back in Oz. It might have been looming and creepy, but the fortress was the only shelter they had. Jasmine didn't need another warning. She went after him. They got up to the entrance with Micha right behind. Jasmine leaned against the stone doorway and tried to catch her breath. The stitch in her side gave her another reminder that she had to get off her ass instead of sitting in a chair all day dealing with her clients' insurance woes.

"You think they're going to let us in?" Leon asked.

Jasmine shrugged. "You got me. Let's hope so we don't get eaten alive."

The doors stood ten feet tall. Monstrous knockers with thick iron rings in their mouths glared at them. The knockers reminded her of a cross between a wolf and a gargoyle. The form they took changed when she viewed them from different angles. She covered her ears as the noise of the wings grew louder. Micha motioned to the knockers. Jasmine nodded, understanding they needed to get inside. He tried to lift one. It slipped from his fingers. Leon rushed to help him. Together, they hefted the knocker up and let it fall to hit the aged iron plate underneath. The cloud of bats swarmed around them. Jasmine pulled her shirt up around her nose and mouth and did what she could to keep her ears covered. Their wings brushed against her arm as they took a sharp turn upward. The attack never came but being encompassed by the mass gave her the heebie-jeebies. Once the colony vanished, Jasmine removed her hands from her ears and pulled down her shirt. The men raised the ring to knock once more. It landed heavily on the metal plate, sounding like thunder. The door opened.

Jasmine waited to hear eerie organ music playing somewhere in the castle. *We're walking into Dracula's castle. Or maybe Frankenstein has his monster chained in the dungeon ready to cause havoc at a moment's notice.* A shudder ran down her back. As Micha went ahead of her, she couldn't help but let her gaze fall to how his ass looked in his jeans. He might have been a jerk to her when they first met, but they'd worked out their relationship. The attraction she had for him flared. It took everything in her not to reach out and touch him. Besides, the energy literally sparked when they touched one another. She found herself falling for Micha. Desire turning toward…

Leon chuckled and shook his head.

"What?" Leon pulled her away from her lustful thoughts as her cheeks burned. She took a look at him. Long, shaggy brown hair framed his face and fell down his back. Big brown eyes gazed at her with amusement. Her body responded to his, the way it did with Micha.

"You look at him how I look at him, with longing. Hoping to see the same gaze within his green eyes. I'm not really a fan of those blue ones he has in this guise. I do enjoy the flesh instead of the burlap-and-cloth version of him. Yet I love him. I never stopped even though he was a world away. Then Micha returned with you. And I can't keep my eyes off you." He took her hand, and green energy passed between them. Jasmine trembled from the sudden shock. The jolt left her as breathless as when she touched Micha. Leon kissed the back of her hand.

"What do you expect to happen between us?" Jasmine asked.

"If this is true, and you are what I think you are, then --" He trailed his finger along her cheek. His touch calmed her fear a little bit. "-- I hope you'll let me make love to you. Hope you feel something for me the way things are developing between you and Micha."

"Are you two coming or are you going to keep whispering to one another?" Micha stuck his head back out from inside the castle.

"Coming," Leon responded, and they went in.

Once all three were inside, the door slammed shut. Jasmine jumped. Leon edged closer to her and she edged closer to Micha, taking relief from his presence. She expected to find a run-down interior or maybe the home of a giant. Instead, a candlelit chandelier hung above them. Sconces with large candles illuminated the room, dispelling any shadows. It seemed warm and inviting. Exotic and ordinary dishes of food were spread out on a long table next to an enormous fireplace, big enough for someone to stand in. Jasmine didn't have a good feeling about the whole thing. Leon started to go over to the table, but Micha grabbed his arm.

"Not a good idea. We don't know what story we're in. The food could be poisoned or an illusion. Best to stick together."

"Do you know where we are?" Jasmine asked.

"Somewhere we shouldn't be." Micha dug out the book and tried to open it, but the tome wasn't budging.

"What's wrong with her?" Leon looked over Jasmine's shoulder, hugging her body like a terrified puppy. Having him this close, she could smell the musk of his skin.

Micha tried again, swore under his breath, and shoved the book back in the sack. "Your guess is as good as mine. She can be a bitch, as you've found out."

"Welcome, weary travelers." The smooth voice came from above them.

A fire burst to life in the massive hearth. Flames touched the underside of the mantle, adding to the black scorch marks on the stone. Leon wrapped his arms around her waist and held on. His nose pressed against her hair and she heard him inhale. Jasmine peered back at him and caught the frightened look in his eyes.

"Excuse us for bursting into your home." Jasmine looked up to see if she could see who was speaking. However, the master of the castle remained in the shadows. Micha shot her a glance, but she took a step away from the two men, so she was in front of them. "We have traveled far and our… carriage broke a wheel. Your castle was the only habitable place we could find."

"It's no problem at all. I rarely have visitors. You're welcome to rest the day. Forgive me, but I was about to retire for the day. Tonight, we shall dine together. Follow me and I can show you to a room."

"Jasmine, what are you doing?" Micha asked. "We don't know where we are or who this is. We have to be careful."

She smiled, turned back to him, and kept her voice low. "I realize that, *Micha*, but we need a place to sleep and get some time to catch up on this new… story. Maybe you can even coax your book to open."

"She has a point, Micha. We need a safe place even if it is for just a few hours," Leon replied. A flush of heat warmed her from Leon's praise.

"You are all secure here. The rooms are not far," the owner of the house called to them.

Jasmine caught the irritability in his voice. "Thank you. We've had a long night walking and traveling. It's so kind of you to let us stay."

She went up the stairs and Micha and Leon followed her. Their host stayed in the shadows as they walked down the hall. Jasmine tried to ignore all the cobwebs. She tried to see who provided them lodgings. He might be a mad scientist, or even better, an old man who might be hunched over and leading them to their doom. They stopped in the hallway as two doors opened on either side of them. "Forgive me, but I only have two rooms available for you to sleep in. If you'll excuse me, I must retire for the day. You can tell me of your travels when we dine later tonight."

Jasmine looked to where their host had been, but his form no longer filled the shadows. At the end of the hall, sunlight streamed in, showing off all the dust particles floating in the air. "Do you think we're okay to stay here?" Jasmine edged closer to Micha.

"Let's go into this room." Micha pointed to the room on the right. "I don't think it's a good idea for us to be separated."

Leon closed the door. "With all the food downstairs, it almost seemed like he expected some company."

Micha sighed and sat down on the large bed. Another cloud of dust blossomed into the air. Jasmine coughed and tried to blow it away. "I don't know, Leon," said Micha. He tried to open the book again, but it remained closed. "Stupid bitch. Why don't you open up and show us what story you've dropped us into?"

The book answered by sending a surge of green energy along Micha's hand until he pulled it away and sucked on his fingers before waving the pain off. Jasmine bit her lip to keep from laughing. He shot her a look and shoved the book at her. "Why don't you give it a try and see if she wants to impart some of her wisdom to you? She seems to like you more lately."

Jasmine took the book and stroked the velveteen cover as green energy crackled along her hands. The volume trembled. Jasmine didn't understand why Micha and Leon referred to it as a she. For some reason, the book thought she was important. As the emerald energy inched along Jasmine's arm, it sank deeper into her skin. It left a green-gold residue on her nails.

"Are you going to be nice and open up? We really need to know what's going on. Want to give us a clue?" Jasmine caressed the spine. It took a moment, but it opened.

"Wow. I've never seen her open for anyone else," Leon commented. "Does it mean what I think it means?"

Jasmine glanced at Micha and saw his mouth pressed into a grim line and his forehead creased. "We don't know for sure yet," said Micha.

"Really? She's pulled to both of us. It has to be only one thing," Leon responded. "Don't you want to believe it?"

"Ahh, guys, what are you talking about? I'm right here."

"It's nothing," Micha replied.

"It has to be something. Come on, Micha. Don't shut me out now. I thought we were past you being an ass." Jasmine glanced at Micha hoping he would give her a straight answer.

"Jasmine, now isn't the time to get into it. We need to be sure we're safe here. Can you please see what her pages say?" Micha asked, trying to change the subject.

Jasmine didn't like being kept in the dark. She had a feeling the topic went with why she was attracted to both men. Not that she minded. She was getting used to the strangeness of being with them and who they were -- the Scarecrow and the Cowardly Lion. What blew her mind was how much she had to fight the craving to touch Micha. The sex they'd had together made her all hot and bothered as she thought about it. And the idea of what it would be like with Leon as well inched into her mind.

Warmth flowed deeper along her arm until it reached her shoulder to calm her nerves. Whatever magic the book imparted her, this time it felt as though the energy lay almost within her ability to call upon. Of course, she had no idea how.

"Jasmine?" Leon touched her other hand.

She jumped and realized he sat on the other side of her. The energy raced between them. Jasmine pulled in a breath and looked up into his honey-colored eyes. She leaned in and brushed her lips across his. Leon swiped his tongue along her mouth. He caressed her cheek and pulled away.

"We can't do this now. We need to focus on the book," he whispered.

Jasmine shook herself from the pull between them. *Leon's right. We have to concentrate on what the book wants and not on my infatuations.* Lust was one thing, but it was more important to see where they were. Micha slid his hand along her thigh. She looked over at him and saw the hunger she felt reflected in his eyes.

"Right. The book." Jasmine cleared her throat.

She took in another breath and calmed her raging emotions. "Do you mind giving us a little slice of what we're doing here?"

The hardcover's pages rustled in her hands. They flipped back and forth until the book settled on a blank page near the middle of the volume. Micha let out a frustrated sigh. Cursive writing looped on the empty sheet, forming into words. Jasmine read aloud what the book had to say to them.

"Greetings, fellow characters. You're wondering why I've brought you here. Your questions will have to wait as other events have to fall into place first. You're safe for the day. The story won't change until later. The mighty lion can go exploring as he wishes to satisfy a hunch about the world he's in. He also wishes to separate himself from the one he loves and the potential of who the ordinary girl is. The ordinary girl has more questions than answers at the moment, but soon her curiosity will be satisfied. The most important thing to do is spend some much needed time with your Prince Charming."

"This isn't some fucking fairy tale," Micha growled.

The letters on the page began to fade.

"Wait, can't you give us some more information? I'm sure Micha's sorry for what he said. Aren't you?" Jasmine glanced over at Micha.

"Yes, dearest, you know I love you. I'm only frustrated at the turn in the tale. Can't you give us a clue?" Micha trailed his finger along the edge of the book.

The tome quivered in Jasmine's hand as though it giggled, and Jasmine read out loud, "My prince, your apology is accepted. To some this is a fairy tale. It depends on who's reading it. The knowledge you need will come. Enjoy the day with your ordinary girl because she is special -- else why would I be talking to her?" The book slammed shut.

"She's not going to say anything else until she wants to let us know more." Leon got off the bed and walked toward the door.

"Are you really going to explore?" Micha asked. "You don't know what you're going to find. There could be traps. There --"

Leon kissed Micha quickly. Jasmine watched the scene and had to admit she was somewhat turned on. "She said we're safe for now, and I need to see if I'm right about this place. Spend some time with Jasmine while you can. I know you want to. We can get reacquainted later."

"Fine. Be careful," Micha acquiesced.

"I'll be in the room across the hall after I do a little investigating. Don't worry, I won't touch the food." Leon left the room.

Jasmine turned to Micha. "Are you sure we're going to be okay?"

He slid his hand along her cheek. "She says we will be, and I've never doubted her. Leon's right. I do want to spend some time with you." He kissed her lightly. "You're a lot stronger than I gave you credit for. You're taking all this in stride. Even when I turn into a jerk."

She smiled and turned her head into his palm. The soft caress of his skin along hers made her wonder how he ever became flesh and bone instead of stuffing and cloth. One day she figured he would tell her his story. "You…" She searched for the right words to describe how she felt about him. It was more than an attraction now. "You're more than what L. Frank Baum wrote about in his series of books. You saved my life.

You're special in your own way, and I -- I think I'm falling in love with you despite you being a dick sometimes. Guess you're growing on me."

"I think you're growing on me, too." His fingers trailed along her arm and kicked her excitement into high gear.

Micha mashed his lips against hers. Jasmine sucked on his bottom lip as his hands worked on the zipper of her jeans. He plunged his tongue into her mouth and cupped her breasts. She tugged at his shirt, but Micha stopped and pulled it off, giving her a glimpse of his magnificent chest. He had a rockin' body she could ride all day. Jasmine ran her hands over his chest, feeling how fine it truly was. Again, she found it tough to believe he'd started off as a bag of cloth strung up on a pole to scare away crows.

A moan broke from her lips when he sucked on her throat, sending small bolts of pleasure shooting through her. The tingles started in her center because she was so wet for him. She needed to have his cock inside her. The growing thirst had to be quenched. Jasmine undid the button and zipper on his pants and rolled them down over his hips. The outline of his cock rested against his groin ready to be used and touched. When she trailed her fingers over his erection, all she could hear was his deep groan.

"I need you," Micha groaned.

"Good, I need you too. Fuck me," Jasmine commanded.

Micha scooped her up, spun her around, and pinned her against the bed. She wrapped her arms around his neck and her legs around his waist. He ran one hand over her panties. He tugged on them until she heard cloth tearing and then his hand cupped her pussy. His thumb found her clit as he worked it in a swift rhythm. Jasmine leaned her head back and lost herself to the quick orgasm that swept her over the edge into oblivion.

Jasmine squeezed her eyes shut and rocked with tingles alighting on all her nerves. The cries she tried to suppress tumbled from her lips. She tightened her grip around his neck and moved her hips in time with the pace of his fingering. Micha buried his face in-between her breasts and licked a line from one breast to the other and sucked on her nipple. His lips circled the firm bud and sent another wave of ecstasy through her.

"Stop torturing me."

"I enjoy hearing you moan. It sounds sexy."

"Ass."

Micha chuckled before taking her other nipple into his mouth and biting it. Tiny pinpoints of light exploded in her mind's eye. The throbbing in her pussy only grew worse. Her body trembled with another orgasm, and he was not even inside her. "Now. Please." She pressed her nails into his nape until she heard him suck in a breath.

"That hurt," he muttered.

She opened her eyes and flashed him a quick smile. "I wouldn't have had to do that if you'd shoved your cock in me."

"Like this?"

He thrust inside her and she was complete. Having Micha plunging into her, hitting her G-spot each time, was like Christmas and her birthday all wrapped into one. Jasmine hugged her legs around his ass to keep up with his frenzied pace. Each time he drove into her, lights flashed in her mind, and it seemed she would crack into tiny pieces.

"Fuck, you feel so good," he cried out and buried his face between her breasts once more. He licked a trail over to her other breast and dove into her one last time before a deep growl erupted from within his chest. It reached the primal side of her. Jasmine succumbed to the bliss.

Her head fell backward. When Micha kissed her neck, she dissolved back into the reverie.

"Don't think we're done yet," he whispered to her.

Jasmine clasped his face between her hands and kissed him again. He trailed his hands along the curve of her spine. She pinched one of his nipples and Micha squirmed. She raked her fingers over his sides and took a nipple in her mouth. He slid his fingers through her hair and held her to his chest.

Jasmine stiffened. The tension in his body rode along his skin like it was her own. After a second, she kissed a slow line across his chest and took his other nipple in her mouth. He tasted good, like rain on fresh hay. He tugged on her hair, drawing her away from his chest. Jasmine stared into his blue eyes and saw them change to green. Micha pressed his lips to hers once more. She returned the kiss with a ferocity that surprised even her. He sucked in her bottom lip. She gripped his arms, feeling the lean muscles in his arms. Jasmine pushed her breasts into his chest. Nothing else mattered more than having him inside her. Micha took his jeans all the way off. Jasmine appreciated the rest of his sculpted thighs and calves. Her mouth watered. *Come to momma.* He flashed her a lopsided smile and knelt before the bed. He planted his lips on top of her foot and flicked his tongue along the line of her ankle. From there, he kissed up her calf, moving along her skin, to the bend of her knee, where Micha bit lightly.

Jasmine jerked her leg away. "Sorry. I'm ticklish."

"I'll remember where for later."

"Later? If you keep being an ass, there won't be a later."

Micha kissed the top of her thigh and inched his tongue a little closer to her downy patch of curls.

"Maybe."

Jasmine took his hand. She ran his index finger along her lips before drawing it into her mouth. She wrapped her tongue around it and sucked. Her gaze never left those baby blues as he tried to keep a stoic expression. Micha took her hand and held it to his dick. Jasmine cupped his balls with her other hand. He squirmed when she squeezed them gently. She slowly worked her fingers along his cock. She saw the muscles flutter in his abdomen. She released him and walked her fingers over his stomach. Now it was his turn to pull away.

"I want you, Jasmine."

She kissed him again, this time slower, and brushed her fingers along the line of his throat. Jasmine glided them across his collarbone and settled on his chest. She slipped one hand lower and clutched his cock again. She moved her free hand over her breasts and fondled her nipple. Micha licked his lips. He lowered his mouth to her right nipple while his other hand slid down Jasmine's belly. When he slipped his fingers along her folds, Jasmine was already wet for him. Micha discovered her clit and rubbed. She tried to hold back the moans erupting from her lips, but it was nearly impossible. The pressure of his thumb going in circles drove her toward orgasm. It wasn't going to take much to get her there. Her hips rocked forward.

She gripped his cock and pumped it in time with how fast he fondled her. "Oh shit, Micha."

He drew in a ragged breath, and then withdrew

from Jasmine. She groaned her disapproval. "You didn't have to stop."

He didn't answer, but flicked his tongue lower until he parted her legs and found her slick pussy. Micha plunged his tongue into her wet depths. She gripped the blanket and went along for the ride. He dug his fingers into her hips and doubled the speed at which he pleasured her. Jasmine pressed her nails into his head and pushed her hips into his face. "I need you."

He thrust his tongue into her one last time and returned to her lips. Jasmine kissed him back hard and straddled him. All she wanted was to have him between her thighs. She locked her knees around his hips and guided his cock inside her.

She ran her fingers over his arms, feeling his strong muscles. Jasmine held on while he intensified his pace. Each time he drove inside her, she wanted to crawl out of her skin. The energy between them was building. Micha cupped her breasts before feathering his hands over her lower back to cup her ass while she rode him. Her pulse thrummed under her flesh. He drove into her one more time and captured her lips.

Jasmine rose up and cried out. Her muscles clenched around his dick for a final time, and their screams echoed in the bedroom. Jasmine held him to her for a few seconds. So close she could feel the echo of his heart. It was a soothing feeling she wanted to keep. It lasted a moment before they both collapsed on the bed. She closed her eyes, bathing in the aftermath of her rapture.

Chapter Two

Jasmine stirred and opened her eyes. Micha sat back against the headboard. He had the book in his lap. He stroked her hair and had a strange look on his face. "Everything okay?" she asked.

"Yeah, I hope I didn't wake you. You've been out most of the day."

She sat up and yawned. "No. I guess I needed the rest."

"Traveling between realms can be tiring when you're not used to it. I was watching you sleep."

"I snore sometimes and --"

Micha kissed her to make her stop. "You were beautiful."

Her cheeks seared at his compliment. "I'm sure. You were amazing."

"You don't need to butter me up."

She shrugged. "It's true. She open up again?"

"No. I was waiting for Leon to come back, but he hasn't." Micha glanced out the window. Jasmine glanced over as well and saw the darkness of twilight settling over the castle. Micha frowned. "We should get dressed and head back downstairs and hope he's there. The castle owner will want to talk to us."

Jasmine groaned and got out of the dusty bed. She glanced at her clothes scattered around the floor and didn't think she could wear them again. The backpack she came with lay on the floor. She picked it up and opened the bag. Inside she pulled out another full set of clothes. "I don't understand how magic works or how your magic pen works, but I'm grateful you conjured up these packs."

"They've come in handy. Writing them to give us anything we needed was a useful tool. Magic is unpredictable at times. Like with these bags. They were supposed to only provide food." Micha also got up and pulled another outfit out of his bag. He gathered his other garments and stuffed them into the back. Jasmine did the same.

Leon knocked on the door before he opened it. "You guys ready to go downstairs?"

"Did you find what you were looking for?" Jasmine asked.

"I think so. I'll know for sure when the sun sets completely." Leon brushed his fingers along Jasmine's cheek. "Did you get the rest you needed?"

"Some. Did you get any sleep?" She secured her backpack.

"I had a cat nap." Leon chuckled.

Micha took Leon's hand, gave it a squeeze before he kissed him, and walked out the door. Leon glanced at Jasmine. "You still sure you're okay with me and Micha?"

Jasmine touched his tanned cheek. The green energy raced along her arm and warmed her insides. She trembled and held in a moan as the pleasure consumed her. The idea of Micha and Leon together didn't bother her. They had been in a relationship before they met her. Somehow, she was being drawn into something that already existed. "So far, so good."

Jasmine took a moment to gather her thoughts, and then she went after Micha. When they got downstairs, another layout of food welcomed them. A fire burned in the large hearth. Flames reflected off the polished marble of the fireplace. The aroma of the feast on the ten-foot table made her stomach rumble. She recalled what Micha said the night before. The food could be poisoned, and they didn't know who their host was. Eight place settings, all of silver, waited for someone to sit and partake. There were elegantly carved mahogany chairs, a tapestry of a hunting scene on the wall to their left showing men on horses chasing a dragon, and above the fireplace was a shield showing a coat of arms with a silver dragon. The opulence of the downstairs didn't match the dinginess of the upstairs rooms they'd stayed in.

"Ahh… my travel-worn group. I hope my hospitality for the day fared you well. Why don't we all sit together and dine?" their host's voice purred next to Micha.

Jasmine jumped as a hand slithered across the back of her shoulders. She glanced behind her and thought it might be Leon, but he stood next to Micha. "Yes, thank you for letting us stay."

"You're most welcome. We haven't had visitors in ages. Forgive the mess," the owner of the castle said to them.

The hair raised on her nape as fingers slid across her neck. She peeked behind her once more. Nothing. She shivered when nails trailed along her cheek. "It seems like you've gone all out for us. Thank you."

"Yes, thank you. We'd love to thank our host in person for your generous hospitality." Micha touched the bag slung over his shoulder. He took the job of protecting the book seriously.

Leon stepped closer to her, but she felt someone standing next to her. A fourth person hadn't materialized. Something stirred her hair. *It's gotta be the wind.*

"Are you sure? I could be right in front of you, making sure you can't see me. You have an interesting mind. I can't see all parts of it. I tried sampling your thoughts before I retreated to my resting place last night. Don't worry, my dear. Many pleasures await you and your

beaus here. I dipped into their thoughts and found them tasty." The voice glided through her head, trying to burrow further into her brain.

A soft velvet touch skated around her body until she trembled. Heat lit up her insides as the tendril in her mind hit the pleasure spot of her brain. Sweat broke out on her forehead. She bit her lip to keep in the moan and pushed against the fog threatening to take over her mind. Jasmine squeezed her eyes shut and touched her temples. Warmth rushed through her and dark green flashed against the background of her eyes. A shriek deafened her as it hit her mind. She shook her head as the emerald cleared from her vision and the heat disappeared. The room came back into focus. The unseen presence retreated from her mind.

"We should go." They needed to get out of the castle. Their host had made it clear they were on the menu. She would rather take her chances with the enormous bats that had chased them the night before. She looked for Micha, but he and Leon had vanished. Jasmine turned around and took in the whole room. The only footprints in the layer of dust were theirs going up the stairs and coming down. *What the hell? Where did they go? Did they have the same experience with hearing the voice in their minds? It sounded like our host, but how? What did he mean he sampled my thoughts? And then somehow I drove him out?*

The lavish table no longer held the opulent feast. A thick layer of dust encased the wooden surface. A chill peppered the air because the fireplace overflowed with dried leaves. The hearth hadn't seen a fire in it for long time. The thunder of the bat wings echoed down the chimney. Time had eaten away the magnificence of the tapestry, showing off the moth holes unraveling the weave. Stuffing hung out of the chair cushions where some creature had made its home. The shield barely hung on the wall, the metal rusted and the coat of arms faded. Jasmine rubbed her arms against the cold of the abandoned room. The weight of her backpack shifted which reminded her it remained on her back. Something slammed behind her and made her nearly jump out of her skin. *I fucking hate this place.* She thought it was the door, but when she looked back, the book lay at her feet.

Jasmine picked up the tome. Emerald energy raced up her arms and stretched to her chest. It stung like she'd been bitten by a few hundred fire ants. *Why do you want me involved in all this? Where do I fit into this story?* She turned it over in her hands and sighed. *You wouldn't come to me unless I'm your last resort. What happened to the others?* The cover beat against her chest. Jasmine held it so the book flipped itself open to a page with a picture of the castle on it. Script looped itself onto the blank page next to the image as the book wrote its own story. *Maybe it doesn't really matter whose tale it is. It's the road fate planted us on, and the book is giving little spoilers.*

Jasmine sank down on the stairs while the letters brightened. She took in a breath and read aloud…

"As the ordinary girl wondered where her prince and his cowardly sidekick were, fear and uncertainty ran rampant within her. Where were they? Who was the mysterious man or woman who entered her mind and read her thoughts, making her feel as though the pleasures of the world were focused on her? The girl realized their host distracted her to steal the men away. They remained caught in the spell woven by the castle's owner, unable to free themselves.

"Then why was I released from it? the girl thought."

Jasmine pulled her attention from the pages and the exact thought ran through her mind. *Why was I released from it?* She turned her attention back to the text to find the answer.

"The girl wasn't from the same world as either the prince or his sidekick. Her mind worked differently. The otherworldly magic within the girl helped to keep her from the sway of the voice, along with her immunity to the influence of the master of the house." The letters on the enchanted pages glowed green as more magic from the text inched up her arms like ivy. It sank into her flesh, taking root. Jasmine didn't stop reading and tried to ignore the glow flowing under her skin, mapping her veins. "If she could have seen herself in the mirror, her eyes were the same color as the deepest emeralds used to adorn the highest towers in the Emerald City. The extra boost of magic fortified her from the master of the house's power. For the moment, her safety was guaranteed."

She flipped to the next page. The magical text might be the writer of the story, but Jasmine wasn't sure if it was all knowing. Micha hadn't said it knew a bit about the future. If she had a chance to make her own choices, she was going to take it. Or maybe fate wrote the narrative and the book was… the writing on the page caught her eye again. This time she didn't read it aloud, but to herself.

"As the ordinary girl read the enchanted pages, she discovered the book wasn't woven from the threads of fate. The book didn't play by any of the rules of the world she came from. She had to stop comparing it with the mythology she knew. As she had already learned, not all written accounts are based on truth."

Jasmine chuckled. "Touchy, aren't you? Okay, you're not an extension of fate. And you're telling me to shut up and read the story. At least now you're cooperating, unlike earlier today when Micha wanted to know where we were. Wouldn't it have been easier to play nice then?" She addressed the book, and another zap of energy rode her arm until she sneezed. Jasmine figured the book was telling her yes. More words flashed on the page. She continued to read out loud, but softly…

"'You weren't ready to explore this world and know where I brought you. Besides, you and your prince needed a bit of time to yourselves. Your cuddly sidekick needed some time to think about where he landed and what it meant for him. Keep reading if you want to know what happens. It gets juicy from here…

"'Deep within the bowels of the foreboding stronghold, something stirred from a sleep imposed by the master of the castle. Eyes opened and stared into the darkness, seeing clearly despite the blanket of shadows that shrouded the cavern he dwelled in. Even among the damp and the rats, one thing called to him. One scent, somewhat familiar, roused him more. A heavy thud filled his ears. He sensed his master busied himself with other playthings. He licked his lips and thought about sating his gnawing hunger.'"

That doesn't sound good. Jasmine turned the page.

"Once the prince heard the man's voice in his head, he knew they were in trouble. Some invisible force caught his tongue and stopped him from calling out a warning to his sidekick and the woman he traveled with. He summoned all his magic, but it couldn't break the hold this being had upon him. His thoughts went to the book and what the master would do with it if he discovered its true nature.

"A woman's hand slid across his. For a moment, it resembled the woman he traveled with. Her voice wove through his mind. An image of them wrapped in one another's arms popped into his thoughts. They'd shared their love for one another earlier. This creature tried to use the distraction to trick him. The prince tried to fight the influence.

"The prince's current view of the room wavered. The opulent setting faded. He caught the glimmer of the dusty reality. No one had been to the hall in a long time. The downstairs matched the upstairs bedroom they had slept in. He looked over once more to the ordinary girl, who wasn't so ordinary anymore. A strange man kissed her throat. He glanced up at the prince and winked before his appearance melted away and became a woman. The prince couldn't break away from her gaze no matter how much he fought. Something cold burrowed within his mind. Whatever enchantment the creature cast over him took hold, and his soul tumbled away. His last thought turned to keeping the book safe. The prince dug into the bag. The mysterious woman skimmed her hand along his and gripped his fingers.

"'*I don't think so*'", the woman purred within his thoughts. "'*You're all mine now. Silly hunters. You come into my castle seeking refuge. If it hadn't been during the day, I would've given you to my brides. Here you are with only a few stakes. Your story about your coach breaking down. I saw right through it. Did you really think you could dispatch me?*'

"The prince tried not to let his surprise show. Her laughter caressed his insides until his knees gave out. The pleasure he experienced made him wonder why he cared about the ordinary girl's safety. She was nothing compared to the woman before him. Something nagged at him about his companion. They had shared one another. He knew her flesh. She annoyed him to no end, but her personality clicked a longing inside him. The prince had no thought of ever having a relationship again, but with her -- if what he assumed to be true -- it was possible she…

"Who needs her, when you can have me? I'll fulfill every desire you have, hunter. A stake won't stop me," the woman murmured in his ear and mind.

"She released him. The prince's fingertips brushed along something wooden at the bottom of the bag. The smooth shaft ended in a point. It wasn't the book. A sense of relief flooded him. The woman had no idea who they were.

"Don't worry. I'll take care of your companions. I sampled some of your minds earlier today and they were scrumptious. You'll be the first I sink my fangs into."

"A slick, cold tongue flicked along the prince's throat. He tried to feel disgust, but her control overpowered him. Nothing mattered any longer except pleasing this… creature. His lips touched hers. Her tongue swiped across the prince's bottom lip, and he tasted the tang of bitter blood."

Jasmine sat back against the cold wall and tried to process what the book had shown her. Micha and Leon had been taken prisoner. The manuscript protected itself by coming to her and had put stakes in Micha's bag. It was keeping their identities from the owner of the castle. The master of the house thought they were hunters come to kill him. *How can Micha have forgotten he has a magic pen?* Jasmine turned her attention back to the page. The text stopped writing. She tried to turn to the next page, but the book wouldn't let her.

"Come on," she proclaimed. "You gotta give me a hint. This isn't fair. You give me some information and then leave me hanging."

The book glowed green once more, and Jasmine turned the page.

"The one who awoke in the dungeons licked his lips as he stared at the woman. The shadows concealed his presence. When he was this close to her she should have felt him breathing down her neck, if he had breath. But breath and life had left him long ago. He barely remembered what warmth felt like, what anything felt like besides the driving hunger. Her warmth would allow him to feel once more. He reached out to touch her heat and take in the rich scent of her blood. His mouth watered. His fingers brushed against the curve of her shoulder."

Jasmine felt her something touch her shoulder. She glanced behind her but saw nothing. *I'm freaking myself out.* She turned back to the text which stopped in the middle of the page.

"Don't be surprised I'm not showing you everything. Telling you what's going to happen is every editor's worst nightmare." The book slammed shut.

Jasmine tried to open the cover once more, but the tome didn't budge. "Damn thing has a sense of humor like a rock," she murmured and grabbed the strap of her backpack. Her hand brushed along more than fabric.

Fingers.

Jasmine pivoted to face what was behind her. The creature the book had described was not something she wanted to confront on her own. The text wasn't giving her any more information until it wanted to. A man with a hungry look in his eyes told her she was on the menu. She raced up a few stairs to get away from the beast. Greasy silver hair hung in mats around his shoulders. The unwashed smell of body odor and rot clinging to him knocked her back. Once upon a time he had been a man, but no humanity remained in his gaze. Only hunger. He pulled back his lips and hissed, showing off long, pointed teeth. She dug into her bag and her hand closed upon something solid.

Please let it be a weapon. Please let it be a weapon.

She came out with an ornately carved wooden cross. *What the fuck am I expected to do with this? Throw it at him?* The bag was supposed to provide her with whatever she needed. Right now, she needed something to keep this monster away. The creature hissed and hid his face from the relic. It hit her. *I've* read *this book -- or at least something like it -- before.* Jasmine kept the cross extended before her. All the books she'd read flooded back to her. *He's a vampire. Vampires fear crosses.* The stake in Micha's bag could kill the creature along with sunlight. Once the dawn came, she could look for Micha and Leon. They could escape if the vampire hadn't bitten or turned them. The book had revealed a little bit of this being's perspective as the monster awoke from the slumber its master kept it in.

And the master has to be none other than Count Dracula.

Chapter Three

"I see you have me at a disadvantage. You know who I am, but I don't know who you are. This time you can't lie about your coach breaking down," a sensuous voice whispered next to her ear.

Jasmine felt the pressure Dracula put on her brain to bend her will as he had tried earlier. She jumped back when he materialized in front of her. A black ribbon bound the hair at the nape of his neck. A midnight cape draped over his shoulders. The longer she looked, Jasmine realized, it was darkness suspended around him making it look like a cloak. The blackness had a thickness more than any kind of cloth she had seen. His minion remained behind her. Hunger glistened in his eyes. Whatever power held him back was only because of the man before her.

She was trapped.

"It doesn't matter who I am." Jasmine tried to keep her voice even, but her heart rapped against her chest. Ideas of how to escape stacked up and flew by her as her gaze darted around the room. She could jump off the stairs, but there was no place to hide. Outside, the night made it difficult because the vampires would still be awake. She didn't think there was any village nearby that would take her in. Besides, she couldn't leave Micha and Leon to the dark influence of the monsters in the castle.

"But it does." Dracula trailed his knuckle along her cheek. Jasmine tried not to shrink away and stood her ground. Showing him any fear wouldn't do her or the others any good.

"She's mine," his minion seethed.

Dracula's bushy eyebrows arched up as a chuckle sneaked out from behind his thin lips, chilling her soul. "You forget who is master here. She is *not* yours. Everything in this castle belongs to me. I suggest you return to your hovel and take what I give you. This one isn't for you."

The younger vampire snarled at his master and stepped toward her to take possession of her. The count shoved Jasmine against the wall and launched himself at his creation. They tumbled down the stairs. She used the distraction and raced up to the second floor to look for Micha or Leon. Three long hallways lined with doors spread out before her. One hallway showed their footprints from the room where they had slept. The others remained undisturbed.

She glanced down at the landing and saw a trail in the dust leading to the third floor. She followed it. All kinds of creatures could be lurking in the rooms. Jasmine had to find Micha and Leon, get the hell out of vampville, and pray Dorothy hadn't found them. Maybe one day, when they had saved the day, she could go back home. With the thought of home, came the notion she might never see Micha or Leon again. She wasn't ready for that.

A howl of pain hit her ears. Another shriek sent a bolt of fear through her, and she slipped into a room through a half-open door. Sheets covered the furniture. Jasmine gazed around the room trying to find a place to hide. She hoped Dracula wouldn't think to follow their footprints.

"Psst. Over here." One of the sheets fluttered. Leon stuck his head out and motioned for her to join him. Jasmine dashed into the corner and squeezed behind the large piece of furniture. It was wide enough to fit both of them and over ten feet tall. Thankful for the hiding spot, she took a moment to try and calm her racing heart.

"How did you escape?"

"Shh." He put his finger to his lips.

The door slammed open against the wall.

Jasmine peered through the small crack between the pieces of furniture they hid behind. Dracula glided into the room. She no longer saw the beguiling man who had enticed her downstairs. His pale skin was a sickly yellow-gray. Large bat ears stuck out from the sides of his head. Dracula's flattened nose was too big for his round face. Yellowed fangs hung over his thin lips. Patches of brown hair clung to a gray head. The cloak of shadows was actually thin brown wings that dragged on the floor along with a long rat's tail. The count walked upright on disjointed knees and webbed feet. Talons scraped the stone as he walked. Tufts of brown fur covered his chest, revealing a naked torso. In this guise, the count was definitely male. The vampire clicked his claws together as he searched for them. "I know you're here." Dracula's words came out garbled. "I smell you. I hear those lovely beating hearts. Your footprints in the dust proved most helpful as well. You won't escape. The castle and all in it belong to me."

Jasmine retreated against the wall as the vampire came closer to their hiding spot. Leon poked her in the ribs to get her attention. He gestured to the sheet and made a motion of pulling it down. He put up his hand and glanced back at the vampire. Leon counted down with his fingers. When he got to zero, they tugged on the sheet. The dust cloud made her sneeze, but the vampire's roar caught her attention. Dracula retreated from the room and the door banged shut on his exit.

"We're okay here for a little while. Vampires can't stand to see their reflections," Leon said calmly.

The sudden show of courage made him a little

cuter. "Thanks for saving me. How did you escape him downstairs? When his influence died away, I was all alone."

"When your eyes started glowing green, he focused his attention on Micha. I slipped away and came up here to hide. I hoped you'd find me."

"I followed your footprints. My eyes were green?"

"Yeah. Do you have any water in your magic bag?"

"Let me check." She dug into the backpack. Jasmine felt the book and burrowed deeper. Her fingers brushed on some cloth she guessed were extra clothes, but she went deeper. *Could I climb in this thing and use it as a portal to bring me home? Better not chance it. I could end up somewhere worse.* Her hand closed on a familiar smooth container. Jasmine pulled out the water and handed it to Leon. He popped the plastic top with a long black fingernail.

"Something you want to tell me?" She gestured to his hand.

"We all have our secrets. I'd like to keep mine for a bit longer if you don't mind." His eyes glowed golden for a brief second. He touched her hand and the soft gesture tugged at her heart. "Are you okay?"

"I'm fine. It's good to see you're okay. Care to tell me how you knew Count Dracuvamp would be frightened off by his reflection?" Jasmine rummaged for food in her sack and came out with a sub rolled in brown paper. Leon snatched it from her hand before she could open it. She went back in and found another sub-like parcel for her. She opened it to find a roast beef sandwich with feta cheese and spinach -- her favorite. Her stomach grumbled as she ate. Red liquid smeared Leon's lips. Remnants of raw meat clung to the wrapper on his lap. He gave a contented growl and then burped.

"Excuse me. Just what I needed." His eyes no longer shone. His face seemed less animalistic.

"You gonna tell me how you knew about the reflection, or is that a secret, too?" She finished half of her sandwich and saw Leon eying the rest. She handed the sub to him. He dissected it and slurped down the meat.

He sighed and glanced at her, taking a few minutes before speaking. "I've had experiences with them before. I had a hunch this world might have the same creatures I dealt with. My experience was in another place --" He winced. "-- in a separate story. Micha saved me a long time ago. We were both different then. Much has changed, but these creatures are similar to the ones who kept me prisoner. I was their pet. The world where you come from has nothing like them or me except in nightmares or tales you may read. You must understand by now how important the book is, right?"

"It's a portal to different realms. The book is magic and writes its own story. From what I've gathered, each world -- each reality -- has had a book written about that realm. I'm not wholly sure on that part and the book is a pain in the ass because she has a mind of her own. Why do you and Micha call her she, anyway?"

"Tell me about it. I'm sure you'll find out the reason when she wants you to know," Leon murmured.

"You've handled the book even with Micha being all overprotective?"

"She picks who she wants to interact with. She has her reasons. One thing I've learned is, even though the stories are written in your world or in any other, they're not the same even if they seem to be. They're all a little bit unique."

"Millions of books adorn shelves in my world. Maybe even billions. With the way technology is, people publish thousands every day. I can't even imagine where this thing might take us. Some people have freaky imaginations. I read this one book recently about a blood-sucking green alien who blended in with humans by being a rock star."

"How was it?"

Jasmine shrugged. "I'd give it four stars, but I wouldn't want to end up in one of the author's storylines. Never know what she's going to come up with next."

Leon laid a hand on hers. His flesh was warmer than before. He leaned in and kissed her. His lips were soft and his kiss gentle. Her insides melted. He smiled, closing his eyes, and moved his hand down her thigh. Jasmine glanced at his fingers. The tops of his nails were black and sharpened again. His touch comforted her. Leon opened his eyes and looked at her with a longing gaze. "You're the first woman I've touched in a long time. I hope you don't mind."

"I don't mind at all. Don't think about getting frisky up here, though. Never know when Captain Fangs or his minion will come back."

"Get some sleep. I'll keep watch. He won't come back in here. I can hear Dracula downstairs. We can't do anything to find Micha until dawn when they sleep."

"What about his minion?"

"Did either one of them bite you?"

"No. The underling wanted me, but then Drac decided I was his. They went at one another, so I scooted out of there bite-free. Would I have been infected? Stories in my world about vampires -- at least the most common one -- say that a vampire must bite you and exchange blood for the virus to get inside you. Some books say they can't see their reflection and that the sun kills them."

He relaxed against the wall. "Yes. They have no souls, which is why they can't peer into a mirror. Vampires see what they've become -- all rotted inside. They have no heart. The undead can't feel anything. They crave blood as well as emotions and drain a person dry. If they are like the ones in my world, then yes, blood must be exchanged for the infection to spread. I still have problems being around a lot of people. My emotions are difficult to control." He squeezed her leg.

Something dark flashed across his eyes as his expression hardened. This was the animal -- the man -- who stalked her when she found herself in his room for no reason back in Oz. She laid her hand over his that rested on her knee and patted it. "Why don't I take first watch instead?"

Leon nodded. He closed his eyes. His face became more boyish as it rounded into sleep and his cares melted away. The black tips of his fingers retracted and became regular nails. He breathed evenly. Jasmine pulled out the book from her bag to pass the time feeling a little safer with Leon's insight about the vampires. She brushed the tome's velveteen cover. Energy sparked up her fingertips and into her arms. The sudden rush didn't startle her as much as it had before. She learned the book had a purpose for everything. Jasmine would eventually discover what hers was in the overall story. Maybe even wield magic in some capacity.

"Okay, book, please don't be stubborn. Can you tell me if Micha is..." Jasmine's throat closed as emotion choked her up to think Micha might be... Her eyes burned from the thought she didn't want to even admit to herself. "... alive, please?" Jasmine tugged on the cover. At first it didn't want to open, but then it slowly yawned open in her hands. The page number showed one hundred and thirty-four. They were a quarter of the way through the story, but that could change at the book's whim. Jasmine tried to flip back and see if she could garner some more information from the last chapters she might have missed, but the jolt of energy she got numbed her fingers.

"Picky. Picky. Fine. No going backward." Jasmine tried to peer ahead, but the pages were stuck together. The letters glowed an angry green, so she stopped. "Hey, I was just curious. Don't get your pages in a wad." Jasmine patted the book and rolled her eyes. "I'm sorry. I like to skip forward when I read books to see what happens."

"I'm not an ordinary book." The script appeared on the page. This wasn't the first time the book had replied directly to her.

"Yes, I realize whatever you're doing to me has a purpose. You might not be an ordinary book, but you have to remember I'm not used to all this magical stuff. It's bad enough you decided I had to be in this tale, and now my heart is wrapped up in these two guys. Give a girl a break."

"You've had your break. The others need you to step up."

She ground her teeth together and nearly threw the book across the room. The damn thing was giving her lip. "I'm not going to cut and run, whatever you --"

"You thought about escaping for a second, even if

your heart is 'wrapped up in the two guys' *as you said. You'll never get home without me. If I were you, I'd put your big girl pants on and grow a pair."* The letters flashed on the paper.

"I'm well aware that without you I'm not going home. I wasn't going to leave Micha… not after everything that's happened. Leon, well, I thought he couldn't fend for himself, but he's more capable than he's letting on. Besides, I couldn't bear for anything to happen to him either." Jasmine glanced at the sleeping man who snorted and clutched her leg protectively as he whimpered in his dreams. The sweet man had a fierceness underneath the surface, waiting to burst out. *Can he really turn into a full-grown lion?* Jasmine figured whatever he became he would defend her and Micha. The idea of Micha succumbing to Dracula turned her stomach. They had to get to him.

"You can't judge a book by its cover." The text flickered at her on the empty page.

A cry erupted from the bowels of the castle. Leon didn't stir. The book grew heavy in her lap. The pages flipped quickly as they revealed pictures instead of script showing Jasmine the scene which played out involving Micha. The count whipped him mercilessly. He cringed and screamed every time the lash hit his flesh. He bucked in the chains until Dracula stopped and licked the blood from the wounds. Her stomach turned and she looked away. When she glanced back, the count hovered above Micha's neck about to bite into it. The count looked up as though he knew someone watched him. The face Jasmine saw was not the man, but a woman. The eyes and the smile were the same. Her mouth opened wider than normal and a long thick tongue caressed Micha's throat.

The picture faded as text reappeared. Jasmine

trailed her fingers over the vanishing image and a wet spot plopped onto the page. She wiped her eyes and read aloud.

"The prince found himself under the evil spell of the beautiful seductress. He tried to fight the grip she had on him. Her mental command to stay quiet echoed in his mind. When the pain started from the whip licking his flesh, he shrieked. Fire engulfed him each time the creature lashed him. The prince wanted to break away, but chains bound him. Relief came when the whipping stopped. He sagged in his chains. Then he felt the cool presence of the count near him. He heard the slapping sound of the vampire's tongue hitting his flesh and licking his wounds.

"'You're mine. The ones above might have driven me off with the old mirror trick, but they can't save you. By the time they find you, you'll be my disciple. Maybe you'll mind me better than the last one.'

"I'll never become like you. You won't survive this. I'll write you out of existence."

"You hunters always have the best lines. Nothing you do will ever *erase* me. I'll come back. You don't know how many times I've been resurrected."

"Maybe you'll find a way back, but your rebirth won't be for a long time." The prince struggled again, trying to find a way to get to the magical implement in his pocket. He wasn't able to get to the pen to write the count out of his life. Or to free himself so he could escape and get back to his companion and his girl.

The idea of her being put under the fang or becoming a dark creature like the vampire torturing him angered the prince. He enjoyed arguing with the ordinary girl. She looked upon the world she stepped into with wide eyes, and thought about magic the way he used to -- with innocence and expectations. She'd saved his life. The book had given her magic to revive him. The tome had brought them to Dracula's realm for a reason.

If he got out of this, he would tell the ordinary girl why he thought the book had woven her into his story. The volume had led him to others before, but they'd turned out to be the wrong ones. He'd never seen her coming, and she had laced her way into his heart. She might have been an ordinary girl when he first met her, but that was no longer the case. Something extraordinary lived within her. The prince wasn't sure he could utter the word *love*, but it lingered in his heart. He couldn't bring himself to think of what the implications might be if she were the one. He couldn't imagine seeing an end to the long journey he'd been on. Signs already pointed toward her being the one since both he and his sidekick were set upon her. The prince didn't mind the thought of sharing the ordinary girl either.

Jasmine laughed and sniffled, at the same time wiping away her tears as she read the last passage. *He's being tortured and yet he's thinking about me. I guess Micha isn't as much of an ass as I thought. I have to rescue him. Then maybe I'll be able to get an answer to what part I play. Something about me being attracted to both men means something, too. He loves me.* Her heart hitched. Jasmine itched to rush into the dungeon to free him even if the vampires lurked about. To pass the time, she started reading again hoping the book would be nice and show her a shortcut to the cells. Something to make her life easier.

"Sometimes the journey is what makes the destination worth it. Gotta keep the mystery alive." The text appeared on the page.

Jasmine groaned. "Now you're quoting me. Fine. No shortcuts. Show me whatever the next part of the story is, please."

The tome shivered as though amused. At least it didn't send her to some frozen wasteland or down a rabbit hole. Not wanting to give the volume any ideas, Jasmine shifted her thoughts to saving Micha. She didn't know if the evil bitch after them in Oz -- aka Dorothy -- would find them in this reality. The longer they stayed, though, the longer Dorothy had to home in on the book's energy. Jasmine hoped the next place they ended up would be tranquil and they could get a little bit of rest. She wasn't holding her breath.

Jasmine went back to the book to see what part of the story it would reveal. She hoped what she read would be more about Micha, but as she skimmed the page, another chronicle emerged.

"Dracula's minion stood outside the room watching from the shadows. His master stalked the woman up to the second floor after they fought. The count left him bleeding and hurt. The command to leave the intruders alone echoed in his mind, but he found the strength to fight the master's mental directive and go up the stairs. Maybe it was because he heard his master scream after the woman had outfoxed him and then slink away in fear from the second floor. Or maybe he finally had grown stronger than Dracula.

"The subordinate knew something his master didn't know. These weren't hunters. He sensed magic about them. His master had no experience with such things. In another lifetime, the minion used to know how to conjure. Now a different type of power animated him. Past memories tried to reemerge from the time before he became a monster. Something about the woman reawakened buried desires. She reminded him of another. No matter what happened, he couldn't let the count get his fangs into her.

"As the shadows drifted, he went with them a little closer to the door and peered in, hoping to catch a glimpse of the woman again. His eye caught the mirror. At first his reflection showed his unchanged steely appearance and silver hair. Pale gray eyes and skin with a sheen reminding him of metal. Then it changed to the makings of the creature underneath. He could still see the humanity within because he had only taken a handful of lives. Mostly his fare consisted of rats. A green glow shimmered from behind the mirror. *In such a short time, she feels different. Stronger.* He smelled the difference in her, but it wasn't the perfume of magic or the implement she held that intrigued him. The warmth of her flesh sparked his memories and made him want to defy his master.

"The ordinary girl gasped when she glimpsed him through the gap between the furniture. Her companion snored on. Dracula's minion unwound from the shadows and took the full force of the mirror. The vampire held up his hands before him, so she'd see he wasn't there to harm her."

The letters faded. Jasmine looked up and met the vampire's gaze through the slit in the furniture. She gasped as the passage had said. His eyes were no longer hungry, but kind and almost human. He waited in the doorway. She glanced back at the book, but it had closed. Leon snored away, dead to the world. The book showed her the vampire in the doorway didn't want to hurt her. Jasmine slipped the volume back into her bag and got up.

"What do you want?" she addressed the vampire.

"I can help you get your friend back. There's still

time before the count turns him into one of us. He thinks you're hunters come to kill him, but I know you're more than that."

Chapter Four

"Yes," she replied.

His gaze flicked between her and then out into the hallway. She understood he kept looking away from his reflection because the mirror made him uncomfortable. Jasmine slipped out from behind the mirror and made sure the straps on her bag were secure.

"We were brought here, trying to get away from someone worse than Dracula."

The younger vampire laughed, a dry sound with no amusement in his tone. "I don't think there's anyone worse than him. He keeps me as a plaything. His pride and joy are the brides. Mina is first among them. She's already ventured out for the night. If you encounter her, she *will* hurt you."

"I'll do my best to stay away from her. Before this, I never would've thought there was anything worse than your count. Can you help me get Micha back? You promise you won't bite me?"

He sighed. His gray eyes flashed red, but then they normalized. "I hunger, but no. I give you my word I won't sip from you. I will do all in my power to free him and get you out of the castle. When dawn comes, take me with you."

"Won't the sunlight kill you?"

"The count and the others have walked in daylight even though the rays weaken him. I'd rather face the sun than stay another moment in this castle." He stopped and turned back to her.

Leon snuffled again. She giggled at the interruption and wondered if he was dreaming about chasing a white fluffy bunny down a rabbit hole. Jasmine realized how nervous she was. Trusting the stranger was her only option. The book wasn't going to create a magical portal for them to step through. They had to get to Micha before Dracula did anything worse to him.

"Do you wish my help or not?"

"Your help would be appreciated. Let's go."

"Arm yourself if you have weapons."

Jasmine hadn't come in with weapons. A bottle of water wasn't going to do her any good against a vampire. She dug into her bag and came out with something hard and long. A stake. At least she could use that. On the next foray into her magic bag, she pulled out another bottle labeled holy water.

"I'll take the pointy object." Leon grabbed the stake from her.

"I didn't realize you were joining us."

"I dozed off for a moment. Smelled the beast and came back to my senses. They're beguiling creatures. I wouldn't trust this one either." Leon swung at the vampire, but Jasmine jumped in front of him.

"Whoa there, cowboy! He's going to help us get Micha. We need him."

Leon's gaze narrowed. "We only need him for Micha. He's not coming with us." He grimaced. His eyes turned golden again. His teeth looked sharper than they had been before. Leon grabbed one of her hands. She saw black claws had replaced his nails.

"The brides have returned. He will spend time with them until dawn. We must get your friend now. Come with me." The minion beckoned them to follow.

Jasmine chased the vampire through the shadows of the dimly lit hall. Leon growled something and caught up to them. She clutched the bottle of holy water and thought back to some of the cliché and cheesy vampire novels she read as a teenager.

Somehow, she'd ended up in the middle of one. Maybe this world was a compilation of all those books from her realm about Dracula tied together in some way to give it rules, but independent enough to exist outside all of the stories written about Dracula.

Her stomach knotted as the vampire led them down a dark staircase. She didn't know what to call him. The book hadn't revealed his identity and she wasn't going to shout, "Hey, you." Their ally held up his hand to stop them. Jasmine peered over his shoulder. Down below, the count fawned over four women. Each was clothed in rags that barely covered their naked flesh. The only one dressed decently was the one who led the procession of brides. Dracula pulled out something shiny and handed it to the first one dressed in crimson. Micha's pen. The others made a grab for it, but the first hissed at them. The other brides cowered and huddled together before the first.

"We need to get that pen back," she said to the other vampire.

"Why is it important?"

"If they figure out how to use it, they could change things." Jasmine wasn't sure how much information she should give away about the pen.

"Fine. We'll worry about it later. Let's get your friend. Follow me." The vampire dashed across the hall and into the darkness.

Leon caught her waist and pulled her back into him. His breath caressed her neck. They lingered together for a quick second as she found her footing and felt his lean body along her back. His warmth helped calm her fear. Not to mention she could feel how turned on he was by the hard cock pressing into her ass. Something about his scent as she caught his musk and manly scent aroused her in a different way than when she was with Micha. Leon spun her around, so she could see his golden eyes glowing in the wan light. He slid his hands over her ass and pulled her into him.

"Do you really think this is a good time for this?"

He flashed her a cocky smile. "I don't care. I want you to know once we rescue Micha and get to a safe spot, I'm going to ravage you. You're going to be mine. Do you know what that means to one of my kind?"

The question floored and intrigued her. "Ummm… no idea."

"I could show you if you let me." Leon kissed her lightly before he nipped her bottom lip. Jasmine returned the kiss with a quick hunger. As their lips touched, electricity sparked between them the way it did between her and Micha. Being with Leon felt just as right. His question flooded her mind. How would Leon make her feel if he claimed her wholly? The urge to find out flared along her nerves. Leon deepened the kiss and squeezed her ass. His tongue slipped into her mouth and she could taste his sweetness, but sensed he was holding back. Jasmine touched her tongue to his. She used all her willpower to break away from him. Right now, they had to focus on saving Micha.

"Leon, Micha is our objective right now." She ran her fingers down his chest and watched their combined energy play over her fingers. "We have to get this under control. As much as I appreciate you telling me… hmm… showing me how you feel… but you don't need to be the king of the jungle to prove to me you're some macho, take-charge kinda guy and how you feel about me. I know you care."

"My feelings go beyond caring, Jasmine. It's more than love for me. You are what Micha is to me.

You're my mate, and there's nothing I wouldn't do for one of my mates. We'll get Micha back and then you're mine."

Jasmine didn't know what Leon claiming her would entail, but it intrigued her. She brushed her lips along Leon's once more. "I guess we have something to look forward to, then. Let's go save Micha."

She backed away and went after the vampire. Thoughts flew through her mind about what Leon had said to her. *What is it with men? They find the worst times to tell me how they feel. Although I can't wait to get between the sheets with him and figure out what makes him purr.* The idea dawned on her that the book could be manipulating her emotions about Leon and Micha. Maybe having Leon being an animal shifter was the romantic twist to this side of the plot. Jasmine read enough romances in her spare time to know how they worked. The more take-charge Leon got, the more protective he became, and the more the animal burst out. If he lost control, then he might go full lion. She wasn't prepared to deal with his transformation. *I'm going to have a serious talk with the book when I'm done, getting its jollies off -- by throwing me into a romance novel.* Jasmine nearly ran into the vampire at the bottom of the stairs.

The vampire motioned for them to head lower into the dungeons. Jasmine crinkled her nose at the stench of death. Nothing good lived down here. "He's one more level below, but the master has him guarded. It's too late. The Count has claimed him for his own. I can get you both out of the castle, but there's no hope for your friend. He is gone."

"We're not leaving him behind. He saved my life. I owe him. I won't let him rot in some dank cell where he turns into an evil monster. Besides, you haven't lost what makes you a good person. I see the humanity in your eyes. And I don't even know your name."

He flashed her half a smile. "It's been so long I've forgotten it. Thank you for your kind words. Something about meeting you has stirred old memories. Maybe my name's among them. I understand about your friend. You're going to need much more than a bottle of holy water and the stake your companion has to get past the count's pets."

"Leave the monster to me." Leon cracked his knuckles and rolled his shoulders. He stripped off his clothes and handed them to Jasmine.

"What are you doing?"

"Proving to you I'm the king of the jungle. Stick these in your bag." He strolled into the shadows giving Jasmine a clear view of his swagger and his fine ass along with his cock, which she had to admit was impressive. She wondered how it would feel to have him inside her.

Their vampire guide glanced between the two of them. "He's attracted to you. I can smell the difference in him from when he was upstairs to now."

"I kinda got that by the big hard-on he sported when he walked by. His dick all but bowed in my presence." Jasmine pushed the hair out of her eyes and laughed. She stared into the darkness after Leon. *Am I really going to see him turn into a lion? Can I handle that?*

"I can understand why. There's something about you."

"You said that already. Where I come from, you wouldn't give me the time of day. I'm Plain Jane sitting behind a desk, working in insurance all day, and wrestling the guys in my office so they stay on top of things. My boring life."

He touched her arm. "I don't know what this

occupation of yours means, but it sounds as though you don't have much of a life. I would assume that's the problem. You're so used to being locked away you've forgotten how to live. I understand. I've been sealed in the shadows for a long time. A great power is unlocking inside you. Don't put yourself down so lightly. I don't see you as plain at all."

She couldn't meet his eyes and moved away. Getting compliments wasn't her thing. Jasmine didn't want to reveal he'd hit the nail dead on the head. She had let her work consume her. Maybe the vampire told her the truth. The book was unlocking something inside her. *Or the book's having fun with me. It goes around changing my life to fit me into the story it's writing. The storylines are fucked. Even if I'm somehow involved in the plot, how can I trust what I'm feeling for Micha or Leon? The attraction started almost immediately when the book started sharing its magic with me.* It flattered her to know Micha loved her and Leon wanted to claim her as a mate. She hadn't fallen into a book to find a boyfriend, and now she had two of them. Of course, they had to save Micha first. Without him, there was no going forward. If she lost him, Jasmine didn't know if the book would even respond to her if Micha became... *Nope. I can't think like that. We're going to save him, and he's not going to become a monster.*

"My remark has lulled you into silence."

Jasmine glanced up into his light gray eyes and saw the sincerity in them. He might have been a monster, but he had once been a man. Something inside him continued to be human. "Sorry. I was thinking. I'm nothing special. The book is changing me. Forget about me. We need to rescue Micha and make sure Leon doesn't get eaten."

He nodded. "You're right."

A large animal roar shook her to the core. Jasmine raced toward the rumble. Torches popped to life as she went by. The sudden brightness made her wince. At the bottom of the stairs stood the biggest lion she had ever seen. The beast's shoulder came to her waist. Its head reached her neck. A dark blue substance stained its mane. Something slithered away trying to escape the great beast. The lion pounced on it. The creature screamed. He sank his large fangs into the neck of one of the things and tore another hunk out of it. A large shadow bat landed on his shoulder.

Leon roared in pain. *I need to do something.* The rage at being helpless seared her spirit. Jasmine's right palm tingled, and her fingers burned. She glanced at her hand. A green glow emanated from her skin. Leon cried out again. The heat in the center of her hand grew so bad she had to get rid of it as the green light grew. Jasmine threw the energy out of her hand. It hit the shadow creature somewhere near its head. At least she thought it was a head. The shadow bat bellowed. The beast retreated into the darkness as the mass of energy gave it an emerald sheen and it melted from the inside out. By the time the monster hit the darkness, nothing remained. Leon finished off the other shadow bat and turned back to her. Black goo dripped from his fangs.

"How did you do that?" the vampire asked her.

"Not sure." Jasmine tried to catch her breath at the effort of lobbing the energy from her hand. A jade sheen remained under her fingernails. Her fingertips were numb, and it tasted like she sucked on a mouthful of pennies. Her world tilted, but she caught herself on the wall. The vampire slid a hand around her waist to hold her up. Jasmine's head swam, and stars formed into constellations before her eyes. She wondered if this was how Micha felt when he used all his energy to get them to Glen-da back in Oz when the twister was bearing down on them. She had no way of knowing unless they found him. He was somewhere in darkness being tortured by Dracula.

"Are you okay?" the vampire asked.

She nodded, but her stomach decided it wasn't okay. Jasmine turned into the shadows, and what she'd eaten recently came back up. She opened the bottle of holy water and took a swig. It kinda tasted like mouthwash. Once she took in a few deep breaths, her head cleared. Leon bumped his head against her hand. She looked into his golden eyes and smiled. His scratchy tongue scraped along her arm.

"I'm okay. Really. Come on. We gotta find Micha," she said to Leon.

Jasmine ventured deeper into the fortress with Leon on one side and their friendly vampire on the other. She kept the bottle of holy water handy. Thankfully, no vampire jumped them. They got to the cell at the very end of the hall. A single torch threw a little bit of light into the room. Micha lay slumped against a pillar with his hands shackled above him. He looked pale and beaten like he had been tortured for days. She raced in and touched the manacles. He opened his eyes at her presence and lunged at her. Their vampire guide yanked her out of Micha's reach. This was not the man who rescued her. Nothing of the person she loved remained in his wild gaze. They were red instead of sky blue with slitted pupils like a cat's. His lips pulled back to reveal sharpening canines. As he gnashed at them, she spotted two large puncture wounds on his throat.

"I told you it was hopeless. The master's blood has worked fast on him. A turn that would've normally taken days has only taken hours. Leave him and I can help you and your lion friend escape." He tugged on her shirt to get her to leave.

Leon sniffed Micha and raised his paw toward him, but Micha even swiped at him. He uttered a low growl and stepped backward becoming a man as he did. Fascinated, Jasmine watched as his animal form withdrew. The hair retreated until his tanned skin remained. He shrank back down to his human form. It was difficult to believe this lean man could become the hulking lion she had seen. Jasmine took in the crisscrossing scars across his back where someone had lashed him. What had truly happened to him before Micha rescued him from whatever hell he'd existed in before? Her heart went out to the shifter. She understood why Leon didn't want to talk about his past.

"Can I have my clothes back, please? I don't mind you ogling me, but I'd rather give you a private showing when we get somewhere safe."

"Right." Her cheeks burned as she tore her gaze away from his naked form. Digging into her bag, she snagged Leon's garments and felt another tingle as she brushed the top of the book. She pulled the tome out and opened it up.

"If you're going to get snarky on me, I really don't want to read it."

The page remained blank as if the text was thinking about what to say back. Words appeared slowly. *"You can still save him."*

"How?" Jasmine whispered. Hope rose in her throat at the thought of saving Micha until she choked.

"You need the pen and the axe."

"Dracula gave the pen to Mina. I planned on getting it before we left. Figured we needed Micha first."

"We don't have time for you to be reading. Dracula and his brides are coming," their friendly vampire warned her.

The book didn't seem to be in a rush.

"What axe?" Jasmine asked the volume.

"Once you retrieve the Tinman's axe, then Micha can be restored. I will tell you how to use them."

"Who is the Tinman?" Jasmine waited for the book to answer her.

"Dracula's minion. The one who has been helping you."

Jasmine glanced at their vampire companion, not sure she believed what she read. How was it possible he was the other third of Dorothy's threesome? He *was* human, or *had been* human. He wasn't made of metal the way the book said. Then again, as Micha had said, things weren't always what they seemed. "Him? Really? The vampire is the Tinman?"

"Yes."

"But how is that possible?"

"Jasmine, we have to get Micha out of here before the count comes. Trust what she shows you even if you might find it difficult to believe," Leon interrupted her conversation with the book.

"We have to get the pen from Mina. Then we need to find the Tinman's axe. After that, we can free Micha." She glanced at Leon, hoping he might recognize his onetime companion. "Is he the Tinman?" she asked the lion shifter.

Leon shook his head. "He's not the Haley I remember. He doesn't even look the same. The last time I saw him, he and Micha got into a huge fight. The Haley I know wouldn't lift a finger to help Micha in any way."

"The book says the Tinman's axe is here. We

need it and the pen in order to help Micha. How that works I don't know. I'm sure the almighty book will tell me when -- if -- we survive this. The snarky tome doesn't let me skip ahead in the story."

"You'll do more than survive this," a cold breath caressed her throat.

Jasmine dashed away from the wall and turned around. One of the brides had Leon backed into a corner. Dracula stood next to Micha. The other two brides ran their hands down their guide's chest. She wasn't sure if he was the Tinman or not. Jasmine slammed the book shut and tossed it into the corner. The vampires didn't seem to have any interest in the magical volume, which relieved her some. She spun around with only her half-gone bottle of holy water to protect her. Whatever vampire book they were supposed to be in, she was not the heroine. She was the flunky sidekick. No one would ever assume she was the big bad slayer of the fanged beasts. Jasmine thrust the bottle out in front of her hoping to ward off the vampires. Her eyes met Mina's, whose cruel smile twisted into a sneer.

"Do you really think you can defeat me with water?" Mina's British accent made her tone even more sinister. Long brown hair flowed over her antique dress. The torn high lace collar full of clumped earth stuck to her ivory throat. The stink coming from Mina made Jasmine's eyes water. From the dirt and debris caked on her pale flesh, Jasmine assumed they all slept in their graves with the raw earth. Underneath the smudges, Mina's pink lips parted to reveal twin fangs. The ice-cold beauty of her sculpted features and sharp green eyes made Jasmine wonder who this woman had been before she fell into Dracula's clutches. In the book, Mina had escaped Dracula's influence and lived to tell the tale with her husband, Jonathan Harker. Obviously, this wasn't the case here.

Jasmine unscrewed the bottle cap and threw the water at the vampire. Mina screamed when the liquid hit her face. Her hair erupted in flames. She batted at the blaze and spun around into the shadows. The sound of something hitting the dungeon floor as Mina disappeared got Jasmine's attention. Silver glinted in the torch light. Micha's pen. Before Jasmine could grab it, she found herself on her back in a stack of moldering hay with Micha straddling her. Dracula yanked him back and held him as a string of drool hung out of Micha's mouth. Jasmine scrambled to her feet.

"You'll pay for what you did to Mina. This one you care about. He's mine now. You'll be his first meal, and then you'll be mine, too."

She looked into Dracula's cold eyes and saw nothing more than a demon. Nothing remained of the human -- or maybe he'd always been this way. Leon screamed and another bride shrieked. Dracula turned to see what the commotion was. Micha shoved Jasmine back into the wall. He caught her wrists and held them above her head. His eyes sparked green showing her the man she loved remained inside.

"I know you're in there wrestling the infection devouring you. I see it in your eyes. Remember the book. If you give in, you won't be able to keep the book safe from Dorothy."

Recognition came to his gaze. "This bloodlust is so strong. The poison in my veins is changing me from the inside out. I'm trying to hold on, but I hear the song of your blood. I can taste it on the tip of my tongue. Jasmine, I don't have much time."

"The book told me I need the pen and the Tinman's axe to heal you. It seemed to think our vampire guide was the Tinman."

The green flickered in and out of his eyes like a dying candle. His grip on her wrists tightened. His sharpened nails cut into her skin. Micha showed her his lengthening canines. His tongue grew long, and he latched onto her wrist. The quick pain of his fangs cutting into her made Jasmine whimper. The wet sucking sound as he drank from her turned her stomach. Another screech hit the room. Micha released her suddenly and shook his head, coming out of his murderous daze.

"I can distract Dracula long enough for you to get the pen." He jumped off her, leaving Jasmine to catch her breath as her heartbeat returned to normal.

She dashed in the direction of where Mina dropped the pen. She raked her fingers through the debris on the floor not wanting to think what she touched until she found the pen. Jasmine slipped it into her pocket. When she turned back to the action, Micha had a stake above his head while Leon and their vampire guide held Dracula's arms. The count struggled underneath them. Micha plunged the stake into Dracula's chest pinning him down. They released him, but Dracula clutched the stake with a smile on his face.

"You might kill me now, but I'll be back. I always come back." He laughed as he dissolved into ash.

A great shout came from the shadows. Mina rushed at Jasmine. The holy water had melted half of her face and her chest. A black socket leered at her where Mina's eye had been. Holes in her neck showed sections of her throat. She caught Jasmine around the waist in a viselike grip. "You did this to me."

"Let her go, Mina," the count's minion shouted.

Micha's eyes flickered between green and the red

of his hunger taking over. Mina's teeth latched onto Jasmine's throat. Jasmine sobbed, but she stayed focused. She could get out of this. Micha lost his battle with the hunger and lunged. Leon grabbed him in time and held him back.

Mina purred into her ear. "You taste better than you smell. Something I've never had before. I can feel the power in your blood. You love this one, but he's succumbed to the hunger. I'm going to sip from you and let him finish you off. Then I'll make sure his blood resurrects my beloved." Her fangs pushed deeper into Jasmine's throat.

Jasmine reached into her pocket and found the pen. A shooting pain raced up her arm. Her vision turned green for a split second. Her head spun, but she kept her balance. The magic in the pen seemed compatible with her. The metal grew thick in her fingers and turned to wood. Jasmine jabbed the stake behind her into Mina's stomach. The vampire released her and tried to pull the stake out. Micha launched himself forward and landed on top of Mina. He pulled out the stake and then shoved it into Mina's heart. She struggled to get the rod out, but Micha held it in place as her body flaked into ashes. Once nothing remained, the pen returned to its metal state. A blink of green in the corner caught Jasmine's attention. She scooped up the book in the corner of the dungeon. It opened in her hands to a blank page.

More writing appeared as the book told their saga:

"As the prince regained possession of the magic pen, a little bit more of himself emerged from the blood haze. He found it difficult to hold on and fight the hunger surging through him. The prince glanced up at the woman he had sipped from. He recognized her and yet saw her as food at the

same time. Memories of the past of them together swam before his eyes. Emotions warmed his heart, and images of the man who smelled more like an animal flashed in his mind. Together they'd fought another evil. The prince's gaze switched to him. Feelings overwhelmed him about this man. The prince knew him on a deeper level. The memories rushed on him so fast he couldn't grasp hold of them. Dracula's blood worked on his soul, his body, and his mind, changing him into something else. He looked at her... The girl's name came to him.

"Jasmine.

"For a moment, another woman's face -- a woman from another time he also had feelings for -- was superimposed over Jasmine's image. He used to be something else before he was a man. A prince of straw whose thoughts were difficult to form until he sprang to life. The prince studied his companions and saw the lion he used to know. The great beast who had been beaten down by other creatures like the count. And the vampire... No, it wasn't a vampire. His image varied as well. The prince saw a man with an axe wearing some sort of funny metal hat. He traveled in a wagon with more metal surrounding him. The hunger surged forward as something else tried to be born within him. The voice was unclear, but he caught the basic meaning of the whispered words. Fear. Lust. Loyalty. Blood.

"The prince grabbed his head and cried out. The energy of the magic pen waned because it couldn't fight the invading influence. He needed help. Jasmine promised she could help him, but she required something. What did she need? Haley had to know. His axe was like the prince's pen. If he had the axe, he would remember. The girl had to stop being ordinary and help the prince and his companions."

Jasmine looked up as Micha grabbed his head and screamed the way he had in the story. Green energy crackled from the book and wove along her hands and arms. The power lit up the fibers of her muscles and the outline of her bones, leaving her energized. The pain in her throat and wrist lessened as the wounds healed. The book slammed shut. Jasmine shoved it into her backpack with an idea of what she had to do.

She took Micha's hands and forced them away from his head. Jasmine held his face. "Hey, you can't give in to it now. I know you're fighting. I love you, Micha. I can't lose you. I need you to stay with me a little while longer. Can you do that?"

Micha nodded, but the red grew brighter in his eyes. They had to act fast because he was losing the battle. "I'll try. We need Haley's axe. You told me that, right?"

"Yes, I did." They both glanced at the vampire who had helped her.

"Why are you looking at me?"

After what the book showed her, Jasmine was convinced this vampire was the Tinman. As each minute ticked away, they lost more and more of Micha.

"Because you're the Tinman," Micha whispered.

"We need your axe, Haley," Jasmine said to him.

His gray eyes showed no sign of recognition. "I don't know what you're talking about. I'm no Tinman."

"Yes, you are," Micha replied through gritted teeth.

"Are you sure it's him?" Leon asked. "He doesn't look like the Haley I remember."

"Look at Micha. He's already changed in the few hours we've been here. Whatever Dracula did, it transforms him more than just on the inside. The infection strips away everything they used to be. Leon, keep an eye on Micha. Haley, that's what your name used to be. Don't you remember?" She pointed to the others. "They were your traveling companions and your friends for a long time. And then something…" Jasmine thought about the book and how they all were befriended by Dorothy. *Something had to have happened with her which is why they parted ways.* "Something came between you three. Does any of this ring a bell?"

Haley shook his head. "No."

She twined her fingers through his. A jolt of green passed between them. "You said there was something different about me, right?"

"Yeah." He squeezed her fingers a little harder. The green reached his eyes. "I remember something, but I'm not sure. I need more of a taste."

Haley trailed his fingers under her chin. His nails sliced into her skin, but he made no move to taste her blood. He pressed his mouth to Jasmine's. He tasted like dirt, but then the sting from her hands passed over her lips. Haley continued to kiss her as though he drank in her very life essence. He nibbled her bottom lip, trying to get more. When he pulled away, his eyes glowed green. Jasmine felt winded, but not like she would fall over. He stepped away and his skin had a darker sheen. Haley raked his fingers over his face. His eyes were brown, and his face lost the gauntness of being dead. Green energy raced through her veins and made her hands glow. The magic beat under her skin like a second pulse.

"Leon, it's been ages. What are you doing here?" Haley looked around the dungeon as though he had no idea where he was. His gaze met hers. He planted his lips on Jasmine's once more in a quick kiss and spun her around. "You broke me from the spell I've been under. I am at your service. How can I help you?"

"It's Micha. Dracula infected him with his blood. We need your axe to break him free of Dracula's influence. Do you remember where it is?" Jasmine prayed he would know. There was no way to tell how long the effects of the magic would last.

He rubbed his chin. "When I came to this castle, I was greeted by a great feast and a beautiful woman. She… She told me I didn't need the axe, but then the feast vanished. I was… somewhere dark and hungry. My axe…" He spun around looking for the weapon. His eyes settled on Micha. "What is he doing here?" Haley's tone grew bitter.

"Micha saved my life. We need your axe, so we can save him from the same fate you suffered." Jasmine hoped he would understand and want to save his onetime friend.

Haley grabbed Micha's chin and examined him.

"Please," Micha begged him as he spat out the word through his growing canines.

"You're begging me! You wrote me out of the picture and sent me here. I tried to chop my way back, but the portal had already closed. She chose me over you. The count ripped it all away. Let this curse take you." Haley released him and turned his back on Micha.

"You have to help him." Jasmine caught his arm.

He hissed and backed Jasmine up into one of the pillars. "You have no idea what it's like being one of them. Let Micha suffer. What he did to me and her is unspeakable."

"You mean Dorothy?" Jasmine asked.

"Don't say her name," Haley whispered.

"I don't know the details, but… I won't let you walk away! You're going to help me." She hit his chest and a flash of green energy zapped him. The release left her breathless and yet energized at the same time.

"You have no idea what you're getting yourself

into with the book. She turned us against one another. If it's injecting you with magic, then it has plans for you. Once you get a taste of the power, you won't care about anyone else."

"This power the book's given me has broken the spell over you, so that has to count for something. I don't feel like I'm someone else. I'm still me. The book can decide to write you back to the soulless vampire you were. I'm sure you don't desire to return to the shadows. I don't give a shit about the magic. I didn't sign up for any of its bullshit. I'm trying to get home."

"Maybe you are. Maybe you aren't. Maybe you're still telling yourself that because you don't know if you can truly accept you love Micha. You afraid I'm going to bite you?" Haley scoffed.

"No. Even when you were the fearsome vampire you didn't attack me. I trust you won't, but you can't let Micha endure the same hell you did."

"You care for him?"

Jasmine opened her mouth, considering how to answer. She might have told Micha she loved him, and she did feel something for him, but she wasn't ready to talk about her feelings. "He saved my life. If he's a vampire ready to tear my throat out, I can't get home, now can I? Even if you resent him for past events, at least help me help him so I don't have to be stuck with you three for the rest of my life. Questioning me if I care for him doesn't apply in this situation. He's my ticket out of here."

Haley crossed his arms over his chest. "Oh, I think it does. I'll tell you what. I'll get the axe, but I want a couple of things in return from you."

Jasmine didn't like the sound of his proposal. She was certain the conditions weren't going to be favorable. Then again, the book could be adding intrigue to the story. Or just Haley trying to get back at Micha. "What do you suggest?"

He trailed his finger over her throat. "I want another dose of what you have in your veins. I get to bite you. I'm sure you'll enjoy it."

She shivered at the idea of being bitten by him. The thought didn't appeal to her. "Will I become a vampire?"

"No. We have to exchange blood to change you into a vampire."

"You seem to be recalling all this now when you didn't before," Leon murmured.

"Old friend, my memory has become clearer the longer we're talking."

"Fine. You can cut me and take a couple of sips, but no teeth. What are your other terms?" Micha thrashed about. Leon struggled to hold him. They were running out of time. Haley's fingers inched a little lower until they ran along the collar of her shirt. Jasmine shifted away from him, very much aware she needed to shower.

"It's been a long time since I've been with a woman. We'll need a roll in the hay to cement the deal. Would you consent to that?"

"So you can rub it in Micha's face when you're done? Not a chance."

Haley's laugh was almost as diabolical as the count's had been. *Something is seriously twisted in this man.* The idea of being with Haley made Jasmine's skin crawl. Micha screamed again. Leon clung to him as he tried to get to her. Micha foamed at the mouth. The red had bled into the rest of his eyes. His pupils became slitted once more.

"I can't hold him much longer. He's getting stronger," Leon said as the muscles in his neck strained. He lost his grip on Micha for a second. Micha rushed at Jasmine, ready to tackle her. Haley caught Micha and dragged him back to Leon.

"This won't take much more time." He glanced over to Jasmine. "What do you say? Do you leave him like this, or will you take me up on my offer?"

"Fine," she whispered. "But not until I've showered and there's a bed. All right?"

"Let's seal the deal with a kiss." Haley puckered his lips. As soon as Jasmine's mouth touched his, a zap sent her backward into the wall.

Chapter Five

"Guess the book doesn't want us going down that road." Jasmine got up and rubbed the dirt off her jeans. She rolled her shoulders and felt her neck pop, but nothing hurt.

"Damn the book. You swore to me we'd have a go at it." Haley came at her again to kiss her. The twisted look on his face made her see he wasn't going to let this go.

Jasmine tried to dart out of the way, but he had her trapped. Haley forced her hands behind her head as she struggled to get away from him. The itch in her fingers and the greenish glow from the magic in her wasn't strong enough to come out or she wasn't recharged enough. She didn't really understand how it worked yet.

"I will make you mine and he's going to see --"

A whoosh of air went by her as Haley was there and then he wasn't. A low growl echoed in the dungeon. Leon had the vampire pinned to the floor. Tatters of clothes hung on his large animal frame as he shifted. His claws pushed into Haley's throat. The vampire struggled to get up from beneath him. Leon growled and glanced back at Jasmine. She rubbed her wrists and went over to him.

"I don't think Leon appreciates how you treated me. Our deal is off. Get me the axe."

Haley laughed. "I'll never tell you where it is. Micha will rot. He tore the woman I loved from me and now because of his jealousy he will become everything I was."

Jasmine threaded her fingers through Leon's mane and scratched him. "Speaking of Micha. Leon, what did you do with him?"

The lion shifter motioned with his head in the direction of the shadows. Jasmine heard a metallic grinding sound coming toward them. A few seconds later, a green glow parted the darkness. Micha dragged the axe behind him. The red had left his eyes. His clothes draped over his emaciated form. His eyes were sunken in and his face gaunt. He gritted his teeth. His canines hung over his thinning lips. A slender black tongue stuck out between them. Micha shoved the axe at her and took in shallow breaths. His color made it seem as though he was dying right before her eyes. How he held on gave her some hope they could beat this.

"Do whatever you need to do. Get this out of me," Micha begged her.

Jasmine opened the book up. "What do I do? I got the pen and we have the axe."

"The pen can rewrite pieces of the story. The axe chops away huge sections of the plot. The pen is a more delicate instrument than the axe. You need their combined magic to transform him back into what he was because the infection is so deeply rooted. Take the axe first and find the point in Micha's story where the contagion first began. Then you chop away at it."

"That doesn't make any sense. The pollution started when Dracula bit him and they shared blood. If I carve out *any* part of him, I'm going to kill him."

"Magic is unexpected and sometimes unpredictable. You have to trust yourself or you're going to lose him. If you want to get home, you'll do this."

Jasmine wanted to get out of this realm with Micha and Leon intact. She needed them back in a safe place where she could tell them how much she cared for both of them. Getting home seemed to be a goal she would accomplish sooner or later. Jasmine set the book down on the floor, hoping it decided to give her step-by-step instructions. The axe glowed green in the wan light of the dungeon. She picked it up, but nearly lost her grip on the heavy weapon. Her hands itched as she held the smooth wooden handle. The axe grew lighter in her hands, adjusting its weight so she could wield the magical blade. Jasmine studied Micha. A red haze surrounded his body. The largest concentration of the crimson hovered over his heart, his head, and his stomach. Smaller clusters lingered in other groups like hiving ants, but Jasmine felt if she removed the biggest ones Micha would return to normal.

"If I miss, or this doesn't work, I'm sorry. Leon, don't eat me if I accidently kill Micha."

The lion shifter huffed.

Haley laughed. "The axe is attuned only to me."

"We'll see." Jasmine mentally crossed her fingers, toes, eyes, and aimed for the largest chunk over Micha's stomach. On her first swing, the blade sparked as it hit the stone because she missed. She gritted her teeth and swung again. Micha screamed. Jasmine dropped the weapon thinking she disemboweled him. Red flowed from the spot on his stomach where she penetrated the crimson energy. He fell to his knees and clutched his abdomen. "I'm sorry. Shit. I can't do this."

He looked up at her. His eyes reflected his pain, but they were clearer and not as sunken in as they had been before. "You only nicked the skin. The wound hurts because you're attacking the root of the infection on an energy level. Keep going before I lose myself completely." Micha stood up on wobbly legs and waited for her to strike.

Jasmine bit her lip and aimed for the blob over his heart. She tried to swing the blade, so it would slice the energy like cutting butter, but the axe had other ideas. Her fingers remained glued to the handle. She lost control over her arms. They came over her head like she was going to throw the axe and brought it down in the center of the large red blotch. It stuck in the glob of energy in midair. Micha clutched where the axe struck as dark liquid covered his palms. Black tears dripped out of the corners of his eyes and ran down his cheeks like bad clown makeup. He sank to his knees. Wisps of onyx smoke curled up from the center of the wound and spread outward as the magic in the axe attacked the infection. Once the scarlet died away, Jasmine caught the axe handle. She didn't know how she would attack the large globule surrounding his head. Her hands shook. The green under her fingernails glimmered a little brighter. *Trust myself. That damn book had better be right about this.* Jasmine closed her eyes and let the axe guide her. So she held the axe like a baseball bat. Her arms went above her head and struck. The sound of a melon hitting the floor and going splat made her cry out. She thought it was Micha's head and opened her eyes.

A reddish lump the size of a head rolled around on the floor. The energy blob grew tentacle legs and wriggled out from under the axe's blade. Jasmine grabbed the axe and threw it as far as she could. The spider-like creature struggled to get away from the blade embedded in it. The thing shrieked, and died, melting into the floor. Micha collapsed and started floundering as if having a seizure.

Jasmine rushed to him, but the book glowed to get her attention.

"The major influence upon him has been carved out, but you need to write him better and change the scene."

She took the pen from her pocket and clicked the

end and the point came out. Micha used it to change things in the world and about her. She prayed she could do the same with him. She hoped the pen was fully charged because she intended to free Micha of any vampire taint and restore him to the point before they entered Dracula's castle. Taking a breath, Jasmine wrote as quickly as she could. Letters formed in the air. They glowed and faded as she got to the end of her sentence. She thought about what she wrote and added one last line that he would recall everything. Energy heated the metal until she nearly lost her grip on the pen. Micha no longer writhed in pain but stood before her looking healthy as he had before the entered the castle. He shoved the book back into his bag.

The pen cooled. Jasmine felt winded as if she'd run uphill. It took a minute to catch her breath. Micha dug into her backpack and handed her a bottle of water. "You look better."

"Back to normal. Thanks." He flashed her a small smile and turned to Haley.

She wasn't sure if she had just been snubbed. She expected some gratitude. Maybe a hug. Jasmine sipped on the water and tried to push her feelings aside. "What are we going to do with Haley?" She scratched Leon in his lion form behind his ear. It helped to keep her grounded and kept her from obsessing about giving Micha a piece of her mind.

"He comes. The book obviously brought us here to reunite the three of us." Micha wrote something above the Tinman whose hands were suddenly bound in silver manacles.

"You wish!" Haley cackled. "I'm not going anywhere with you."

Leon transformed back into a man. He caught Jasmine gazing at his nakedness and smirked. She looked away and blushed. Jasmine opened her bag and felt around. Her fingers caught on some cloth. She took out some garments and handed the clothes to him. The lion shifter nodded and pulled on his pants. He remained shirtless and without shoes. Micha hauled up Haley.

"You don't have a choice. Those cuffs compel you to come with us. That's the way I wrote them. You won't be needing the axe either." Micha picked it up and handed the weapon to Jasmine. "You mind keeping this for me?"

"Sure. I'm good at carrying stuff," she muttered and stuffed it into her backpack.

"Ahh, Micha, we need to get going," Leon warned them.

"I know. We need to get out of here before Dracula rises from the ashes. I really don't want to go through all that rigmarole again."

"No. The monkeys are here. They must've finally caught the scent of the book's magic."

"How do you know? I don't hear anything," Jasmine asked.

"Heightened senses. Micha, pull the book out and see where she's going to send us now. I hope it's not down a rabbit hole. I don't feel like chasing bunnies unless I'm going to eat one."

"Wait, are you're talking about Wonderland?" Jasmine looked at the lion shifter, fascinated as to what other stories they had already been in.

"Sure am. Almost lost my head. The White Queen is a total bitch."

"We can talk all night about Wonderland and the other places we've gone later. It's time to get going. Leon's right. I can hear them lumbering down the stairs." Micha placed the book on the floor.

As it flipped its pages, Jasmine could feel the warm energy coming off the book. She glanced at her hands. The green glow within her skin grew stronger as the book's power hit her flesh as the tome fed her magic even from afar. Why was it giving her magic? Why was the book changing her from an ordinary girl into an extraordinary one? She wanted answers to all this. She wanted to tell Micha and Leon how she felt and explore where those feelings were going.

She shook her head. *Now is not the time to think about them being naked or how I feel. We have to get out of here. Once we do that, I need to know where my place is in this story. It's obvious the book has plans for all of us.*

Chapter Six

The book stopped on a picture of three men sitting around a table playing poker. The men's faces remained hidden. A large pumpkin rested on top of the round table. She knew enough by now to assume the book had a reason to send them there. Leon touched the picture. He dissolved, breaking up into letters and words until the image sucked him in. Micha grabbed Haley and shoved him toward the tome, but Haley stopped before he could touch the pages.

"They'll find you again. You can't keep me in these or with you forever. I'll uncover a way to escape."

"I don't need you to stay with us forever, just until we get back to Oz. She wanted us all together again. Once the story plays out, then you can do whatever you want. For now, you're coming with us." Micha pushed him and he fell into the book. He offered Jasmine his hand. "Next."

"Where are we going now?" Jasmine slipped her fingers into his, feeling the warmth of his skin. His expression remained unreadable. She wanted to see something in his eyes, but it seemed he looked right through her.

"I have no idea."

"I sniffs it. Down heres a little bits farther," a gravelly voice echoed down the hall.

"It smells like shit. You sure it's down here?" Shuffling footsteps got closer.

Part of her wanted to get a look at the things following them. The other part wasn't ready to see what they were. Micha released her hand. She broke from his gaze and touched the book. It tickled as she deconstructed into words and sentences floating into the tome. Jasmine felt as though she remained together. Her vision blackened for a second. The feeling of falling enveloped her. When the light returned, she found herself in a different space. This time she didn't land on anyone but was in the room with the men playing poker.

"Where the hell did you come from?" the Jack-o'-lantern on the table proclaimed.

Jasmine blinked when the pumpkin's mouth moved. She glanced around and saw Leon in the corner of the room standing over Haley. Micha appeared, holding the book, then stuffed it into his bag.

"How the fuck did you get in here, mate? This is a closed game." The man wearing a black hat with a white feather stuck in the brim stood up and threw his cards down. A long blue beard brushed the top of his chest.

The man next to him stood up. His black cape brushed the floor, but he had no head. The body picked up the pumpkin and held it protectively under his arm. The third man rose. Half of his face was covered with a white mask while the other half was dashingly handsome. His dark, intense stare didn't leave her.

"Hess, you scared the poor girl. Can't you see they've come in for a song?" He spread his arms out and broke out into serenade.

Jasmine giggled.

Micha slung his hand around her waist and pulled her to him. "Gentlemen, I'm sorry to have interrupted your poker game. We won't be joining you. Hess, it's good to see you again."

The Jack-o'-lantern's face scowled. The crooked eyebrows scrunched together and then opened up in surprise. "Scarecrow!. I didn't recognize you with all the flesh. Been a long time. Nice skin suit. When did you get the flesh? Fine squeeze you got there."

Micha smiled. "Thanks, Hess. Had the skin for a while now. Long story."

"We'll have to catch up sometime when you're not so busy." The headless man reached out with a normal human hand.

Micha clasped it. "Sounds good. I'll see you on the other side, man." He pulled Jasmine through the door.

When she looked back, the man with the blue beard winked at her. The four of them left the room and entered an ornate hotel lobby. It was decorated in gold and red with white and black marble columns. Bellhops ran about pushing carts filled with parcels and clothes. Paintings of cherubs sitting on fluffy clouds floated across the ceiling. The blue in the ceiling faded into darkness. Lightning lit up the sky, and the lights blinked in the hotel lobby. Mist floated down and settled on her skin. Something about the air didn't smell right. She caught the hint of sulfur. When she looked back up at the cherubs, they had turned into little devils.

"Micha, where are we?" Jasmine asked.

A man popped out of nowhere. "Welcome to Hel! Exactly where you're supposed to be. Master Scarecrow! You haven't stayed with us for a long time. You've brought the whole gang again. Although, a new woman, I see." The man led them over to the counter.

Jasmine stayed behind and glanced over at Leon, who shrugged his shoulders. Haley kept admiring the women passing by and whistling at them. They sneered and looked away. A woman dressed in a white fur coat floated by. The light caught the bluish sheen to her hair and skin. Jasmine stepped backward into Leon to stay out of her way. He held onto her arm. His touch brought her some comfort.

"Hey, it's going to be okay. At least here we get a break from the monkeys."

"You've been here before?"

"Yeah. Long story."

"There are a lot of long stories in your life. Look, I just saw a dude with a blue beard, the Phantom of the Opera and, I think, the Headless Horseman. These other women walking by don't give me the warm and fuzzies. Is this place a refuge for evildoers or something?" Jasmine asked as she took in more of the guests in the lobby. None of them made her feel at home.

"Not exactly," Leon said to her.

"My. My. We have a hu-u-uman." Another impish bellman popped onto the counter. It was nothing more than a round, purplish creature with a large eye in the center of its face. It balanced on one leg with four hairy toes and two arms with three fingers each.

Jasmine jumped. Leon held onto her a little tighter. She glanced up and got lost in his tantalizing smile.

"Igor, don't scare our guests. I'm assuming you want rooms for the night?" the manager asked.

Micha dug into his backpack and pulled out a small pouch. He plunked it on the counter. "This should pay for our stay. I need two rooms and a place in your cells for my silver-haired friend here. Something light tight so he won't catch on fire. He's a bit different than the last time we were all here."

"You can't hold me forever." Haley growled as

two guards carted him away.

"We'll take good care of him. As to the matter of the two rooms, we only have one of our larger suites available. We're booked up for a convention, you see. It's been in the making for years. The guest of honor hasn't arrived yet, but I can throw in some complimentary tickets for the inconvenience this causes you to share the suite."

"Does it have two beds?" Jasmine asked the desk clerk. She wasn't ready to be wedged between Micha and Leon even in a king-size bed. The notion of sharing them crossed her mind, but she did like the idea of sleeping by herself at least for now. She would have preferred a room to herself, but she wasn't going to argue. All she craved was a bath, some answers, and then sleep. Maybe some food.

"Yes, ma'am. I can get someone to take your bags." He reached for her backpack.

"Thanks, but I'll keep it with me." She held it a bit closer.

"Of course. Here are your keys." The clerk handed them each brass keys with a plastic tag dangling from each of them. "Each key is magically coded to the room. This way, please."

They followed the bellhop through the lobby. The hotel stretched on forever as they walked to the elevator. Other hallways appeared as they rounded corners. Shops for all kinds of goods lined the lobby, turning it into a vast mall. Succulent smells drifted through the space, making her mouth water. She spied a sign above one of the archways directing guests to numerous restaurants. The ringing of coin slots echoed in the distance. It reminded her of a grand casino in Las Vegas. They passed people in dark capes that hid their faces. A woman in a white-feathered cloak stood next to them while they waited for the elevators to come down to the lobby floor. A blast of frigid air came off the woman as she moved into the lift. She caught Jasmine's gaze from under the fur-lined hood and smiled as the doors closed. The woman had an air about her that intrigued Jasmine. Their elevator dinged, and they went up to their suite on the thirteenth floor.

"Isn't it unlucky to have a thirteenth floor in a hotel?" she asked.

The bellhop gave her a look like she had four heads. "Where did you hear such nonsense?"

"I… um… it's not something we normally have where I come from," she stammered.

"You come from a strange place." He opened the door to their suite. They went inside and he showed them around. "This is the main sitting room. The bedrooms are to the left and right. Upstairs is the dining room and access to a rooftop pool. If you need anything, ring down to the front desk and we'll bring it right up. I almost forgot." He snapped his fingers and held out three placards. "These are your all access passes to the convention. They'll get you into all the special events and the after-hours parties. Ring if you need us."

Micha tipped him. "Thanks."

The bellhop winked and popped out, leaving a trail of sulfur in his wake. The door slammed shut, making her jump and leaving the three of them alone.

Leon touched her arm. "You okay?"

"Yes. Fine, I guess. I'm a bit jittery. Those goons after the book caught up to us. Everything that's happened with Haley has left me a bit overwhelmed. What happened between you and Haley? Did you go to the Wizard and ask to become human so you could be with Dorothy? Maybe you got jealous of Haley's relationship with her and wanted Dorothy for yourself. You sent him through the book, and he ended up at Dracula's castle." As Jasmine rattled off her thoughts, some pieces of her puzzle fell together.

"You don't know the half of it. Besides, our past is dead. You only saved me because you want to get home," Micha said through gritted teeth. His eyes narrowed and flashed emerald, but Jasmine thought she saw a tinge of red within the green as well. "My life means nothing to you."

"Not true and you know it. I thought we were beyond you being a dick. Don't push me away…" Hot tears burned her eyes as she wiped them away. "Why don't you consult the book? Or maybe you know I might not need you anymore when it comes to the damn thing. Whatever is happening here, this isn't just your story or Leon's. The book wrote me into it, and you can't stand that. When you were all vampy, I read your story and saw how you felt about me. M-maybe you can't deal with your emotions or maybe how I feel --"

A bolt of green energy struck her chest. She stumbled backward into an overstuffed ottoman and the energy sucked the air from her lungs. Leon caught her and ran his hands along her arms. A few moments later, Jasmine caught her breath. His touch brought her solace. Her heart twisted around as she thought about him and what she had come to feel for Micha.

"I said enough." The vein's throbbed on the side of Micha's forehead. An aura of power flared around him. "I don't want to talk about it. You're right. The book wants us here. It likes you for some reason. Fine, you saved my life back there in the castle and I'm grateful. Enjoy the time here. Get a few souvenirs.

Charge everything to the room. I don't give a shit. Gamble. Eat yourself into a food coma. I'll pay for it later. I owe you that much. Maybe get a new set of clothes. Those are pretty tattered. Excuse me, I'm going to get a drink." Micha walked out of the room ignoring her.

"Don't listen to him. He gets like this sometimes. We've argued over what an ass he can be. He gets caught up in himself. He goes inward and forgets he has a heart." Leon led her over to a chair and helped her sit.

She rubbed her chest to get the feeling back. The lion shifter knelt before the chair and swiped the tears from her face. Looking into those golden eyes melted her heart. Jasmine touched his cheek. "I'm sorry. I didn't say thank you for saving me back in the castle. I should have."

He blushed. "You don't need to thank me. I would've rescued you anyway. No one deserves to become one of those creatures. Look at how twisted Haley's become. Although he was kinda weird when we first met him. I guess time and the infection brought out the evil buried in his soul. You were brave to save Micha."

"I almost killed him."

"You love him which is why you're so angry with him. He loves you, too. Give him a bit of time to come around." Her fingers trailed down his cheek as he slid his hand over hers. The warmth of his flesh felt good after all they had been through. "I hadn't seen him in a long time until you showed up with him back at the Emerald City. I wanted to rush in, but Glen-da made me take a moment. We both watched as the book took to you and… Well, I have to admit I find myself in love with you. You're my mate the same as Micha is."

Jasmine brushed her mouth across his, unable to stop herself. His sweet lips met hers as he returned the kiss. She leaned into him and moaned, enjoying the heat of his body. She relaxed with Leon for the first time since she'd landed in Oz. She slid her hands along his sides. He broke the kiss and pulled away. "Jasmine, are you sure about this?"

"Aren't you the one who said you wanted to show me what being your mate means?"

"I did, but we just got here. I thought you might want to unwind a little bit. We don't have to jump right into bed."

"I could use a shower or a bath." She bit her lip and held out her hand. "You wanna join me?"

"I'd love to." He took her hand and then swept her up off her feet.

Jasmine squealed and wrapped her arms around his neck. Leon carried her into the bathroom. He set her down on the cool tile floor. She let out a low whistle as she took in the room. All white and black marble with a tub the size of a small pond. Next to it was a shower stall large enough for three people. Stacks of towels sat on shelves next to both along with two robes hanging on a door.

"I could live in this place." She went over to examine the colored bottles of different sizes lined up on the counter. Jasmine lifted a stopper on one of them and caught a citrus smell. Leon picked up one with a bubbling purple liquid in it and had her smell it.

"Would you try this one?"

Jasmine inhaled a mixture of lavender and vanilla. "Do you like it?"

"Very much. I love how you smell better, but…" He shivered and licked his lips. "I can imagine how this smells mixed with your scent. The idea makes me mad for you."

"Why don't you put it on me?" She winked at him and set the bottle on the rim of the tub. She turned toward him and stripped off her shirt. Once it hit the tile, her top dissolved and vanished. Leon kept his eyes glued to her as she took her bra off and ran her fingers over her breasts. She fingered the button on her jeans. Leon gave out a little growl and grabbed her wrist. He brought her hand up to his lips and slid his mouth down around her finger. She noticed the tips of his nails were black and pointed. He dragged his teeth along her finger. The sharpness of his teeth made her shiver along with the feeling of his rough tongue. He let her finger go and placed her hand over his heart where she could feel the gentle thud under her palm.

"This is yours now. You hold my heart."

"I thought Micha did, too," Jasmine murmured as she moved her other hand along his chest feeling the raised scars along his flesh. Her heart hurt at the thought of him being tortured.

"He does, but so do you now. I hope you don't mind sharing." He dragged his finger along her jaw until she looked up at him. "Why are you sad all of a sudden?"

Jasmine forced a smile and touched one of his scars. "How could someone do such a thing to you?"

"In the reality where I'm from, vampires -- slightly different creatures from the ones at Dracula's castle -- rule the realm. Humans are prized possessions since there are so few of them. Shifters exist as slaves to the vampires. Micha, Dorothy, and Haley dropped into the dungeons. They saw me being whipped and Micha rescued me. He wasn't the man you see. He was the scarecrow. Even back then, I knew he was the one for me by his smell. It didn't bother me he was stuffed with straw. I'd seen stranger creatures in my territory. The masters whipped me for any reason. We were food sources, slaves, and sometimes used for other things. Micha took me with him. It took Micha a long while to accept how I felt for him, even though the book had showed him. I took my time with him. He loves you, but give him a little while to accept his feelings… to let it sink in. Nearly becoming a vampire jarred him more than he wants to admit. Don't take it personally."

Jasmine forced a smile and thought about what Leon said. It made sense Micha would feel he had lost his identity to the vampire infection and didn't have time to compensate for coming back to himself. She couldn't fathom what he had been through. Maybe what he was still going through. "You're right. We all need some time to relax. If he needs to get a drink and chill out, I'm good with that."

Leon brushed his lips across hers. "So am I. Besides, it gives me time with you." He cupped her cheek. "Have I told you how gorgeous you are?"

Jasmine snorted. "Yeah. I smell like dank dungeon, have God knows what in my hair, and my clothes are covered in… ick."

"Then take the rest of them off so we can get you clean, and I can rock your world." Leon stepped away from her and stripped off his pants. As they hit the floor, they disappeared. Jasmine wasn't sure if she was coming to enjoy magic or finding it irritating. She also undressed and stood before Leon naked. The lion shifter walked around her slowly touching her shoulder or tracing his fingers along the curve of her back. Each time his nails left trails across her flesh, she shivered. He slipped his hands around her waist and pulled her back into him. His cock pressed into her ass. Leon scraped his nails along her full figure. His lips nibbled along her throat and the line of her shoulder.

"You taste like sage and smell like pomegranate," a growl rolled out of him. "I could eat you up." His nails poked into her hips. Leon bit at her throat. Each time his teeth pushed against her flesh, Jasmine waited for him to bite her and she wanted him to.

"Am I the main course?"

"You are. First, let's get into this bath." Leon stepped away from her and turned the taps on until the tub was full. The water steamed. He climbed into the tub and sank in up to his waist. He offered her his hand as she stepped down into the water. The warm water felt good as she went in. "Sit here. I'll make sure you're good and clean."

"Leon, you don't have to…"

"Shh… Let someone pamper you for a change." Leon sat behind her on the bench seat, and she slid down on the next step down. The warm water made her feel more relaxed, then Leon began to massage her. His fingers dug into her muscles along her shoulders and moved down her back getting the places where she was bruised from being thrown around in the dungeon. Warm water cascaded over her head. The deluge broke her out of her trance, and she sputtered. She turned around quickly and saw the playful gleam in Leon's eyes. She punched him in the arm.

"Not funny."

"I could've dunked you, but I didn't think you'd appreciate that."

"Not really." Jasmine rolled her eyes and splashed some water at him. She went over to the edge of the tub and grabbed the bottle he wanted her to use. She didn't mind wearing it for him. She gathered a little bit of the purple liquid in her hands and rubbed until it foamed. Leon snagged the bottle from her before she could protest.

"Remember I said I would do this for you." Leon dragged a washcloth over her shoulders and between her breasts. He made sure to slide lower until he washed the insides of her thighs. Jasmine trembled. He left her yearning for more of his touch.

Jasmine turned toward him and brought his mouth down to hers. She plunged her tongue into his mouth, not wanting to wait any longer. Leon met her lips with an intensity she hadn't felt in him before. She ran her tongue over his teeth and felt their sharpness. He bit down, trapping her tongue, until she tasted blood. Jasmine gasped and pulled away. Leon's eyes shone golden in the light. She scooted a little bit away from him on the seat. He prowled closer with a small drop of her blood on the corner of his lips.

"You fear me. Why?"

She shook her head. "I think it's the way you're looking at me or the way you kissed me -- like you were going to eat me up."

He flashed her a half-crooked smile. "Your blood tastes good. I would *never* hurt you, Jasmine. I want more of you. What can I say? You bring out the animal in me." Leon held out his hand. His nails were black studded claws. "Trust me."

"I do." She slid her hand back into his. His other hand glided along her back and he began to lower her into the water. Jasmine almost fought him, but instead she let Leon dunk her under the water. She came up and Leon guided her to sit back between his legs. He took another bottle and something cold splashed over her head. His hands massaged her scalp. Jasmine let out a contented sigh as more warm water came over her head to rinse out the shampoo.

"You smell all clean now," Leon whispered in her ear and nuzzled her neck. His hands slid over her breasts and pinched her nipples.

Jasmine moaned. "What about you?"

Leon bit her a little harder. "I'll take a dip when we're done. Right now, I want you. I want to claim you. Make you truly mine." He glided his fingers down her stomach until he found her clit. Jasmine arched her back as he rubbed her. His lips trailed down her throat until he nibbled her shoulder. She ran her hands along his legs, feeling the muscles in his lean calves. He tortured her slowly. Jasmine closed her eyes and gave herself over to the pleasure he brought to her. Green glowed in the darkness behind her eyes. She could feel the warmth and the energy mounting, along with the pleasure coursing through her. Jasmine dug her nails into his calf as Leon nibbled on her shoulder. Sudden pain from him nibbling on her shoulder throttled her toward an orgasm. She opened her eyes and cried out as the warmth hit her. Green energy flared over the water from her hands. The energy played over the walls and made the lights explode. It also lit the wicks of candles in the room until their flames burned green.

"Amazing," Leon murmured. He ran his tongue over her shoulder. Jasmine shivered again as she felt a small amount of pain.

"How did this happen?" Jasmine exclaimed. The emerald flickers from the candles reflected off the white marble causing the shadows to dance.

"I don't know how magic works, but I know from being with Micha it can come out when strong emotions are involved. I'd say you had a strong reaction to my bite."

"You bit me?"

He licked her shoulder as his rough tongue found the spot where he marked her. Jasmine trembled at the pain. It shot straight to her clit again leaving her breathless and throbbing for more. She needed to have him inside her. "I had to mark you as my mate. Now no one will make another claim on you. Except Micha. You'll bear my mark from now on. Each of my kind always marks their mates."

"Do you really think I'm going to come upon another lion shifter who is going to want me?"

Leon growled and his eyes narrowed. "Let's not even think about it. You're mine and no one else can have you."

"Down, boy. I love the both of you." Jasmine glanced at her shoulder and saw the green energy already stitching the wound back together, but a scar remained from his teeth.

The lion shifter claimed her lips one more time. "You love me?"

Jasmine shifted around and wrapped her arms around his neck. His cock pressed against her thigh. The words had slipped out before she realized she said them, but it was true. She loved both him and Micha. *Wonder what the book is going to make out of this.* "I do. Now you're going to fuck me like you promised." She stroked his cock and slipped it inside her.

"Yes, ma'am." He thrust into her as the water splashed around them. Jasmine kissed his throat and tasted the salt on his skin. He claimed her lips as his hands grabbed her ass. They moved together and the energy in the room brightened as she got closer to coming. Each time he plunged into her, it felt as though she were rising to some new height she hadn't reached before until it felt as though they were floating in the air. Jasmine threw her head back and gasped.

"What?" Leon gasped. His fingers dug into her ass.

"Look." The world around them appeared to have frozen. Darkness surrounded them. Tiny lights appeared like stars. They sparkled until she recognized the constellations from her realm.

Leon slid into her one last time as Jasmine kept watching the lights while he brought her to the crest of the orgasm. The stars burned brighter. She snuggled into her new lover's arms and felt the tears in her eyes. Leon wiped them away.

"Did I do something?"

"No, I never thought I'd see my constellations again. My grandmother taught me to see the shapes in the stars when I was a kid. When I first landed in Oz and saw the stars I didn't recognize, I knew I was lost."

He kissed her cheek. "I guess now you know you've been found. Besides, I'll make sure you're never lost again."

Chapter Seven

Jasmine listened to Leon snoring lightly. He lay sprawled out, nearly taking up half of the huge king-size bed. She smiled at the night they had together and how quickly her feelings for him had emerged. She should have blamed the book. Maybe she would later when it all sank in. They were on the run from Dorothy and her flying monkeys because Dorothy wanted the magic book they possessed. In her head it sounded impossible. Yet here she was, in love with the Cowardly Lion and the Scarecrow. They had escaped Dracula's castle in one piece. Well, maybe not in one piece. Micha had caught the brunt of the vampire's wrath. She hadn't seen him the rest of the night after he burst out of the hotel room.

Leon snorted again. Jasmine got out of bed and headed to the bathroom. Feeling a sudden chill, she grabbed a robe in the bathroom and went out into the sitting area. The dark suite made it difficult to see, but after a moment a light switched on.

"What the hell, Micha!" Jasmine jumped.

"Sorry. I didn't want to wake you or Leon."

She glanced at him and saw the bags under his eyes and the weary expression. It was more than him not sleeping. "Are you okay?"

"Seems like you and Leon got to mix it up."

Jasmine sat across from Micha. His insensitive blue stare bored into hers. "We made love, if you must know. He marked me for his mate. Said he wouldn't mind sharing me with you, of course."

"Great! Now we can all fuck and it will be spectacular." He leaned back in his chair, but his expression remained dead.

"What the hell is wrong with you? Are you

suddenly jealous? Is that why you're being an ass? You asked me back in Oz if I minded if you and Leon were together, and I told you it was fine. Now are you --"

Micha threw something that whizzed by her head and smashed something across the room. "I don't care if you fuck Leon six ways from Sunday. It has nothing to do with you and him." His eyes sparked green at his growing rage and more red appeared in his gaze.

Terror spread in her heart. She prayed this didn't mean what she thought it might. Jasmine laid her hand on top of his. He flinched away from her. She nearly took it as an insult, but remembered what Leon said earlier about giving Micha space for what he had been through at Dracula's. "Tell me what's bothering you."

He closed his eyes and pinched his nose together. "What's bothering me? What's bothering me is I want to rip your fucking throat out and fuck you while I drink you dry."

Jasmine's mouth went dry. A bit of fear climbed up her throat, but she tried to remain calm. "I thought we got all the infection. I mean I wrote you back to normal after I chopped everything out of you with the axe. Have you checked the book to see what she says?"

He opened his eyes and they burned red. He snarled showing her his growing fangs. "The book won't open for me now. She's won't even let me near her."

A sudden thud landed between them. Jasmine pulled her hand away. She watched Micha, but his expression didn't change. Jasmine took the book and green energy raced along her arms giving her a jolt. "Let's see if she can tell us what's going on."

She opened the volume to the middle of the book. Blank pages stared back at her for a few seconds until the writing appeared.

"What's going on with Micha? I thought I got all of it." Jasmine asked the book.

Writing flashed along the blank page. *"A small piece was left that neither of us saw or anticipated. I have been watching the plot lines to see where this twist will take the story. What has rooted within Micha can't be taken out. It's only roused when he's around those he loves. The beast can be sated by the blood of his mates. The infection has wound into his very being and tied to his soul. It can't be written out or changed in anyway. Sometimes even I can't see the curve balls."*

Jasmine glanced over at Micha and saw the beast in his face. However, he didn't look dead like he did before. She wondered about something based on what the book said. "If we can tame the hunger, will he return to normal?"

"Normal? I was never human to begin with." Micha spat. His eyes remained crimson. Jasmine bit her lip and then looked back at the book.

"Yes, but it is only beauty who can tame the beast." The words winked out, leaving the page blank once more.

"Gee, talk about getting into the fairy-tale shit." Jasmine rolled her eyes and set the book on the table. "She's being a bitch."

"You think? So, Beauty. How do you tame my beast?" Micha asked.

How could she conquer the hunger inside Micha without having him kill her? It seemed he was barely holding on, but he didn't look like a walking corpse. She couldn't be afraid of him even if her heart hammered in her chest. She recalled how he had made love to her back in Oz and how she felt about him. Jasmine pushed the table out of the way and knelt before Micha. She pulled the hair away from her throat. She placed her other hand over Micha's heart and felt it beat at a slower pace.

"If there's only one way to soothe your beast, then take what you need. I trust you, Micha."

His fingers trailed over the bend of her throat. "You have no idea what you're asking of me. I remember the taste of your blood from before and it makes me --" He licked his lips and quaked. "-- It makes me want to drink all of you."

She leaned up and brushed his lips with hers. "I trust you. I trusted you in Oz and when you brought me to Dracula's castle."

"Look what happened when we got there? I turned into a monster. I don't want to hurt you. I don't care what the book says. I know what I feel. I'm sorry for reacting the way I did when we first got up here. I didn't mean to lash out at you. I thought I was free of the infection. The more my feelings for you surfaced, the more the monster returned. I couldn't be around you or Leon because all I wanted was... I'm sorry."

She undid the tie on her robe and let it drop to the floor. His eyes grew wide and he let out a low growl. Micha's lips found her breast as his hands scraped over her back. Jasmine trembled, but she didn't give into the dread pounding in her brain. Instead, she slid her hands over Micha's chest and straddled him. She could feel his cock straining to get out. She kissed the top of his head as his lips moved to her other breast. Micha raked his teeth over her nipple as he tried to stuff more of her breast into his mouth. She trailed her fingers along his cheeks to get his attention. When he looked up, even though his eyes glowed red, they were lined with tears.

"I need you... I..."

She felt the fight within him. His eyes wavered from green to red as he fought whatever was inside him. Jasmine tugged on his shirt. Micha didn't fight her as she pulled it over his head. Next, she tugged on his jeans until he wiggled them down and his dick sprang out. She ran her fingers along it until he growled.

"I'm yours," she whispered.

Micha licked his tongue along the center of her chest until he came to her neck. He grabbed her ass and squeezed. He bit along her shoulder where Leon had marked her. "I smell him on you. Taste him on you."

"Good thing you're his mate too, or you might be jealous."

He responded by thrusting his cock inside her. Jasmine gasped. Having Micha inside her awakened her magic as he moved in and out, biting her with his normal teeth over the mark where Leon had claimed her. Micha's lips worked up her throat as he pumped into her. She tried to keep up with his pace but found herself out of breath. Green sparked in her fingers as it had with Leon when they were together. She let the energy grow, not really sure how to control it or if she really could. It washed over Micha. He groaned. She dug her nails into his shoulder. Micha licked her throat. As he hit her sweet spot, Micha's teeth fastened onto her neck.

Jasmine screamed as she came. This didn't feel like how he bit her when they were in the castle. This was different. Sure, he drank her blood, but he wasn't slurping it down. The hunger was controlled. For whatever reason, it turned her on. Green energy flowed over both of them. Micha pulled away from her, out of breath. His eyes lost the red and blazed green. The magic crackled around them until Jasmine rested her head on his shoulder. Micha trailed his fingers down her back.

"Whatever you did, it worked. Thank you," Micha murmured against her ear.

She slid out of the chair, grabbed her robe, and felt the magic in her working on the bite wound. It tickled a little bit, but the encounter left her feeling satisfied. "I guess the book was right about taming the beast." No trace of the vampire remained in his expression. This was the man she loved.

"However, you did it, I want to thank you and tell you…" He took her hands. He looked her in the eyes. "I love you, Jasmine."

A smile spread over her lips as the words she had read before actually came from him. "I love you, too."

"There's more to it than that. It's one of the reasons I've been short and distant with you from time to time. Leon marking you for his mate cemented it all together. It means you're the one I've been looking for. You're the one who is going to save Oz."

She wasn't sure what to make of his statement. The confession floored her. "What do you mean, I'm the one you've been looking for?"

"He means because both of us are in love with you, and you're the one to stop Dorothy." Leon leaned against the wall and rubbed his neck.

"You knew this about me all along?" Jasmine asked.

Micha shook his head. "No. The book has led me to others in the past she felt might be the one. Man or woman. Sex didn't matter. Besides keeping the book away from Dorothy's goons, I've been looking for the one for a long time. There were other signs. I'd fall in love with them and so would Leon. We'd have to mesh together beyond just getting along. When we first met, I didn't think anything of it. You were so annoying. But I couldn't deny the attraction I had for you the longer I was around you. Then you told me how the book gave you its magic to revive me. It wrote you into our story. I saw the way Leon looked at you. I knew then, but I couldn't admit it to myself."

Leon came up behind Micha, kissed him quickly, before going behind Jasmine and rubbing her shoulders. She let out a sigh as he hit the right places. All of what Micha said answered a few of the questions rattling around in her brain. "What about the magic? Is that all part of your plan, too?"

"I don't know. The book never revealed anything about how filling you with magic would affect the storyline. She's never mentioned in the past just how we're supposed to know if the person was The One. Whatever it means, she's not ready to reveal the plot twist."

Leon kissed her throat and licked a line up her ear. "She will when she's ready. It's the same reason why she brought us here and dropped us in at Dracula's castle. Things are escalating now we've found Jasmine. She's brought Haley back because, whatever this is, it's leading up to confronting Dorothy."

Jasmine sighed and thought about what she had learned. Micha had finally answered some of her questions. She had turned into the heroine of the story. Or the would-be heroine. Now all they had to do was wait for the final act. All she knew was she had Micha and Leon with her. They were safe for now. Glad for the brief reprieve, she looked at the two men who loved her. They would be there for her the way she was there for them. No matter what the book threw at them next. The longer she stayed in the story, the more it really did feel like some sort of strange fairy tale.

Spelled for Love (The Accidental Fairy Tale 3)
A Women's Urban Fantasy Romance
Crymsyn Hart

When the magic book deposits Jasmine, Micha, and Leon at a villains' convention, all Jasmine wants is some time to unwind before their next adventure. Getting to be alone with her two mates means the world. All the while, the magic within her starts to go out of control.

Meanwhile, the evil Dorothy enlists some of the villains at the convention to kidnap the trio. Jasmine finds only her magic can save the men she loves and all of Oz. The only thing standing in her way is herself. She needs to accept her fate or all could be lost.

Chapter One

Jasmine Thorne took in a long breath. The masseur found all the right spots on her back. Under the hands of this magical genius, she felt like putty as her cares melted away. All the thoughts of having to save Oz from the evil Dorothy faded. If she ruminated about her mission too long, it gave her a migraine. Wrapping her mind around the idea that she was in love with the Scarecrow and the Cowardly Lion seemed easier to fathom than taking on a storybook heroine who had turned into the villain. At least the Tinman was in the hotel jail, so she didn't have to worry about him. They had brought him from Dracula's castle through the magic book. He'd been turned into a vampire, but still hell-bent on getting back to Dorothy. She had no idea why she was the one Micha's magic book picked to save Oz.

The massage therapist hit another place on her shoulders. Jasmine groaned and pushed her troubles from her mind.

"Ma'am, excuse me."

A shake roused her enough that Jasmine realized she had fallen asleep during the rubdown. She yawned and looked up at the small woman who had made her forget her current situation for a little while. "Sorry. Must have drifted off."

The woman gave her a warm smile. "It happens."

"You are amazing. Thank you." Jasmine sat up slowly and rolled her shoulders. She held the sheet to her chest as the woman exited the room. Jasmine hopped off the table and slipped her clothes back on.

She thought about her agenda for the rest of the day. Nothing except dinner with her two men and maybe a night of lovemaking. The convention they had free passes for would start tomorrow morning. The tickets came with the room for the inconvenience of only having one room when she'd wanted two. The manager had given them all-access passes. Jasmine didn't really know what the convention was for, but Micha, her Scarecrow, and Leon wanted to check it out.

Jasmine left the spa and wove through the hotel lobby clutching the brass key to her room in her hand. The ornate lobby was decorated in gold and red with white and black marble columns. Bellhops dashed about pushing carts filled with parcels. Paintings of cherubs sitting on fluffy clouds floated across the ceiling. The blue in the ceiling faded into darkness. Lightning lit up the sky and the lights blinked in the atrium. Mist floated down and settled on her skin. She caught the hint of sulfur in the air. When Jasmine looked back up at the cherubs, they had turned into little devils. She stopped by a placard with arrows directing her every which way to get to restaurants, the casino, or the dozens of shops in the resort. A red marker on the screen showed where she was. Jasmine pressed it.

"Welcome to Hel, right where you're supposed to be," the high-pitched voice from the screen startled her. She touched the screen and the image enlarged so she could get a better look at her location inside the hotel. The whole complex was bigger than a Las Vegas casino. She had gotten turned around as some of the elevators didn't go all the way up to the thirteenth floor where they had a room.

"It's all a little confusing, don't you think?"

A blast of cold air hit the back of Jasmine's neck. She turned to see where the sudden chill emanated from. A woman in a white feathered cloak stood next to her. Another gust of frigid air came off the woman as she pushed on the touchscreen. It blinked and mapped the way to elevators Jasmine needed to get to.

"You're on the thirteenth floor. This should do it." She caught Jasmine's gaze from under the fur-lined hood. All Jasmine could see were her piercing blue eyes and the turn of her smile.

"Thanks."

"You're most welcome. I'm sure I'll be seeing you around, Jasmine."

She turned to address the woman, who had already been swallowed up by the crowd. Jasmine returned to the room, wondering how the woman knew her name. The idea of magic got on her nerves. It wasn't like she knew how to use the power the book gave her. Jasmine got back to her suite and closed the door. An arm came around her waist and spun her around before she could get her bearings. She jumped. A blast of heat came out of her hands as she pushed away whoever had grabbed her.

"Hey, ouch! What was that for?" Leon's voice brought her back to reality.

She glanced at her warm palms. Both hands glowed green from the magic within her. This wasn't the first time the power had come out on instinct. *Hopefully, the power will manifest when I need it the most.* She rubbed her palms along her jeans until a tingle remained in her fingertips. Jasmine flashed him an apologetic smile.

"Sorry. I didn't mean to zap you." She helped the lion shifter up. Everyone knew Leon as the Cowardly Lion from the *Wizard of Oz* books.

Leon pulled her into his arms and planted his lips on hers. The softness of his mouth made her melt against him, forgetting all about how he pounced on her when she entered the suite. Her fingers trailed down his naked torso, going over the raised scars on his flesh. Her thoughts suddenly turned to them being alone and her on top of him. He worked his way along her throat as his hand snaked under her shirt and cupped her breast. Jasmine moaned as though he were reading her mind.

"I could eat you up," he murmured.

Jasmine stroked the bulge of his cock through his jeans. "I just put my clothes back on."

He pulled away with an over exaggerated pout on his full lips. "Don't you want me to take them off again? Don't you want me?"

She squeezed his dick. "I didn't say that. I need a second. I had a strange encounter downstairs with a woman. It's left me a little shaken. She knew my name."

Leon's golden eyes narrowed. "What did she look like?"

"She was wearing white and had a blueish tint to her skin. Her eyes were the strangest color blue I'd seen. Cold radiated off her. She helped me find my way back to the elevators because I got a little lost. She said she'd see me later."

Leon ran his hands over her arms. The touch comforted her. "This woman might be the real reason why we're here. The book has her own ideas of why she does what she does."

"Why who does what?" Micha stepped into the room drying his dirty blond hair with a towel. Even wet it hung past his shoulders. His defined chest made her lick her lips. She could see the outline of his cock along the towel around his waist. Micha kissed her and pinched her ass until she squealed.

Leon chuckled. "We were talking about how the

book has her reasons for placing us into the realms she does. Have you had a chance to check her today? Jasmine had an encounter downstairs with a frosty woman," Leon told him.

"Not yet." He dropped the towel and went over to his bag where the book remained safely. Micha dug it out and handed Jasmine the tome. The velveteen cover warmed in her hands as bolts of green inched along her arms. The buzz from the magic was something she had come to anticipate. Jasmine slid into a chair and studied the book. It was the size of a dictionary, but not as heavy. She ran her fingers along the spine. The volume shivered in her hands and yawned open without giving her any fuss. Blank pages stared at her.

"Are you going to tell us why you brought us to the hotel?"

I could tell you or you could find out for yourself, the tome replied. Jasmine could almost read the sarcasm in the words.

"I don't think Jasmine's in the mood for your games. You might've written her into the story, but she shouldn't have to deal with your bullshit," Micha responded.

You've been dealing with it for all these years, dear, the book answered him as the text flashed green.

Jasmine glanced at Micha and saw the frustrated look in his blue eyes. They changed color to green before he took a calming breath and they went back to blue. "Look, the guys told me how I'm supposed to save Oz from Dorothy and some other reasons they know I'm the one."

There's more to it than what they've divulged.

"Great, are you going to let me in on the little secret?" Jasmine asked.

If I were to tell you, then what's the point of you experiencing the story? I don't need an editor hacking away all my good lines.

"You do your fair share of writing the scenes. Why don't you give us some indication why we're here? I'm grateful for the reprieve, but how long is this mini-vacation going to last?" Leon inquired. "If you're not going to answer me, can you at least let Jasmine know about this strange woman who approached her?"

All shall be revealed soon enough. You needed the bonding time. All those on the darkened vine are not as deeply rooted in the darkness as they appear. Sometimes you need to trust those who offer you a poisoned apple. As the words on the page faded, the book slammed shut.

Jasmine groaned. She didn't expect anything more from the mysterious magical pages. The book never gave her an easy answer. She needed to live the story to see how it would play out. "Well, that's been helpful." She ran her fingers through her brown hair.

"It was worth a try." Leon kissed her neck once more. She trembled at the desire his action stirred within her.

Micha chuckled, stuffed the book back into the bag, and tossed it onto the sofa. "I wasn't expecting anything different. We have to find out why she wants us here. It has to be more than her wanting us to get acquainted. Not that I'm complaining. We've needed the time together."

He slid his arm around Leon. The lion leaned up and kissed him. Jasmine watched as their mouths met. Leon got up and led him back to the sofa. She looked away as Leon slipped his hand lower on Micha's waist. Leon moaned. She trembled at the throaty sound. Jasmine drew in a quick breath. Micha told her when they first got to Oz, he and Leon had a relationship before he was forced to leave Oz with the book. She told him she hadn't minded. Seeing them together turned her on. A blast of warm breath slid along her neck.

"You want to join us?" Micha asked. He nipped her ear.

She looked into his burning green eyes. The wide smile on his face reinforced the invitation. Leon winked at her. He offered her his hand. "Be with us."

Jasmine took in a deep breath. Being with both of them at the same time made her a little apprehensive. She bit her lip as a small bit of fear went through her. Micha slid his fingers along her collarbone pushing her shirt down.

"You already know we both love you. This is just another evolution of where our relationship is heading." Micha sucked on her throat and cupped her breast. He pinched her nipple until she quivered. She glanced up and met his lips in a hungry kiss as passion ignited in her. Micha pulled her up from the couch. He took her hand and brought his mouth around her finger.

She pressed her thighs together at the sudden rising desire Micha stirred in her. Leon's rough tongue swiped over her wrist as he nipped at her flesh. Jasmine found herself caught between her two beautiful men. She closed her eyes and leaned back against Leon. His hard body reassured her. Leon pushed the hair away from her throat and kissed her slowly marking his territory. Micha took one of her hands and kissed her palm. Once his lips touched the skin, a jolt went through her. His mouth enclosed her finger, slowly sucking it in once more. She opened her eyes to watch him.

"He can pack quite a punch," Leon whispered.

Micha released her finger and trailed his hands down her sides. "I'm packing more than that."

Her head spun being with both of them. A small pain on her neck from Leon biting her reconnected her with her body. Micha had stepped away from them. Leon held her tight, sucking on her neck where he claimed her for his mate. Her body hummed with desire for them.

"I so want to fuck you." Leon scraped his nails down her back.

Jasmine bathed in his bliss, but then pushed herself away from Leon. She sauntered over to Micha and trailed a finger down his chest. Jasmine stopped at the sprinkling of hair before it delved under the towel around his waist. She placed the tip of her tongue on his nipple, barely touching it, but flicking over the hardening bud. With her free hand, she rasped the pad of her fingertip over the other nipple. Micha pulled in a labored breath. She met his gaze. Gradually, Jasmine let more of her tongue touch his nipple, slowly, circling around it, feeling the subtle ridges of the puckering skin. She flicked her tongue over his pec until her entire mouth enclosed on it. She barely pressed her lips upon his supple flesh. The groan that left his lips made her look up and meet his smoldering gaze. His eyes changed color again to the red of the vampire in him.

She trailed her thumb over the ridges of his muscles. Magic arched between them in vibrant flashes of jade. Then she brought her teeth to his nipple, biting it until his fingers wound in her hair and he pulled her to his lips. His tongue hungrily sought entrance into her mouth. Jasmine met his tongue in a fevered French kiss, intermingling their saliva until she pulled away to catch her breath. He was breathing heavy, too.

"Where did you learn to do that?" Micha murmured.

"I still have a few tricks up my sleeve," Jasmine teased.

"I'd like to see some of those, too," Leon whispered against her ear.

"Good." She leaned up on tiptoe and licked the lobe of Micha's ear before nibbling on it. "Just imagine what I can do with your dick." She tugged on his towel until it fell to the floor. Then she slid her hand over his erection. Next, Jasmine sauntered over to the bedroom and passed Leon. She pulled her shirt over her head and dropped it outside the door.

Her men looked at each other and then at her. Smiles spread on their lips. They stalked over to her. She undid her bra and threw it onto the bed. She unbuttoned her jeans when Leon grabbed her and threw her down onto the king-size bed. He straddled her. She craned her neck up and pressed her mouth to his. He kissed her slowly. His lips were soft against hers and she tasted a hint of honey. Jasmine wound her arms around his neck, pressing her breasts against his chest. The bed depressed and the springs creaked. Micha settled behind her. His hands slipped along her sides and cupped her breasts. His fingers grazed her nipples slowly until they hardened.

"What do you want?" Micha asked.

Leon's golden eyes reflected the light. He lowered his head and brushed his tongue along the valley of her breasts. She cried out when Micha twisted her nipples. Her back arched. She felt both men pressed against her. Both their cocks were hard. One against her back, the other touching her stomach through Leon's pants.

"I want you both inside me. I want you both to

fuck me."

"You've never been claimed from behind. It could hurt you," Leon whispered. "I don't want you to be in pain."

She touched his face, seeing the concern for her wellbeing. "I won't be. I'll be with the both of you." She kissed him and turned to bring Micha to her lips as well. His lips were fuller than Leon's, but more firm in a way. He captured her lips while Leon unwound himself from her body. She lingered in the kiss for a few seconds before Micha pulled away, too. Her eyes were glued to Micha. Below the dark patch of hair, his cock jutted out. She reached for it, but Leon caught her hands and pulled them behind her back.

"What was that for?"

He gave her the devilish smile she had come to love. She felt Micha's hands on the waist of her jeans unzipping them the rest of the way. When he touched her clit, a zap of pleasure wound through her.

"Damn, you're already so wet," he murmured next to her ear.

She squirmed while he rubbed her buried bud faster. Leon stood up and moved behind her. He wound his arm around her, anchoring her to the bed, and grabbed hold of his other mate's cock. Micha's eyes widened. Jasmine's muscles clenched, and she came without hesitation. She rested her head against Leon's shoulder, trying to catch her breath. Leon pumped Micha's length, slowly caressing him. There was a shifting in weight on the bed. A groan left her lips when Micha nipped at her throat. She could feel the points of his fangs pressed along her flesh. Micha's hunger had awoken. Her panties were drenched. Both of the men were naked.

"Stand up, Jasmine."

She tried to, but her legs wavered. Leon held her up. Micha slid his fingers down her hips, pushing her jeans and panties completely off. The air helped to cool her now she was naked. She glanced down and saw Micha on his knees. He lifted her foot gently and kissed along her calf. Leon thumbed her nipples, rolling them in circles and hardening them even more.

"I'm going to take you from behind," Leon murmured. "I don't want you to feel any pain. Are you ready for both of us?"

Jasmine heard his words, but as she touched Micha the magic within her sparked. Green trailed down his flesh until he shivered. Jasmine could feel their connection as though their feelings were becoming hers as well. Micha bit her inner thigh a little harder.

"I need you," Micha groaned. "I need to taste you and fuck you." He raked his fingers along her calves. "The magic is binding us together. I can feel your pleasure and Leon's. Oh fuck!"

"I'm yours, completely."

Micha kissed the inside of her thigh, trailed his tongue lightly over her clit, and slid his body along hers. She shivered. Micha claimed her lips. Leon released her hands. She rested her palms lightly on Micha's chest, feeling his heart beating slower than normal because the vampire was in his nature.

"And you're ours," Leon murmured to her.

Jasmine gasped when something cold slid along her backside. She tried to turn, but Micha caught her chin. He locked her gaze with hers. She whispered, "What is --?"

The coldness ringed her asshole.

"It's the lube. It will warm in a moment. It's a wonder what magic can conjure." Micha sat on the bed and scooted back against the mass of pillows. Once he was settled, he grabbed his cock and held it erect for her. "Ride me, Jasmine."

Jasmine nodded, feeling Leon's acceptance and anticipation. She glanced behind her and saw his smile. She climbed onto the bed, straddled Micha, and let him plunge his cock inside her. At the first thrust, he rested his hands on her hips. His eyes closed. Their combined enthusiasm overrode her senses. The magic between them ran under her skin and along Micha's. The very energy enhanced her nerve endings. Each time he touched her, it overwhelmed her with passion. She didn't know how it worked, but she went with it. Jasmine ran her hands over his chest, feeling the smooth, warm skin.

She began a rhythm, drawing him in and out of her pussy. Each time Micha went into her, she sank more into the bliss that enraptured him. Then it expanded when he shifted his hand and rubbed her clit.

"Micha, more," she begged.

He didn't increase his tempo. With his hand on her hip, Micha slowed her motions. The intensity of her coming orgasm mounted the longer Micha rubbed her bud.

"Are you sure you can handle both of us?" he asked.

"Yes. Yes," she whispered.

Her nails left trails on his chest. He cried out when she orgasmed, feeling her ecstasy, although he didn't seem close to coming. Micha stopped massaging her clit and drew her down to his soft lips. His lack of body heat felt good against her fevered flesh. While he kissed her, tasting her, Jasmine sensed Leon behind her. She kissed Micha harder and sank into the desire shredding her insides. She kissed along his jawline and nipped at his throat. He groaned when she licked behind his ear. He thrust inside her faster. She had found one of his arousal points. Jasmine sucked on the small spot, enjoying Micha losing control and plunging into her quicker. Before she could take full advantage, Leon spread her legs wider, then clutched her ass cheeks.

Leon filled her ass gradually. He pulled out and slid back in a little more at a time. Micha had slowed beneath her. He was taking in her experience. His expression remained locked in concentration. Jasmine didn't feel any pain from Leon's entrance. Not even when he moved with her. It took her a moment to realize all three of their hands were entwined. The sense of completion she had was unlike anything she had ever experienced.

"I need you to come for me, Jasmine. Once more," Leon whispered in her ear.

He kissed the line of her neck. He broke their embrace and slid his palm over her chest. She took in a breath and felt the hunger building in Micha. She reached around and cupped Leon's face, bringing her mouth to his. She darted her tongue over his lips, brushing against his sharpened teeth. His eyes glowed and his face seemed more animal than human. He held onto her and his nails were blacked and sharp.

Leon thrust into her again. He was going to come. So was Micha. He cupped her breast and squeezed it. Leon kissed along her neck, reclaiming the spot he marked her as a mate. The rise of her climax overtook her the moment Micha spilled into her. At that exact instant, Leon came, too. Jasmine cried out, feeling the pain of Micha piercing her flesh with his fangs and drinking her blood. She rode the small death wave while her lovers continued to pump into her, and he sucked her blood. Jasmine closed her eyes and gave over to everything. The love she had for her mates encompassed her.

"I love you both," she said to them.

The magic they shared unwound and sank back into her skin, leaving her feeling warm and fuzzy as she drifted in the bliss they shared together. Leon pulled away from her and dropped to one side of the bed. He draped his arm around her and pulled her closer to him. The heat from his body warmed her. Micha wiped the crimson from his lips. His eyes faded back to blue.

"I don't know what I'd do without you two." Micha stroked her cheek and smiled.

"You'd still be an ass," Leon joked.

"What do you mean still?" Jasmine poked Micha's chest.

"I'd be lost without either of you. I might not say it all the time, but I'm glad you are both my mates. I love you," Micha answered.

Leon purred as he nuzzled her neck. His breathing evened out and his hand cupped her stomach. Micha stared into her eyes and traced her lips. "Are you okay?"

"I'm fine. My magic... our magic bound us together... I could feel your desire. There wasn't any pain, just..." Jasmine closed her eyes and shivered. "... just you."

"I'm glad. You should get some rest. We have the convention tomorrow."

The comfort of sleep tugged at her eyelids as she smiled, not able to answer because dreams called.

Chapter Two

Jasmine shimmied her way out from between her two men. Leon snorted and Micha murmured in his sleep. She didn't know how long she had slept, but after their lovemaking she felt like a new woman. Her stomach rumbled. She headed into the bathroom and climbed into the tub. The steam in the bathroom smelled almost like cotton candy and vanilla. After her soak, she went to grab a towel. On top of the bath towel, Jasmine found a green dress along with shoes and undergarments to match the gown. *What the hell? Where did these come from?* Jasmine held the dress up to her body. It appeared to fit. She placed the garment back on the counter and tried the bathroom door. She turned the knob, but it wouldn't budge.

"Micha!" Jasmine shouted and pounded and the door. She gritted her teeth and slammed her palm on the wood. A flash of green energy blasted over the door and dispersed around the room.

She turned around and saw there was, next to the dress, a white feather with a note.

Your presence is requested for dinner by Her Royal Highness, the Erlqueen.

Great! More fucking magic. She touched the feather and a sting of cold gripped her fingers. The chill reminded her of the woman she met in the lobby. It appeared she was being summoned. The only way out of the bathroom was to put on the dress and see what this Erlqueen wanted. Jasmine put on the undergarments, slipped the dress over her head, and zipped it up. The green dress had a Mandarin neckline that hugged her neck, then plunged between her breasts. This was not the type of thing she wore every day. Jasmine admired her reflection. Green energy flowed under her skin and gathered at the hollow of her throat into an emerald. Her hair lifted off her neck and twisted itself up into an ornate hairstyle. It bound itself with a comb with another emerald in the center of her locks as she could see it from the mirror behind her. "I have no idea how that happened, but it looks great. If this is part of the hotel service, I could get used to this." She glanced down at her feet.

"If you gave me the dress, oh great fairy godmother, what about some shoes?" Jasmine said sarcastically to the empty bathroom. A moment later, a pair of shoes popped out of thin air onto the counter. She tried them on. They matched her dress and were flat. They were the most comfortable things she had ever worn. *At least they aren't glass.*

Jasmine picked up the note one more time and wondered why a queen had invited her for dinner.

"There you are. I was beginning to wonder if you had received my invitation."

Jasmine glanced up from the note. Somehow, she had been transported from the bathroom to a glassed-in patio from which she could see the dark landscape outside. The woman from the lobby gestured to the open seat across from her and sipped her champagne. The table was set with only two place settings. The queen wore a sleek dress made of black metallic scales. Her pale blue skin gleamed against the inky fabric. Light blonde hair rolled down her back in ringlets. A silver necklace with a yellow stone at the center hugged her throat.

"How did I get up here?"

The queen laughed. "Magic, darling. I felt you even before I came into the hotel. You're one of the most powerful beings I've ever encountered, and that's saying something with all these dark creatures under one roof. You shine like the emerald at your throat. Oz knows how to make them. Or at least it used to. Sit. Sit."

Jasmine touched the jewel and felt it throb with a life of its own. "I think you have me confused with someone else. I'm not from Oz, but I did visit there. This magic thing is all new to me. I don't even know how to use it. Why did you lock me in the bathroom?"

The queen gave her a sly smile. "I couldn't have you running to your companions. I needed to get you alone. Forgive my antics -- I meant no harm. Sit, please."

Jasmine sighed. The woman wanted an audience with her. She had to endure this before she could go back to Micha and Leon. This meeting could be the whole reason the book brought her here. Jasmine had to see it to the end, so she sat across from the Erlqueen.

A butler popped out of nowhere with a tray. He set the dishes down and removed the domes. On the plates were steak and some green vegetable doused with sauce. Water and wine filled the glasses. Jasmine poked the food with her fork.

"Not hungry?"

"It's not that. You think I'm from Oz, and say I'm the strongest person in this place. You're a queen and I'm nothing. Surely, there are others in the hotel who deserve to be sitting here."

The queen cut into her steak. Blood ran over the white plate. She took a bite and licked her fingers as the juice slid down her fork. Her tongue flicked along her sharp nails. "You really don't know, do you?"

"No, Your Majesty, I don't. I appreciate the dinner invitation and the dress. I'm clearly not who you think I am." She started to get up, but the queen grabbed her wrist. A surge of purple energy wrapped around Jasmine's hand and traveled up her arm. The warmth of the emerald zigzagged from her neck and flashed down her arm. The green tendrils wound around the purple threads until it choked them out. The threads of magic dissolved and the emerald tendrils faded until Jasmine could pull her hand away, leaving her breathless but not drained.

The evil queen removed her hand and sat back with a smug smile. "Girl, you might not know what you're doing, but I've just proven my point. That should've turned you into one of my nightingales. You defended yourself. Just then you were all Oz and now you're all human. Very clever. Whatever switch you turn on, it certainly works. Let me guess -- it's that damn book. She knows how to protect the things she wants."

Jasmine felt the blood drain from her face. "What do you know about the book?"

"Dig into your steak and we'll talk. It's not poisoned. I don't stoop as low as some other wicked queens. I have subtler ways, and I have no desire to add you to my menagerie. I wanted to speak with you is because we have a common foe. When I saw you with the Scarecrow and the Lion, I assumed you knew why you were here. And you arrived just in time too."

Now her curiosity was piqued. "Knew what? What are we in time for?"

"What's been going on with Dorothy. She's driven out all the magical creatures and people in Oz. Didn't the Scarecrow tell you?"

"He hasn't told me much about his past relationship with Dorothy." Jasmine cut into her steak. She tasted it and found it was well done -- the way she liked it.

The Erlqueen drummed her nails on the table.

Each *click-clack* agitated Jasmine a little more. "If you're here with those two and the book, then you're here to topple the evil bitch. Dorothy has sucked out all the magic from Oz. She used to be a good egg, but something snapped in her. Many of the magical inhabitants of Oz became refugees and defected to other realms. The Scarecrow and the Lion sided with the inhabitants of Oz and tried to stop Dorothy. The Tinman sided with her. A great battle ensued, leaving the Scarecrow to escape with a book that opens to other worlds. She's found a way to tap into other realms' magic and drain it. That's why we've gathered here under the guise of this villains' convention. A few others and myself are hoping to defeat Dorothy once and for all."

Jasmine nearly choked on her steak. "Wait, you mean we're here to take out Dorothy?"

"It makes sense. Now you're here, we can discuss it with my counterparts. Your boys will have some ideas."

"How about we relax while you're hatching your evil schemes? I need a break before I take on an evil bitch."

The queen broke out into laughter. "I like you. Your naïveté makes you a breath of fresh air. You need to sit down with your Scarecrow and get some answers. I'll tell you what I know because you're involved in this. Anyone of us would love to get our hands on that book, but it only works for special people. You may not've wanted to end up in your own fairy tale, but sometimes you don't get to choose your fairy godmothers. They're pesky things, by the way. Fairy tales aren't all they're cracked up to be. Neither are the characters in them. Stories start with 'Once Upon A Time' but there's so much to the tales that haven't made it into your mythology. The convention lasts through the weekend. I'll find you before the it ends." She stopped and looked at Jasmine. "You love them, but you're still unsure of your place. You need to resolve that before your power can be fully realized."

Jasmine took a couple more bites of the steak and lost her appetite. Her thoughts moved back to Leon and Micha. "I don't think my heart is an issue. They both know I love them, but I don't know how to use this magic. As you said, my life isn't a fairy tale, so I'm not expecting a prince. Although, I do wish there was an instruction manual to the magic."

The Erlqueen chuckled. "I leave you with this piece of advice. Don't get caught up in your mind. Give up that control and go with it. Magic might be unpredictable, but once you learn to grasp it wonders can happen. Being with your lovers might trigger something within you that you didn't know you had."

Jasmine held in a smile as she thought about being with them both. Her magic had bound them closer together. She couldn't help but think how strange and complicated her life had become. "I think it already has."

The Erlqueen plucked a feather from her dress and crushed it between her fingers. She blew the remnants at Jasmine. "Think about what I said. This feather will bring you closer to your goal. Go down and join the ball."

"What ball?"

"The one for the villains' convention. Why do you think I picked out the dress for you?"

She ran her fingers over the silky material. "Let me guess. I'm going to turn into a pumpkin if I'm not back in my room by midnight and some dark prince will find one of my shoes."

The Erlqueen gave her a small smile and flicked her fingers. A cold breeze enveloped Jasmine. She shivered and the world blurred around her. Her feet hit something solid. When her eyes focused again, Jasmine found herself in the hotel lobby in front of a mirror. Her reflection showed the green dress, but now she had some added makeup. Dark emerald eye shadow accentuated her eyes with lipstick to match giving her a sinister look. *Guess I need to fit in with the other baddies.*

People bustled around her in all types of garb. A sign near the mirror pointed toward the ballroom. She followed it until she heard the music playing. She wasn't sure she could trust the queen. *Maybe she's telling the truth. If Dorothy is trying to take over other worlds and get their magic, then I understand why the queen would want to take her out.* Jasmine sighed and got in line to enter the ballroom.

"Ticket, please, miss," the usher requested.

Jasmine was about to say she didn't have one, when it appeared in her hand. Her fingers had a little chill to them. She handed it over to the usher. "Here you are."

He let her pass. The room was filled with women in flowing dresses and men in tuxes. Some of them were not even human but were different creatures she couldn't classify. The luxury was not something she had witnessed before. Someone grabbed her arm and whirled her onto the dance floor. It took her a moment to realize she was looking at a man with a mask on half his face. The exposed half showed a handsome man. His beguiling smile made her wonder what the true story was about the Phantom of the Opera.

"You look ravishing, my darlin'. I could serenade you about how your beauty is more lovely than the music of the night."

She giggled. "You sure do know how to compliment a woman."

The Phantom spun her so that when she came back around she accidently grabbed his mask to catch her balance, and ripped it off. He growled and threw her away from him. Not before she got a glimpse of the twisted mass of flesh hidden beneath the mask. "You bitch." He raised his hand to slap her when someone caught it.

"I wouldn't if I were you." Micha had the Phantom's wrist. "Find someone else to enthrall." Micha took her hand. Once their flesh made contact, a surge of energy joined them. Warmth entered her heart. Something lifted within him when his eyes glimmered green and he smiled. He seemed more relaxed than he had been before. There was no hint of the red in his gaze, showing the remnants of the vampire. "You look amazing tonight."

"I appreciate the compliment, but didn't you wonder where I was when I wasn't in bed with you two?"

"I saw your note about shopping for the ball. We're safe here, so I wasn't worried. If anything happened, you'd handle yourself." Micha brushed his lips over hers.

"I didn't leave a note."

His eyes narrowed. "Then what happened?"

"I got invited to dinner with the Erlqueen." Jasmine pressed against him as the music slowed. He stopped in the middle of the dance floor and looked at her.

"Who did you say?"

She opened her mouth to say what happened between her and the queen, when he covered her mouth with his. Jasmine returned the kiss and let herself get lost in his caress as he worked his lips over her cheek and nipped on her throat. Being in his arms let her relax. "We should talk about this outside."

"Why?" Jasmine peered into his green eyes and felt herself falling into them. The room grew hot. She needed everyone to stop crowding her. Micha touched her cheek to get her attention. Her head spun and the blood pounded in her ears. She broke away from Micha and dashed toward the nearest exit, taking his advice about getting outside.

The cool breeze made her shiver on the balcony, but she could breathe. She gripped the stone railing and gazed into the garden trying to clear her mind. Several stone statues stood guard along the path leading to the hedge maze. *Why does he know about the Erlqueen?* Jasmine gazed up into the sky and stared into the blackness. In one direction a great fire burned against the ebony horizon. On the opposite side, a bright light like a spotlight lit up the sky. Without any stars, she couldn't find the comfort she normally did in her own realm.

"Hey." Micha touched her shoulder.

Jasmine jumped and faced him. Micha pushed a strand of hair away from her face.

"Why did you run away? I asked you about going outside, but I didn't want to make you run off."

"Sorry. It got a bit too crowded in there. Why did you not want to talk about her in there?"

"Too many prying ears."

"You really weren't worried about me when you found the note?" Jasmine asked, wondering if he had that much faith in her defending herself when she had no idea how to call upon her magic.

"Of course, I was worried when I couldn't find

you. Leon and I searched the suite. I checked the book. She decided to be nice and showed me your conversation with the Erlqueen."

It was difficult to take everything at face value when not everything in the story was the way she thought it would be. "If you read about it, then you know why she wanted to meet me. She thinks I'm here to help stop Dorothy. Maybe the Erlqueen enchanted the book."

Micha opened his jacket and showed her the book in his pocket. It had shrunk down to the size of a regular paperback. "Let's go someplace a little quieter. Nothing can charm the book. She'd rewrite the spell if anyone tried." He brushed his lips across hers. Jasmine melted a little. He led her deep into the hedge maze past the few people who lingered at the entrance until they were quite alone. They rounded a corner where Leon sat calmly on a bench in a small alcove. He smiled when he saw them.

Leon scooted over for them to sit next to him. Jasmine settled in the middle. Leon slid his hand over the material on her thigh. He leaned in and ran his nose along the curve of her throat before pressing his teeth into her flesh. Jasmine whimpered as her heart started racing. His light touch lit up her skin. The lion shifter nipped before pulling away, leaving her wanting more.

"There's my beautiful mate. Micha consulted the book, and she showed us I was supposed to meet you out here. After that she clammed up. I explored the halls but didn't catch your scent."

Micha sat on her other side. He trailed his fingers down her arm and brushed her breast. Leon inched up her dress until he could touch the flesh of her thigh just above her knee. Jasmine squeezed her thighs together and tried to think straight. Leon glanced at Micha. He rubbed his hand over her knee. Micha pulled the book from his pocket and set it in her lap. It grew back to its original size. Leon placed his hand from her knee over Micha's hand. She glanced between them and caught the loving look they shared.

"Shit. Have you guys gotten a little bit of alone time? I hadn't even thought about it. I mean we've all shared… but you two." Jasmine was trapped by the book and their hands and she didn't mind. It made her feel wanted to have them touching her and see the love in their gazes. Micha played his fingers over the back of her hand, trailing green lines of her magic from under her skin that made her shudder.

She needed to tell them about what the Erlqueen said. Unless the book revealed their whole discussion. All of it overwhelmed her. Maybe this was happening because it was fated to happen. The odds were she wasn't going home until her story concluded. The book wasn't allowing her to jump ahead in their story. *The queen said I had to settle the matters with my heart before I can realize my power.* It seemed so simple when she just had the wrong car at the beginning of her story before she ever met Micha and found out the rental company had screwed up.

"Don't worry about us getting some alone time. We can do that when this is all over," Leon told her.

"I think it's time to see if the book will tell us her agenda. We need to see what's coming next. Are you game?" Micha asked.

"If we can see what's going to happen, sure. Let's see what she's got." Jasmine forced a smile, hoping to get more answers.

They placed their hands on the book's cover. A surge of power singed her hand and spread deeper within her. Jasmine sneezed at the wave. Green tendrils sprouted from the book and wound around their wrists binding them together. The glow from the vines grew until it blinded her. The cover of the book changed material under their palms. It lost its velveteen softness replaced by the suppleness of new leather. The power flared once more, lighting up the bones in her arm as the vines shivered and fell off. When they lifted their hands, a large golden "O" interlocked with a "Z" and an emerald in the center stood out on the leather cover.

Another jolt of energy shot up her arm. The impact lifted her a couple inches off the bench, but the two men held onto her as the power passed into her. Jasmine could see the power behind her eyes and feel it in the gem at her throat. The book opened to the first page. Gone was the "Once Upon A Time…" beginning. Text appeared on a blank sheet.

Hello, Jasmine. Please forgive my boys for how they've acted. They each had to be sure you were the one as you already know. It's nice to finally meet you. I'm Gertrude.

"Gertrude. You've had a name through all this, and you're telling me now? Is that why you've been jerking my chain?" The sudden surge of anger she felt toward the text made her want to tear the pages out.

Once the boys accepted you, and you were able to conquer Micha's new thirst, I thought it was time to reveal my true nature.

"It's taken you long enough. Who are you, really?" Jasmine asked.

I'm the Wizard.

"Seriously? I thought the Wizard was a man and not a book."

"Dorothy was never the witch's prisoner. After she had drained the magic from Glen-da's sister -- the

Good Witch of the North -- and killed her, she stole the Wicked Witch of the West's power and the book." Leon nuzzled her neck and nipped at it.

Jasmine bit her lip and pressed her legs together. "You can't do that if you want me to concentrate."

"I can't help it. That dress shows off a lot of your skin and you smell wonderful." He bit into her neck harder. Jasmine grabbed Micha's hand and squeezed it.

"Leon, let her be so Gertrude can talk. Jasmine needs to finally know the truth." Micha stroked the back of her hand while Leon pulled away but remained seated next to Jasmine. When she inhaled, Jasmine caught the heady animal scent of the lion. It made her head spin and her body tingle.

"Let me tell you a story. Read this aloud and understand why you're so important."

Jasmine took in a breath and focused on the words scrawling on the page. They spelled out a very different story than the Wizard of Oz from her childhood.

Chapter Three

Glancing at Micha and Leon, Jasmine read aloud from the magic book. "By the time Dorothy was rescued, she had gotten a taste for the magic of Oz from the Wicked Witch of the West. Micha and the others never knew she had become the witch's pupil and not her prisoner. Once they rescued her, Dorothy emerged from the castle with the witch's magical book. At first, nothing was amiss, and the book helped Dorothy and the others. She allowed them to step through her pages and into other worlds. However, as time passed, Dorothy changed. She fell in love with the Tinman and used her newfound powers to fashion him a special axe.

"The Scarecrow adored Dorothy and would do anything for her. The Cowardly Lion pined for his mate, hoping Micha would see that Dorothy didn't really care for him. It hurt Leon to have his mate toss him aside. Leon asked the book to see if, anywhere in the story, Micha would come back to him. Gertrude peered into the future and saw the worst turn of events. To help counteract the diabolical state of affairs caused by Dorothy, she spun a tool to rival the Tinman's axe. Gertrude told Leon of the collapse of Oz and swore him to secrecy. Yet there was a bright spot. A prophecy of one who could restore Oz to its greatness and heal his heart.

"Leon didn't want to believe what Gertrude told him. Then Dorothy went one step too far. She commanded the Tinman to slaughter the people of Munchkinville because they had made an unflattering crack about her. Micha snapped out from under her spell. He stole the axe and cleaved a hole in their dimension to another realm. He shoved the Tinman through the rift, but not before Haley grabbed the axe and brought it with him. Dorothy punished Micha by turning him from straw into a real man. After the astonishing transformation, Dorothy had the brilliant idea that magic could change her into what she so desperately wanted to be. She concocted a scheme to touch upon the very magic woven into Oz and its citizens. She devised a way to pull magic from the world around her and from its people, killing thousands.

"Gertrude finished spinning her weapon by using words and ink. She imbued it with her own magic and got some help from Glen-da to create a magic pen to rewrite what was possible. Then she helped smuggle citizens of Oz out of the city and into other worlds that would be safe for them, so Dorothy would not claim their magic and their lives.

"Dorothy came with her minions for the Wizard's power. Leon swore to protect the Wizard. Glen-da and the Scarecrow fought off her flying monkeys. Dorothy started her enchantment, but Glen-da came back with a spell that threw Dorothy out of the castle. Glen-da drove out their enemies and set up a force field around the city to keep Dorothy out.

"Together, they formulated a plan to secret the book away from Oz. Dorothy discovered their plot and sent a handful of monkeys through the gateway. The Scarecrow ferried Gertrude away to Earth. Over the years, Micha eliminated the monkeys one by one until only two remained. Leon mourned the loss of his mate, but he understood the sacrifice Micha made. Gertrude tried to find an answer in her pages to rid the world of Dorothy or write in a few story changes. However, she couldn't erase the prophecy in her pages. She found she *could* influence story lines the way Micha's pen did.

If she was ever going to become human again and rid Oz of Dorothy's evil wrath, then the prophecy had to be fulfilled. Someone who had the lineage of Oz in their blood was needed. This person had to be able to unlock the book and reunite the two long-lost loves.

"The prophecy told of an ordinary person who found themselves in a fairy tale even if they didn't want to believe that. The Scarecrow scoured the Earth, always on the move to keep the book from Dorothy's evil monkeys. If he stayed in one place too long, the monkeys could catch the book's scent. As he roved the world, he found ordinary lads and maidens who almost fit the bill. None seemed to be right. Gertrude began to think no one would ever be found. Micha lost hope in ever returning home. He pined for Leon and prayed he could return home soon.

"Much time passed. Wars raged on Earth. Nations were born and torn apart. Micha pressed on, keeping the book safe and using the magic of the pen sparingly as it took a while to recharge. Gertrude steered him toward a few targets, but none clicked with the book. Micha decided to take a break from the search. Then his car and Jasmine's were switched, and he had the opportunity to meet her. Neither he nor Gertrude saw her coming. Things took an even stranger turn when the monkeys destroyed his car. The only way to save himself and Jasmine was to get to Oz, but oh my, how things had changed."

* * *

Jasmine stopped reading and looked up at the two men. "So Dorothy devised a way to pull magic from the people of Oz and the whole land. What made her so power hungry?"

The book, Gertrude, revealed she could only be opened by someone whose ancestors had come from

Oz. Her fingers itched to turn the page and find out more.

Of course, you have questions, Gertrude answered Jasmine's thoughts. *It's understandable. For you to defeat Dorothy, you need to control your magic. In order to awaken the magic, you needed to open your heart to your mates. I gave you the push, but you need to grab a hold of it. You've awakened the lion within Leon. Micha has opened his heart to you. You are the one the prophecy within my pages spoke about.*

"I can't be the one." Jasmine voiced her disbelief even though, deep down, she knew everything added up to her being the one Gertrude spoke about.

What more proof do you need? the book asked.

She shook her head. "None, I guess. So what's next? Are you going to tell us how to defeat Dorothy?"

"It'd be nice if you gave us a straightforward answer, Gert." Leon slid his palms along Jasmine's shoulders. Jasmine shivered as his nails dug into the fabric of her dress. The warmth of his hands broke through to her skin.

I'm not going to be much help to you when it comes to Dorothy. I don't know the ending to this story. I can write what I want to happen, but there are forces beyond my control as to how this plays out.

"Of course, they are." Micha trailed his fingers over the pages.

"What do we do until the story changes? What do we do about the Erlqueen?" Jasmine asked.

Enjoy yourselves. The words flashed on the pages.

Leon kissed the top of her head. "I think we take her advice. Want to join me in the room, Jasmine?"

She turned back to him and smiled. Being in his arms sounded wonderful, but she wanted to clear her head. "In a few minutes."

He separated from her. "Sounds good. Gert, you coming back up to the room or are you going to stay with Jasmine?"

We're going to talk for a little while. I have a few more things I think she needs to see before you can have her back. Micha, why don't you go back with Leon? The book closed and stayed in Jasmine's lap.

"Later." Leon touched her cheek and winked at her. He tugged on Micha's arm. He got up from the bench in the maze and looped his arm around Leon's waist.

"See you later." Micha dragged his finger along her collarbone and gave her a cocky smile as his eyes flashed green giving her a promise of what was to come later.

Once her men were gone, the book shimmered and the velveteen cover returned. Jasmine opened the text again and found the pages were full until she came to a blank chapter. It felt like she was back to square one even though she had more information. She hung her head in her hands and held back some tears because her two men were counting on her to get it together and take down Dorothy. She ran her fingers over the pages. The green streaks under her flesh were like veins of magic. *This magic within me means I'm related to someone from Oz.* Her mother's family grew up in Maine and her father's parents emigrated from Italy to Nebraska. She didn't know much about her great-grandparents on either side.

"Can you show me who I'm related to from Oz?" Jasmine asked Gertrude.

Lines came together and colored in to illustrate a young girl being pushed through a curtain where people welcomed her. On the other side of the drape was New York City at the turn of the twentieth century. The picture changed. It showed an older version of the girl who resembled an image of her great-great grandmother on her mother's side. This was who she had gotten her magic from.

"What kind of person was she?" Jasmine asked.

She was an ordinary girl born into a family of merchants. Her father crafted jewels for the highborn of Oz. She was found to be magical and Glen-da was about to take her under his wing. It was a proud moment in the family. Those with magic were highly regarded in the North and South. That's where you inherited your magic from. Stronger than her, too.

"You've been awakening the magic within me, but how do I control it?" Jasmine raked her fingers over her face. She didn't want a part in this war, but she was already in it. She rubbed her fingers together. Sparks came from her fingertips. Her heart felt like it was torn in two. Her mind said one thing and her heart said another. The Erlqueen told her she had to set her mind aside and follow her heart. "We're in the middle of a villains' convention. I'm certainly not one of those. What if you're wrong and I'm really not the one?"

Get out of the headspace of you being an ordinary girl doing paperwork in her office. You're not that woman anymore. Technically, you are *a villain when it comes to Dorothy. She's been searching for me, but she can't find me here. There's too much magic shrouding this place.*

"Where are we, anyway?" she asked.

In a place between here and there. Between light and dark. It's a place where she can't get in unless she's invited. I'm not sure about any of her minions. They are arduous to track these days because they've become more human than monkey.

"Those are the flying monkeys with the Wicked Witch of the West that came after Micha and I?"

The very same.

"Such a lovely bird away from the nest. What are you doing out here alone and reading in such horrible light? You should be inside with the other exquisite ladies, dancing the night away."

The weight of the book evaporated from her lap. She was left with a man before her with a long hood obscuring his face. The magic under her skin zinged along her arms and centered in her palms. The man stepped back. "Whoa, pretty lady. I'm giving you a compliment. You shouldn't have to be out here all alone with the shindig in the hotel."

"Thank you, but I'd rather be by myself."

Jasmine left the hooded figure behind and wandered farther into the hedge maze. She felt like she was in the hedge maze from *The Shining*. Pressure built around and within her until it seemed her heart would burst. She got to the middle of the hedgerow and found a pool. She glanced around and only had one way in and one way out. Rustling starting around her. The verges had closed off the opening behind her. A faint light shone from the pool, and someone popped out of the water. Her arms rested on the side of the pond. Big blue eyes stared up at Jasmine. Blonde hair dripped water and curled around a heart-shaped face. A seashell bra covered her breasts.

"Hello," the woman said.

Her iridescent skin shimmered in the light. Her skin wasn't flesh but scales. "Hello. Who are you? Why did you trap me in this labyrinth?"

"I didn't trap you here. I'm not sure how I got here myself. I was swimming, and then I saw this light. I swam toward it and you were on the other end. You look sad?" She pushed her blonde hair back from her head.

Jasmine sank down on the bench before the pool. The woman in the pool had a long fishtail where there should have been legs. Something snapped in Jasmine. "I'm not sad. I'm just trying to process all the information I've learned. It's overwhelming to discover everything I thought about my family wasn't true."

"Sometimes family isn't all that it's cracked up to be. I'm sure you'll get a handle on it."

"They want me to go into battle using magic I don't know how to use. Where I'm from magic doesn't exist. I'm at a loss here."

The mermaid lifted out of the water on a large wave. Jasmine waited for it to slosh over the pool, but it froze. The mermaid sat atop of it, so they were eye to eye. Her skin glistened.

"Doesn't that hurt? You know -- the seashells against your nipples. Chaffing or anything?" Jasmine asked.

The mermaid looked down at the seashell bra. "My attire isn't the point."

"Sorry. I always wondered from the pictures, but yes, you're right."

"What does your heart tell you? I've always listened to mine."

Jasmine thought about what she knew about books and remembered she had read a story about a mermaid. "Yes, but didn't one of your kind turn into sea foam because the prince didn't love her back?"

"If you're going to be rude about it, I'll leave." The mermaid dove off her frozen wave, back into the pool, and disappeared. The water sloshed over Jasmine and left her soaked.

"That sucked."

"You can't trust mermaids. Their heads are full of sand and sea shanties." A dark voice came from the pool.

Jasmine peered down into the pool. Something dark spread into the water. A face formed in the murky water. Glowing malice gazed back at her from yellow eyes under the water. *I'm getting a little tired of this fairy-tale shit.* "Are you here to tell me I have to say 'Mirror, mirror on the wall' to get you to talk?"

The presence in the pool laughed, shaking the shrubs. "I haven't done the mirror gig in a long time. I'm pulled to the strongest witch around and you're it."

"I really don't want to be. I'd rather figure out how to call upon my magic before I have to do battle with a tyrannical teenager. At least, I think she's a teenager."

"After serving many diabolical women, I have a bit of knowledge I can impart. This place is full of power-hungry civilians. If you cross one, they'll come back on you threefold. Gathering so many here in this space has taken years as they are outside of their respective realms."

"Did you get recruited as the spokesperson for this convention?"

"Let's not talk about that. I'm here for you right now. You might have been enlisted to fight, but you truly wish to return home."

"I can't go home. They need me to fight Dorothy."

"You have the power within you to go home *now*. They don't *need* you. Wouldn't you rather be back in your realm, enjoying the comforts of your own castle?"

It'd be nice to go home and put this all behind me. But then, I'd never see them again. She wasn't ready to not have Micha and Leon in her life. She loved them. "I don't live in a castle."

"You get my drift. Your home where you don't have to worry about any flying monkeys chasing you. Where you can be comfortable without fighting any war."

A warm feeling wove around her as she thought of her home. The image of her apartment appeared in the water. It would be easy to step through the pool and return to the world she knew. Her fingers tingled from the power within her. She touched the surface. The image shimmered. The texture of the water changed until it felt as thin as a bubble. She could easily cross dimensions and be back in her apartment wrapped up in a blanket, sipping tea and watching her favorite show. Her life would return to normal. Leon and Micha had kept the information from her. They did say they would try to get her home. Maybe they didn't know she had the power either. *I'll bet Gertrude does. That bitch is keeping the information from me, so she can get her own way and write the story she wants. Just like Dorothy when she had the silver slippers. She had the way to go home all along.*

"Wouldn't it be nice to go back to your home and sip tea? Maybe curl up with a good movie. Then you can go back to your friend and tell her some animal messed with your campsite. You don't have to worry about Leon and Micha anymore. They don't need you. They're happy to be back in one another's arms."

The soothing voice lulled Jasmine into a sense of serenity. *Who cares about Leon and Micha?* They'd been lying to her the whole time. *They don't love me.* That part was obvious because who could love her? *No... That's not right. I know they love me.* They said it, proved it with their touches and the way they made her body light up.

You're fooling yourself. They don't love you. They don't want to get back at Dorothy. They want the power all to themselves. That's the only reason they have the book and you. They know they can control you.

She took in a breath to clear her head. Her mouth filled with water. Something cinched around her wrists as Jasmine gripped the edge of the pool and tried to pull herself out of the water. The voice she thought was her own thoughts whispering in her mind turned into a sinister one as the laughter spread. Jasmine panicked. She tried to escape, but the restraints around her wrists tightened. Jasmine couldn't call for help. Stars dotted the edge of her vision. This thing was trying to kill her! Anger flared to fill her with a greater heat than she had felt before. She held onto that rage and directed it toward the phantom in the pool. A scream pierced her mind. She jerked herself out of the water. The vines around her wrists snapped. The pool blackened. The shriek echoed through the grove.

She backed up until the back of her knees hit the bench and she sat down. Someone called her name. A large lion broke through the hedge with Micha on his back. A zap of green hit the center of the inky pool.

"You won't defeat me. You think that weakling's going to push me out?" A shrill voice came from the water.

"You're going down, Dorothy," Micha screamed.

"That's what you think." Her voice faded away.

Leon bumped Jasmine's knee and sat before her. Micha sank down on the bench next to her. He touched her shoulder. "Are you okay?"

"Cold." She shivered within the water-logged dress.

"How about we get you inside and warmed up?" He led her inside with Leon, as a lion, protecting her as they went up to their room. Jasmine tried to undo the zipper on her dress, but her fingers were too numb from the cold to grip it.

"Here, I'll do it," Micha said to her.

"Go ahead. Thank you for saving me," she replied.

Micha stopped halfway and sighed. "You're welcome." He finished with the rest of the zipper. Leon walked in with a large towel for her while he remained naked. She wrapped it around herself but didn't feel any warmer. "What happened to you down there?"

"Gertrude told me some things about my family history. I needed a little time to digest the information. Dorothy popped in and started messing with my head."

"I don't know how she found her way in." Leon took the towel from her and slid the material along her limbs, warming her up.

Both men fawned over her to make sure she was safe and dried off. Micha got a robe for her so she would be warm. Part of her told her they were doing it because they needed her to defeat Dorothy. Another part knew she loved them. That was the slice she listened to. Life wasn't black-and-white the way it could be in a book. The words that created their story weren't easy to read because they weren't trapped between pages. They were alive. She finally had the courage to rip out of that paper prison she had been living in.

"Guys, it's okay. Tempers were high. I let her get under my skin." She touched Leon's hand. He stopped and so did Micha. "Besides me being descended from someone in Oz. Micha, you have power along with the pen and now the axe. You could use them to change the story with Dorothy."

"Those are all good points." Micha trailed his finger along her collarbone. "Gert has given me some magic over the years, but not enough to take Dorothy down. There's barely enough magic in Oz to keep it going. That's why when the cyclone was coming for us, I used the pen. You were hurt. I depleted its magic to heal you. The usage drained the magic from me until I barely clung to life because it also exhausted my life force. Years ago, it would've been nothing. I've tried to change the story line with Dorothy to kill her myself, but I've been unsuccessful."

"Gertrude showed us the prophecy in her pages. Nothing could change it. In Oz, people assumed I was a coward because I hung back from a fight. They were afraid of my lion form so I learned to stay contained in my human flesh. I pined for Micha while he traversed Earth keeping the book away, but you brought him back to me." Micha kissed Leon quickly before touching her cheek. His flesh burned against hers. "Will you come over to the mirror? We want to show you something. It's another reason to prove why you're the one."

She nodded as they led her over to the mirror. The jewel at her throat had vanished. Leon took her hand in his and laid it over her heart. Micha slipped a hand over theirs. Green energy crackled between their joined hands. Jasmine arched her back as a bolt of power rode her spine. She kept her eyes locked on their reflection. Green energy streamed through all three of them. Micha's features changed slightly to reveal the scarecrow underneath with the stitched brown mouth and the buttons for eyes. Leon's reflection showed the lion behind the human mask.

"The magic within all three of us shows we truly are brought together by fate. Gert has a spell that will destroy the containers Dorothy's storing the magic in. With no magic to bolster her, she'll run out of power and be human," Micha told her.

She played her fingers over their hands watching the lines of green move through them all. "If we focus her spell on whatever's collecting the magic, then won't it be sucked into this battery as well, leaving her even more powerful than before?" Jasmine asked.

Micha pecked her throat. "We overload the collector. What magic has been stolen will be returned to the land. At least, that's what Gert hopes will happen. She can push the magic to where it needs to go. Hopefully, there'll be enough where she can turn herself back into a person instead of a book. It'll be nice to have to stop protecting her."

"Without you, we wouldn't be complete. We love you," Leon purred.

She closed her eyes and enjoyed the sensation of them touching her. Magic sang within her. It reached out to both men to bind them all together. She wanted answers. She had gotten them. Jasmine turned and claimed Leon's lips in a quick kiss. Then she kissed Micha. "I love you, too."

Chapter Four

Jasmine released their hands and walked behind Micha. She trailed her hands over his shoulder blades down over his back until she encompassed his waist. Jasmine took one breath and caught the scent of fresh hay. She felt for the buttons on his shirt and undid them. Halfway down, Micha caught her hands. He took a step back and undid the rest, stripping it off so she could watch. When he went to pull down his pants, Leon grabbed his hands and stopped him.

Micha looked at her as Leon went to his knees and inched his pants down so his cock sprang out. Jasmine wasn't sure she should stay. She backed away a step to give them their privacy.

"No, Jasmine. Kiss me." Micha held out his hand to her.

She undid the belt of her robe and let it fall to the floor. She took his hand and twined his fingers with hers. Micha captured her lips in a quick kiss before he let out a moan. Jasmine felt Leon's hair tickling her stomach. She glanced down and watched as Leon drew Micha's dick into his mouth. His head bobbed as he sucked. She threaded her fingers through Leon's shaggy mane. He didn't stop pleasuring Micha. Her Scarecrow held onto Leon's shoulder. He stared at her while his eyes went from green to red. He hissed, showing off his fangs. Jasmine saw the hunger burning in his eyes. She offered him her wrist. He grasped it and kissed inside it, but he didn't bite.

Instead he groaned and his breath hitched. "Leon, that's it, babe." He gripped Leon's shoulder harder and leaned forward on his feet. His lips pressed into her wrist so she could feel the fangs through the thin skin. Their hardness turned her on. His eyes blazed as Leon stroked Micha's hip. Micha cried out one more time and shivered as he came. Green energy flared from him over to her. It left her with a shiver of pleasure. Leon turned around after pleasuring Micha and rubbed his cheek along her thigh. She threaded her fingers through his hair. His fingers slid along her thigh as he opened her legs. His tongue flicked across her flesh as he found her pussy. Jasmine moaned when she felt his rough tongue delve into her slit and found her clit.

"W-what are you doing?" she asked Leon, trying to stay balanced on her feet.

He kissed her thigh. "Whatever I want."

Micha pressed his fangs into her wrist until his lips locked around her flesh and he drank her blood. "Oh, fuck."

Leon worked her clit with his rough tongue. His fingers went along her inner thigh until they slid inside her. She grabbed Leon's shoulder and held on as his tongue grazed over her. Micha sipped on her blood. Green flowed down her arms and crackled over both her and Leon. She bit her lip to keep the warmth from spilling out even more. Micha dragged his tongue over the wounds on her wrist.

"You taste so good," Micha crooned and then captured her lips. Jasmine quivered as she came quickly from Leon's tongue and his hands plunging into her. Micha held her close as Leon kept on torturing her until it felt like the magic within her was going to burn her alive if she didn't get rid of it.

She broke away from Micha and took in a deep breath. "Micha, I…"

"Shhhh… push it into us. We can take it. It's what we're here for." Micha kissed her throat.

Leon looked up at her and trailed his tongue

along her stomach. He placed kisses here and there until he stood by her side and took her other hand. Jasmine pushed the warmth from her hands and along their connected palms. The energy climbed into them and sank into their bones until the warmth left her and Jasmine felt as though she was in control of herself again. She breathed one more time and the power within her dissipated. She glanced up at her two men and saw how amazing they were. The magic she passed to them glowed under their skin. She could feel the connection between them only growing stronger.

"That was something," Jasmine said to both of them.

Leon trailed his fingertips along her arm. "Yes, it was."

"Are we going to take this back into the bedroom?" Micha asked.

Jasmine grabbed her robe and slipped on. She kissed each of them. "You two spend some time together." Her stomach growled. "I'm going to order room service and find something to watch. I'm starving."

Micha chuckled. "Using magic can do that. You sure, love?"

She glanced between the two of them and nodded. "I'm sure."

Leon kissed her again and nibbled on her. "Thanks, Jasmine." He grabbed Micha's hand and led him into the bedroom.

She grabbed a menu and looked over room service to decide what she wanted to eat, glad to give her two men some time alone.

* * *

Jasmine opened her eyes. It took her a moment to recall she was in the middle of the bed. Leon snorted next to her. His arm was flung across her chest. Micha's head rested on her side. His legs dangled off the bed.

The book appeared on her lap and opened. *I'm not writing this part of your story if that's what you're thinking.*

"I wasn't thinking that. I did before, but I know this is part of my story you couldn't change."

Glad to hear it. Please don't tell the boys, but I'm running out of pages.

"Why are you telling me this?" Jasmine whispered so she wouldn't wake her lovers.

The pages rustled together. *In order to channel the magic to defeat Dorothy, you need the emerald on my cover. I had a feeling about you from the beginning.*

"Is that why you protected me from those monkeys at the campsite?"

Yes. I went on a hunch you were the right fit.

"Good thing you put all your eggs in my basket. What now?"

Meet with Hess, the Erlqueen, and their third. I don't know who it is. They wouldn't tell me.

"You set this all up?"

Been planning it for years. That's why I brought you to this place. They've been the worst affected by Dorothy's encroachment on their realms. They want her out of the picture as much as anyone else. The other villains are here because well... this is an unprecedented event. This hotel is neutral ground. Meet with them this evening. I have something planned. Until then, enjoy the boys.

She thought about what Gertrude wrote. "I did enjoy them."

You needed to come together for the magic to take root within you. Now you can kill Dorothy.

"Thanks, Gert." Jasmine wanted to say more, but

Micha stirred. The book dissolved and returned to its hiding place. He gazed at her and smiled.

"Morning." He crawled over and kissed her. "How are you?"

"I'm fine."

He trailed his fingers under the sheet and over her breasts until she giggled. "Good. I didn't know if we'd hurt you. Leon likes to bite."

"I didn't do any of that last night." Leon brushed his mouth along her cheek, then leaned over and claimed Micha's lips.

Jasmine felt her cheeks flush as they kissed. Watching them was sexy as hell and it turned her on. "I'll leave you two alone. I'm going to take a shower." She shimmied out from between them and went into the bathroom.

After she washed up, Jasmine grabbed her bag and found clothes inside. What she pulled out was a black skirt, a black blouse, and a pair of combat boots. "What in the world is this?"

"I think we're supposed to fit in as villains. What do you think?" Leon asked as he came out dressed in a leather vest and tight black jeans wearing knee-high combat boots.

Micha appeared in hip-hugging leather pants with a red shirt. Both fit the part. "I feel ridiculous. I was never Goth."

"What's a Goth?" Leon asked.

"I'll tell you later." Micha wrapped an arm around her waist.

"You look lovely. How about we go mingle?" Leon slipped his hand around her waist.

Jasmine kissed Micha's cheek and then Leon's. Weight shifted on her head. She broke apart and found the mirror. Her hair had darkened into a shade of green. Her lips were adorned with black lipstick. Dark eyeshadow painted her lids. Her backpack had turned into a small black purse she could sling across her chest with a studded metal skull on the cover. She wore a choker with metal studs with a square-cut emerald in the center.

"Whatever Goth is, it's damn sexy," Leon purred.

Jasmine shook her head as the three of them went to join the rest of the villainous crew.

Down in the lobby, Micha handed them each a lanyard. "Remember, we need these to go anywhere."

Jasmine took a program and glanced at the schedule of panels to see if any topic caught her eye.

How to Kill Your Goody Two-shoes in Three Simple Steps

"Falling with Style" -- How not to appear totally inept while honing your Villaincraft

Succeeding Without Minions: A Streamlined Approach

Poisons and Which Foods Best Mask Them

Living Your Best Life Through Fear and Intimidation

Different Kinds of Magic and How to Wield It.

"Any of these sound good?" Leon asked.

"This *Different Kinds of Magic and How to Wield It* sounds interesting. You want to come with me?" Jasmine asked.

He hooked his arm through hers, and they sauntered off to their panel. Micha went his own way. As they walked the halls, Jasmine was surprised to see how many people -- creatures might have been a better word for them -- had shown up. She and Leon walked by things with eight legs and tentacles. Leon kept her close as something else slid by that left a slime trail. It seemed to be a creature akin to a snake mixed with a slug. Another invisible thing whacked into her. Smaller insect-like creatures flew together in a swarm that could have been bees, but they all had mothwings. Hallways were so packed that she could barely move. They made it to the panel which didn't have many people in it. The speaker floated a foot above the floor. His long black hair hung down around his shoulders. He clacked his fingernails together as he waited for the doors to close. Once they did, his purple skin tone lightened to pale green.

"Greetings, comrades, you're here to learn about the different kinds of magic and how to wield it. My specialty is touch magic. All I have to do is brush against you and I can make you do anything I wish. Touch something of yours or your enemies and they are mine.

"Many of you control your magic with incantations, word magic. Other forms are sex magic, or forming the spell by thinking. In these two hours, you're going to delve deeper into magic and see a few demonstrations."

Jasmine listened to the sorcerer talking about the different kinds of magic. She slipped her hand into her purse and came out with a notepad and pen. As he spoke, she started to take notes about all the different kinds of magic. She found it all fascinating even if it was geared toward evildoers.

After the seminar, Jasmine's head buzzed. She headed out into the hallway and a woman holding a leash led around some green blobby monsters chained in a line, each wearing a red T-shirt stating Minion 1, Minion 2, all the way down the line until the baker's dozen of minions had walked past them.

Leon left her after the two-hour panel. Micha joined her for a couple of panels until she was on her own in the last one listening to a man speak about how to sacrifice a virgin in more than ten different ways. Jasmine walked out. Pretending to be a bad guy tired her out and the boots hurt her feet. No one bothered her. Being amongst all the malefactors, she could feel their darkness rubbing on her like sandpaper.

Jasmine grabbed a cup of water and settled into a corner to observe the people talking in the hallway. A flurry of activity started. People flattened against the wall. Trumpeters announced whoever was coming. The rooms emptied. Everyone applauded as the bodyguards came through with the guest of honor. The Erlqueen stopped in front of Jasmine and held out her hand.

"I've been looking for you."

All eyes went to her. Jasmine wanted to shrink into the wall, but she squared her shoulders and went before the queen. One of the queen's attendants stepped in front of her with his spear and pointed it at Jasmine.

"Kneel before the Erlqueen, peasant."

Jasmine glanced around the room at the shocked stares directed toward her. The queen smirked, waiting for Jasmine to make a move. Micha started toward her, but Jasmine gave him a slight shake of her head. She had to step up and let them know she could take on Dorothy. Jasmine didn't know how to use her magic, but it kicked in when she felt threatened. The words from the panel she attended on how he described working with magic came back to her. Magic was a living thing within them that had to be utilized. If not, then it could consume you. Power lured them into the darkness because it easily corrupted. Some of what he said made sense because Jasmine had seen the power running through her skin. The sorcerer said to get a hold of it early, then you could choose the path you wished to walk. What he said about forming the outcome of the spell in the mind and seeing it through made sense. Magic bent and changed the world around her. Sometimes magic needed a catalyst like a physical joining which he referred to as sex magic. The whole room erupted in laughter because they all seemed to know exactly what he was talking about. Curses that needed something of a person to do them harm. Using magic to change shape. Needing a sacrifice to spark the spell because the energy from the kill would fuel the ritual. If sacrifice was not done, the incarnation could use the energy of the person casting it. Which made sense to what Micha had told her about him forming the doorway in Oz. It helped her understand some things that hadn't been explained before.

The guard waited for her to genuflect before the queen. Instead, Jasmine sought the tingling inside her she associated with magic. Jasmine envisioned turning the guard into a shrub. It might not have been very imaginative, but it was the first thing that popped into her head. The energy built in her hand and raced out of her palm. The blast propelled the sentry through the wall behind them. Someone screamed. Jasmine gathered the rest of her strength and followed the path she'd created to find the guard flattened between the window's glass panes. His form slowly changed into a tree growing toward the sunlight.

It had worked. Although, not in the way she had anticipated. Other villains gathered around her. "I bow to no one." Jasmine turned on her heel and walked out to face the queen. "Is there something you wanted of me?"

"I was done for the day and hoped you'd accompany me to dinner. You and your two men.

You're the talk of the convention. Everyone's going to be discussing that move for a long time."

"You summoned us?" Leon went to one knee before Jasmine, picked up her hand, and kissed the back of it. She ran her nails through his hair and enjoyed the sensation of having him bow before her. It was empowering. Micha knelt on her other side, took her foot, and licked the side of her boot. He looked up at her and winked.

"You have some sexy underlings. Join me for dinner before we all get mauled by the crazy horde." The Erlqueen gestured for them to stand and her bodyguards to follow. People clapped in the halls as they walked by. Micha and Leon stayed behind them as Jasmine walked beside the queen and the group went into a private dining room.

Two other people sat at the table. One she recognized as Hess, the Headless Horseman. She could only see the back of the other person's head. The Erlqueen sat by Hess. Leon and Micha sat next to the unknown occupant, leaving Jasmine to sit between the queen and Leon. The mystery guest pushed the hood of their cloak off their head. Micha and Leon retreated backward from the table knocking over their chairs. Leon hissed. His claws grew, and he nearly lashed out.

"What is she doing here?" Micha asked pointing at the woman with disbelief in his eyes.

"You're dead," Leon growled.

The woman appeared to be in her mid-thirties with fair skin and hair so black it looked like she'd just dyed it. Her twisted smirk made the butterflies in Jasmine's stomach turn into bats and almost sent her away from the table. Jasmine stared right back at the woman. Her two companions were ready to pounce on her.

"Who is she?" Jasmine asked.

A corner of the woman's mouth came up. "Oh dear. It's nice to know someone here doesn't know me. Hel was correct -- you're a powerful thing, aren't you?" She left her side of the table and came toward Jasmine, but Leon and Micha jumped in front of her.

"You won't touch her," Micha seethed.

The woman put her up her hands. "Okay, boys. You don't have to tell me twice. It's good to see you, too, Micha." She ran her hand over Micha's arm and winked at him.

Jasmine caught the disgusted look from Micha. "Who are you?"

"I'm the one Dorothy melted, dearie."

The Wicked Witch of the West. The one that Dorothy supposedly had killed by throwing water on her. Her skin wasn't green, and she was very much alive. For whatever reason, her death had been expertly faked. The door opened. A waiter came in with a rolling cart filled with dishes. All went silent except for the squeaky wheel that made Jasmine cringe like nails on a clean chalkboard. As Jasmine looked at the waiter, she realized it wasn't the wheel, but his metal fingernails scraping along the side of the tray.

"That will be all. Leave the cart there, please," the Erlqueen told the waiter. He lifted his head. Jasmine got a look at his scarred face as he left the room. "Hess, would you mind checking to be sure the food isn't poisoned?"

The Headless Horseman rose and set the pumpkin head on his neck stump. "With pleasure, Kala." He lifted the dome on each tray, took a fork, and tasted a bit of the dish. After the last bite from the first plate, his grin turned into a grimace. The orange skin of his pumpkin head turned brown and shriveled. He dropped the squishy jack-o'-lantern onto the floor. It broke apart into slimy pieces and liquefied. Hess's body pulled out a handful of pumpkin seeds from a hidden pocket in his cloak. He pushed one of the bigger seeds into the gaping wound on the stub of his neck. A green sprout grew from the stump and formed into a large pumpkin. Hess grabbed a knife from the tray and carved eyes and a mouth again.

"All poisoned. Be careful of anything else you eat from the kitchen," Hess replied.

"Someone knows I'm here," the Wicked Witch whispered.

"Impossible. I made sure your arrival was cloaked. Not even Hess knew you were coming," the Erlqueen said to them.

"Even so. We should make this meeting brief. Boys, it's so good to see you again. Jasmine, I know you want to know why I'm here. Dorothy was supposed to have killed me. Obviously, she didn't. I had to fake my own death," the Wicked Witch of the West replied.

"Why?" Micha asked.

"Because Dorothy was getting too powerful. She planned to kill me one way or another. She assumed she'd drained all my magic. What she didn't figure into her plan is that an experienced witch stores their magic in case it's needed later. Dorothy duped you boys into thinking she was the best thing since sliced bread. Haley was head over heels for her. You, Micha, the bag of walking straw given life by my magic, had fallen in love with her, too. She had all Oz twisted around her little finger with that mutt of hers. Blown in by a freak storm and landing on my helpless sister."

"You and your sister terrorized the citizens of Oz. Now you're telling me you were beloved by all,"

Jasmine snorted.

She wasn't buying this bullshit. Jasmine didn't appreciate the witch making eyes at Micha. Prickles of power flared through her until her arm glowed. She pressed her nails into her skin as images of what she wanted to do to the woman wove through her mind. The heat of the magic filled Jasmine. The witch's mouth twitched into a smile. Her eyes flashed in amusement. Jasmine glanced at the Erlqueen. Her expression said she was waiting for Jasmine to lash out. A green ball formed on Jasmine's palm. It would be easy to make this horrible woman shut her mouth and stop making eyes at her man.

The seductive lure of the magic called to Jasmine. She opened her fingers, but Leon touched her shoulder. The pleading in his eyes made her back away. She snapped out of her rage. Yet the magic persisted. It needed an outlet now it had been stirred. It plunged down her arm, but she fought against it, trying to find a way to reabsorb it. Micha caught her around the waist and kissed her. The magic crept up her throat. The heat hit her heart and moved over her tongue. It charged her up and she wanted more of it as she squeezed her thighs together. The moan she wanted to let out was swallowed by Micha's kiss. She pushed against him as he pulled the magic from her until it felt like he sucked the air from her lungs. He broke the kiss and rested his head against her forehead. He trailed his lips down her cheek and nibbled on her ear. The sexual charge between them almost made her throw him down on the table and fuck him in front of everyone.

"Don't let them see your weakness. They want you to give in to the temptation of the power. The Erlqueen wants you to become like her. She lost her heart a long time ago. Please don't go down that road," Micha whispered to her.

"I don't know how to handle this."

Leon nuzzled her cheek. "Don't let the power use you. You have to tame it. Magic is what warped Dorothy. I don't want that to happen to you."

Jasmine squared her shoulders and faced the other villains. "You escaped Dorothy's wrath after she kept you prisoner. Where did you run to?" She tried to push off the display. The others didn't say anything, but the amusement in the witch's eyes made her uneasy.

"I escaped to the very place where Dorothy had come from. You asked about the book. I had to embellish a few things and change others around when I wrote *The Wizard of Oz*. Making up the persona of L. Frank Baum was simple. The people in your world are so gullible. They wanted more so I wrote multiple books until I grew tired of it."

"How could you pretend to be a man?" Jasmine asked.

She smiled. "I didn't pretend to be anything. I was a man. I shifted my shape and lived different lives, exaggerating things here and there. By then, I had stored enough magic, when I needed to shrug one life off, I became someone else. Your world was wonderful. I enjoyed many lives, even bore a couple of children. During that time, Dorothy had been in Oz for more than one hundred of your years. I made the book more of a modern setting to fit in with the times I was writing in. You need to kill Dorothy before she sucks every last ounce of magic out of the place. Glen-da is using the last of Oz's magic to keep the city standing. I can get you into my old castle without Dorothy knowing. I never told her about all the secret passageways."

"I don't think so," Micha snorted.

The door handle jiggled. The Erlqueen plucked a feather from her dress. It turned into a shadow bird and flew through the door. It came back in twice the size that went out. The knob shook again a little more fervently. The third time the whole door rattled. Something was determined to come in. The bird settled on the Erlqueen's shoulder and rubbed her cheek. Before she could say anything, the door exploded inward. The shock of the explosion knocked Jasmine to the floor.

Chapter Five

Something heavy landed on top of her. She tried to get up, but then was covered in darkness.

"Stay quiet and stay down," the Erlqueen whispered next to her ear.

She wanted to answer, but the commotion around her continued. The voices and the snarls made her wince. The Erlqueen gripped her hand and forced Jasmine to stay down when she heard Micha cry out and Leon roar in pain. When all went silent, the queen removed her cloak revealing the chaos of the room. The table was overturned. Hess's pumpkin head was smashed on the floor with a silver sword driven through his heart and spikes through his hands pinning the Headless Horseman to the wall. The Wicked Witch of the West lay on the floor. Leon stood in the center of four bodies as a lion with blood on his muzzle. His sides heaved. Blood matted his fur. The dead looked like some mixture of monkey and human.

"Dorothy." A low groan came from the Wicked Witch.

Jasmine knelt by her. "She did this?"

The witch nodded. "Finally killed me. Stop her before she destroys Oz. Take this. It's --" She pulled something from around her neck and pressed it into Jasmine's hand. Her hand went limp before the witch could explain what it was.

Jasmine half expected it to be a key, but it was a black crystal the size of her thumb. It warmed in her palm and dissolved into her flesh. She jumped like something had stung her. Black flowed into her veins until it mingled with the green of her magic. "What the fuck was that?"

The Erlqueen grabbed her arm and squeezed it

like a tourniquet until blackness arched outward and singed the queen's fingers. She pulled them away and sucked on them. "Shit. You're more of a match than the others ever figured out."

"What does that mean?" Jasmine asked.

Leon came over and trailed his fingers over the same spot where the Erlqueen had touched. "She's right. The Wicked Witch's magic couldn't have reacted as it did unless you were related to her in some way."

"That's impossible. Gert showed me a picture of my great-grandmother. The Wicked Witch told us she'd lived other lives and had children. The timing couldn't be right."

"Not unless one of her children had children and you're related that way." The Erlqueen let go of her arm.

Jasmine didn't have time to think about the magic and the theory she was related to the Wicked Witch of the West. If that were true, well… what did it matter? *I can't go down that road right now.* Her gaze swept the room. "Leon, where's Micha?" Panic rose in her stomach. He couldn't be gone.

"I tried to stop them, but there were too many. I killed three. Hess got another two before they overwhelmed him. They pounced on me, and I lost sight of Micha when he was fighting Haley. Somehow, Haley escaped the dungeons and pulled those damn monkeys through. They must've brought him to Dorothy which means they have the book. Jasmine, I can't let anything happen to him." The plea in his voice over losing Micha made her angry.

She took his face between her hands and kissed him. "We'll get him back. I promise. Whatever we have to do. I don't want to lose him either." She wasn't going to let Dorothy or Haley get away with this.

"He's right. You have to get Micha back. Dorothy will need him to open the portal to your world. She'll empty him of his power and then use it to fuel her diabolical plans. Once she has the gateways open, she'll drain the magic from all the lands she goes to. You need to stop her." The Erlqueen handed the feather cloak to Jasmine. "This will get you to where you need to go. I can't follow you there. Jasmine, doing this will make you the *ultimate* villain. If you don't want to succumb to the magic within you, remember to control your emotions. Use the cloak outside. Good luck and kick Dorothy's ass." The Erlqueen's shape changed into a nightingale. The window burst open and she flew out.

"Looks like we're on our own," Leon said to her.

"Looks like. We have to go after them."

"She's going to expect that."

Leon pulled Jasmine from the room. They walked into a corridor of dead convention goers and the flying monkeys that had hunted them down. People sobbed in the lobby. Jasmine and Leon moved through the carnage and into the elevators. The lurch of the lift made her stomach turn. Jasmine barely made it back to the room where she lost the last thing she ate. Leon handed her a towel. She wiped her face and caught her breath after what she had witnessed. She quickly went down the list of everything she knew. Micha was kidnapped. She had a black feathered cloak to get her and Leon to Oz. She might be related to the Wicked Witch of the West. That wasn't the important thing. They had to stop Dorothy. "Any ideas for a plan?"

"Do you have any regular clothes in that bag of yours? I want to be more comfortable. Some food, too. We need to keep our strength up. You especially if we're going to fight Dorothy."

Jasmine wiped her eyes, gripped the counter, and looked at herself in the mirror. She felt a million years old. Her body ached. Leon was right. She needed to be in comfortable clothes and eat to keep up her strength. As she thought about it, her purse morphed back into the backpack she had before. Jasmine pulled out a set of clothes for them both. Farther in, she came out with two brown bags. Her fingers nicked on something sharp. She grabbed a hold of it and pulled out the axe. "At least we have something they don't."

Leon set it on top of the cloak. "Yeah. That's a good thing." He took one of the brown bags and dug into it. Their meal consisted of a turkey sandwich, an apple, and a brownie. Jasmine stripped off her clothes and pulled on her jeans. She stopped when she noticed Leon staring at her.

"What?"

He swallowed the rest of his food. "Nothing. You're beautiful. Can't a guy take the time to admire his mate?"

"You should think about how we're going to get into the castle or wherever Dorothy's keeping Micha, freeing him, and then killing her. You can ogle me later."

Leon shrugged. "Can't help it." He pulled her close and kissed her. "I love you, Jasmine. Never forget that."

Her throat closed at the statement as emotion overwhelmed her. Jasmine pulled her shirt on and then devoured the food. The act itself allowed her to focus on chewing. It allowed the world to stop and let her calm down. Leon rubbed her shoulders which helped her relax more. It slowed her mind so she could concentrate on their next move. They couldn't stay in the hotel for long. Dorothy was likely to come back for them.

"Who do you think told Dorothy the Wicked Witch was here?" Jasmine asked as she poked at the apples. After being around the villains and learning poison could be in anything, it made her a little leery of the fruit.

"I've been thinking that myself. Micha wouldn't. Haley was in the hotel dungeons. Gertrude said someone had to be invited into this realm. It must've been someone here."

"Do you think it was Hess or the Erlqueen?"

"No. I think it was someone closer to home. Someone who has been waiting for the right time."

Leon got up and stripped off his clothes. It was her turn to regard his physique. Her first impression of him was completely off. He was not the meek man she'd thought him to be. He was stronger than he let on and had sacrificed a lot. Leon trailed his fingers over his jeans leaving ragged scrapes in the fabric with his nails. A pained expression went across his face. "I think it might've been Micha."

"Why would Micha invite Dorothy here? After everything he's done to keep Gertrude away from her, it doesn't make any sense."

"I don't have any other explanation. Nothing about this makes any sense." He brought his fist down on a table, cracking it.

"He was with us in the room the whole time. He defended you until you were both overpowered. He hates Dorothy. Micha wants to return to a home where there's no more war. It can't be him." Jasmine slipped her hands down his chest feeling the firmness of his pecs. He held onto her hands and kissed the back of one of them. Jasmine couldn't help the fluttering butterflies in her stomach from his touch. She kissed the side of his neck tasting the tang of him. Leon's groan turned into a purr. He turned his head and caught her lips, nibbling on the bottom one.

"If things weren't so pressing, then I'd take you right now." Leon looked up at her with his golden eyes that held the world for her in that moment. The tickle of her magic played over her lips as she deepened his kiss. Leon groped one of her breasts before he broke away. "We can't do this now."

She sighed and put distance between them so she could think as the magic receded. Each time it rose, she got better at controlling it. This time it was easier to grapple with it as the wellspring within her opened wider. Maybe it was the infusion of the Witch's magic that helped her gain more control. Being away from Leon helped her to breathe and to focus. "I'm sorry."

"Nothing to be sorry for. It's difficult for me to stay away from you or Micha. The pull is alluring and it's not your magic. It's all you." Leon leaned against the wall and ran his finger over the axe blade. "Maybe we're looking at this all wrong. Haley remembered who he was. You did that. You brought him back. Albeit, I think I rather liked him as the vampire who wanted to help us. He turned into a heartless bastard."

Jasmine giggled. "That's funny."

"Why?"

"Because in the book the Tinman has no heart. At the end, the Wizard gives him a silk heart filled with sawdust and puts it in the Tinman's chest."

"I really have to get my hands on a copy of this book you're talking about. I heard the witch say they made a film about it, too."

"Sorry, I forgot you don't know what a movie is."

His smile widened. "I'm just kidding. I know what movies are. Glen-da has some extra magic sometimes. He keeps her eye on Micha, so we discovered them. At certain times, he was able to talk with him and Gert. Sending messages back and forth. It was Glen-da's way of helping Gert look for descendants who came from Oz and directing them to certain potentials. We've been at this for a long time. Sometimes it gave us time for Micha and I to talk. It wasn't much, but it was something after being apart for so many years."

"After all the hardship you guys have gone through, then you know it wasn't Micha. It had to be Haley. He must've found some weakness in the dungeons. Or someone decided to help him. There were two other men in the room we popped into when we arrived. One of them could've done it. It seemed like they knew who you were. Before Dorothy went batshit, you guys were traveling to different places."

"Gert allowed the three of us to visit different realities. It was fun at first. I went along to keep an eye on Micha. He was so smitten with Dorothy. Dot was so saccharin. Something about her made me sick. I couldn't let anything happen to Micha. Back then he was only sticks and straw, but I loved him anyway."

"Gertrude said Dorothy turned her into the book. Why was she helping you?"

"The Wicked Witch changed her into the book. Maybe after all this time of being nothing more than leather and paper, her memory's started to fray at the edges."

Jasmine nodded. "She told me I was her last hope because she's losing her magic." She gathered up the axe and the cloak and stuffed them into her backpack. She slung that around her back and tugged on Leon's arm. "Let's go find out who let Haley out of the dungeon and let those monkeys in."

They took the stairs to avoid the carnage. Leon stayed close to her. Others passed them going down with suitcases in their hands. Leon tugged on the basement door. Several corpses fell backward from the door. One of them she recognized as being the Phantom when his masked head rolled off the pile and settled by her feet. Leon kicked it out of the way and helped her over the other bodies. The hallway had four cells and a small office at the front. Jasmine heard whimpering as they passed the office. Leon went on ahead.

"Wait. Wait. There's a girl here." Jasmine called him back and went behind the desk.

"Please don't hurt me." She held up her hands to ward off any more attacks. Her face was scratched, and her arms were bloody.

"We're not going to hurt you. We need to know how the monkeys got in here," Jasmine asked.

She pointed toward the cell at the end. "They came out of there."

"Did anyone come and visit with the man in the cell?" Leon asked.

She nodded. "Two people. A man with a mask on half of his face. Then another with a blue beard and a huge feather in his hat. They came down together, but they got into an argument. I couldn't hear what they said. A great wind came through the cells and the monkeys flew out. They killed everyone and took the man with the blue beard. The guys tried to stop them. I hid."

Jasmine handed the girl a tissue from her bag. "It's okay. You're alive and that's all that matters. Thanks for your help." Jasmine looked up at Leon.

"Blue Beard and the Phantom let him loose."

"I wonder what they were arguing about," he said to her.

"Does it matter? We know how Haley got free."

"No. It doesn't matter. Come on. Let's get away from this place. The death…"

They left the holding cell area and went out into the garden. The cool air helped clear her head. "We'll get him back." She reassured him and squeezed his knee. Next to them the bushes rustled.

Leon jumped to attention and growled. "What is it?"

Something dashed by in the shadows in front of them. Leon looked behind her and then she saw another figure dart by on the other side. Her power flowed under her skin, but she was too frightened to focus it. "What is that?"

"Stay here. I'm going to go check it out." Leon started to go off in the direction of the shadows, but she caught up to him.

"You're not leaving me alone in this place. I know how it works in horror novels. You leave to go exploring and someone gets killed. I'm not about to have that happen." Jasmine slipped her arm around him.

"No one is going to kill you tonight or any other night. I don't like the looks of this garden." Leon pushed the hair from her eyes and kissed the tip of her nose. "We need to get out of here." Leon tugged on her arm. They traversed the corridors of the hedge maze moving toward the center.

The foliage rumbled as they walked by. Leon was right. Something had turned. The atmosphere weighed on them. Taking a breath took twice the effort. Her skin tightened over her bones as though she were being stretched. She held onto Leon and stumbled as the shadows crept in. Ivy slithered over the pruned hedges. The verge wasn't as neatly trimmed as it had been earlier. Haphazard branches stuck out the farther they got into the maze. Her lungs were on fire with each breath. She grabbed her throat. The world tottered. Leon went on before her, but she couldn't call to him.

Jasmine fell to her knees and out came a squeak. Leon turned back around. His appearance wavered. He smiled as he held her hands. His golden eyes changed to silver filled with darkness. His caring face melted away to reveal that of a long, gaunt face with a bushy blue beard. He revealed his teeth or just the one tooth in the center of his top gums that was ready to fall out. His clothing changed to all black and ragged. His shirt smelled like death.

"Hello, sweetness. Don't you look tasty."

She shook her head to clear it. This had to be a bad dream, or some vision brought on by magic. "Leon," she forced out.

"Don't worry, little chickee. You'll be reunited with your pussy again. Dorothy wants to see you. Once she's done with you, then I get to have you all to myself. You're so pretty. I can't wait to see your lips wrapped around my c --"

Her head spun until she fell over onto the stone floor that was no longer the dirt from the hedge maze. As she went down, Jasmine caught a glimpse of castle walls and a woman in shadow. As the world turned, she went with it.

Chapter Six

Jasmine jolted awake when something cold was thrown on her. She sputtered as the water went up her nose. She took in a huge breath and coughed. When she opened her eyes, she tried to move, but her hands were bound above her head. The heavy weight of the chains hurt her wrists and the rattle made her wince. Micha was also chained across from her, but far enough away to be out of reach. Red marks riddled his torso and blood stained his shirt. He hung unconscious in his fetters. She could have sworn she saw straw sticking to some of the blood. Leon groaned next to her. He was barely aware and stuck between forms. A low laugh came from the shadows. She squinted to make out who was before her. The silhouette of a curvy woman stood before her.

"Don't worry about your boys. We'll have some more fun when they wake up. I hoped to talk to you so I didn't have to carve you up. Although it could be fun. You have some lovely unblemished skin. I'd love to see what your magic does to it. You could end up with some very nice tattoos. Maybe some nice green lines. You'd be pretty with a few spirals." The woman came into the light. A green dress clung to her form with a low neckline showing off her pale skin. Red hair curled around her shoulders that glimmered like blood. Under the pale skin, black swirls rose along her flesh and sank back down again. She twirled a knife on her fingertip.

She didn't like the idea of being carved up for anything. Jasmine tried to remain calm. How she was going to escape this and then save Oz from Dorothy. "Are you the great and powerful Dot everyone is so afraid of?"

The woman shook her head. "Hardly. I'm surprised you don't recognize me."

"Sorry. You don't look familiar, but then again I'm not real friendly with anyone who chains me up and threatens to torture me."

"You stepped inside me and read from my pages. I was the one who awakened your power."

"Gertrude? Y-you're human. How did you --?"

Gertrude smoothed her hands over her dress and admired her figure once more. "Become mortal again? Dorothy had a little bit of magic to spare and she needed me human. It was so tiring being a book and getting carried around all the time. The shit I had to come up with."

"What do you mean you had to come up with? I thought you hated what Dorothy had become. Why are you helping her?" Jasmine tried to sort it all out from what she had been told. She had been duped along with Micha and Leon. Maybe everyone. Gertrude was so good at telling tales she had learned to spin a few yarns along the way.

"Oh, I wish. Is that what I told you? I'm sorry. The Wicked Witch turned me into a book before she came to this realm with her sister. I'd been her slave for years. The Wizard got a hold of me. He used me to see the future and learned his fate. He knew Dot would turn on him, but I didn't let on how much I had seen. I learned I could influence the way of things. I never told him about the prophecy."

"You used Dorothy to become human again? Or you just got crazier as the time got on?"

"Funny. There were a lot of factors, but I kept things quiet about Dorothy coming and what might happen. As I said to you in the pages, I'm not fate. I can influence some things. Even now, I can see the rips in the realities and how to bend them. That didn't leave me. I was a book too long." She showed off her arms and black lines swirled around her flesh. "The ink of the world imprinted in me forever."

"What do you need me and the others for?"

"Gertrude has many reasons why she needed them. I have better ones, but you're the true prize." Another woman with a squeaky voice stepped into the light. If this was Dorothy, she was not what Jasmine expected.

Dorothy stood up to Gertrude's waist. Her nose and chin came to a sharp point as though they were chiseled by a blunt tool. Scars whirled her skin into off shapes and left a twisted appearance. Dorothy was no more than eleven or twelve at the most. She might have looked young, but her blue eyes reached into Jasmine's soul and stole her will. Dorothy smirked and released her. Jasmine kept her gaze on the floor studying the cracks after that. Her magic hadn't stirred. It had become a bit addictive and she wanted to find it again. She glanced up at the cuffs.

"Why am I your prize?" Jasmine asked.

"Gertrude, love, will you give us a minute, so I can talk to Jasmine?" Dorothy asked the other woman.

Gertrude brushed a quick kiss over Dorothy's lips. "Of course, dear. I'll check on the chamber and see how it's powering up."

Dorothy waited until Gertrude left before she addressed Jasmine.

"This chamber will allow you to cross between worlds? Or does it lead straight to hell?" Jasmine tried to summon the energy, but it remained dead within her.

Dot lifted a few feet off the ground until she was eye to eye with Jasmine. Her sharp nails scraped down

Jasmine's check. The grit of her skin made Jasmine cringe. "The chamber is not your concern. Gertrude has a knack for magical things that need a bit more finesse than I do. I really do hope we can do this without me having to hurt you. The boys... mmm... it's been a while since I saw the boys. They didn't want to tell me the things I needed to know. Since you and I are both from the same realm, I figured we could talk nicely."

"Nicely? You tried to drown me last night. You have me tied up and you want me to play nice!" Jasmine couldn't believe what she was hearing.

"I misjudged you. I apologize. Gertrude set up the conference, but she didn't know the Wicked Witch remained alive. When I hit Helena with the water, she melted. At least she got that part right in the book. I guess Helena used some of her stored magic to lay low. She certainly fooled me."

"Yeah, I never figured I'd be meeting *the* Dorothy from Kansas and her little dog Toto. You and I both know all this small talk is you buying time."

Dorothy snapped her fingers. The shadows peeled away and reassembled into a mastiff with drool hanging from the sides of its mouth. An overbite showed off its curved canines. Its claws scraped the stone floor and left gouges in the bricks. She petted the mutt. "Good boy, Toto. Do you like your new chew toy that Momma brought you?"

Toto hacked up a hairball and spat out a hat with a long feather. Toto bumped against Dot's leg until she scratched behind his ear. His hind leg thumped against the floor. He rolled over, exposing his belly. She rubbed it until his tongue lolled out. "Not the Toto you were thinking of. He's gotten a couple of upgrades over the years because he asked for them. He didn't start off as the wimpy little terrier Helena would've made you think he was. He was a mutt my father didn't want me to feed, but I raised him. When we got here, the magic affected him, too. He turned into a big dog the size of a Great Dane but filled out like a Mastiff. He didn't let anyone get near me. He got a bit more in tune with the magic here, and it changed him in the ways he wanted."

"Great. Nice dog. What do you want with *me*?"

"You're the key to opening the portal. I can go home."

"So you can rule Earth?"

Dorothy's expression grew somber. Jasmine wondered if the ordinary girl remained under all the twisted flesh and she really did just want to go home. Maybe she had gotten lost somewhere in the power that gripped her. Jasmine kinda felt sorry for her and wondered what she'd do in the same situation if she had been left in a strange world with only her dog. If all accounts were real, then Dorothy did land on the Wicked Witch of the East. She and Micha had been in the house when they first landed in Oz to take shelter after nearly being eaten by a plant monster. Everything she learned before stepping into Oz and the realm of Dracula was that nothing was what it seemed. All her family history she knew growing up was also a lie. Well, not really a lie. She wanted to believe what Helena told her about being related wasn't true, but when the Wicked Witch shared her power with her, Jasmine had no doubt they were connected. Toto whined, and the hardened expression returned to Dorothy's face.

"Ruling the world we've both come from isn't my first priority. The thought crossed my mind. I've been watching the politics and it's too messed up even for me. No, my dear, I want to drain its magic. Your realm doesn't understand mystical things. I've seen your scientists try to study strange phenomena and call it science of the paranormal. They have no idea what they're really getting into. So much raw energy. It could fuel my work for decades."

"Okay, so you want to get some energy from Earth and use that to rule the world. That doesn't tell me why you need me or why you've tortured Leon and Micha." Jasmine glanced around. Leon looked at her, listening to their conversation.

"Ahh… yes. You -- a descendent of Oz and Earth -- are the only one who can open the gateway. Not between just Earth and Oz, but every realm. The strange combination flowing through your veins makes you very special. It makes sense because you're related to Helena. She was also from another world. She and her sister landed in Oz, and it changed them. I want to go home and grow again. This body isn't all that it's cracked up to be. I love Haley, but I've never been able to *be* with him. Do you know how difficult it is to love someone and not be intimate?"

"Why not use the silver slippers and get yourself out of here?"

Dorothy smirked. "The Wizard melted them down to make the pen he gave to Micha to make him smarter. Gertrude helped the Wizard craft the pen. Even imbued it with her magic. The other was turned into the axe Haley carries. Haley didn't have it when Blue Beard rescued him from that awful dungeon. Micha didn't want to give me the pen, but he finally did after a little bit of convincing. Leon swears he doesn't know where the axe is, but you do. Blue Beard said it's in your magic bag." Dot twirled her wrist and held up the backpack. Jasmine felt the blood drain from her face. If Dorothy had the axe and the pen, then there was no telling what she could do.

"Did it ever occur to you if you do go back to Earth, then you'll age and turn to dust?"

"Of course, it has. That's why I need the pen so I can rewrite part of my story. If the pen doesn't work, then I can chop out portions of my life story with the axe and fill the gaps back in. I don't plan on dying once I go back to Earth. Besides, it'd be nice to see some of the sights. Maybe check out the old homestead and pay my respects to my aunt and uncle."

"I bet they'd turn in their graves at the bitchy little cunt you've become," Leon growled.

Jasmine shot him a look hoping that he would stay quiet.

Dorothy sauntered over to him. Toto remained at her side. "Leon. I know you never liked me. You only came on our adventures to look after Micha. I respected that, and I put up with it because he was like a little puppy dog nipping on my heels. I made it quite clear I had no interest in him, just Haley. Micha had the pen and Gert, so I humored him. She wasn't too keen on me in the first few days until we got to talking and realized we were kindred spirits. She wanted to become human again and I wanted to age. Gertrude investigated the future and she saw a way to do it. Nevertheless, the stars had to align with that tricky prophecy within her pages. Try as she might, she could never change it. We waited all these years for everything to come to fruition. Now she's been freed. You brought my Haley back to me. I have the pen *and* the axe. Glen-da barely has a leg to stand on. With these tools, I'll take down Emerald City and the rest of the magic he sits on and nothing you can do will stop me."

"Stop *us*. I don't see that happening." Haley appeared from the shadows. He put his hand around Dorothy's shoulders and kissed her with a passion that made Jasmine throw up a little in her mouth. It was bad enough Dorothy looked like wizened grandmother.

"Of course, darling." She ran her finger down his chest. Sparks of power fell to the floor. Haley shivered and glanced at Jasmine. "Love, I'm a bit peckish. Do you mind, or do you need her intact?"

Dot flashed him a wicked grin. "A couple of sips to ease your hunger won't hurt. I do need her to think for herself."

Haley's cool demeanor changed as his eyes reddened. His mouth dropped open as he showed off his growing fangs. "I'm going to enjoy this."

Jasmine whimpered as his canines grew. The monstrous appearance of the vampire came out. He flicked his tongue along her throat. She tried to shimmy away from his pointed tongue, but even as she craned her neck the slimy appendage moved across her flesh. Leon roared. Haley turned and hissed. It happened so quick she barely registered the pain when he struck. His mouth locked onto the wound and he pulled. She'd grown used to Micha taking blood from her during their lovemaking. It pained her a moment and then it was euphoric.

Jasmine wailed. Agony gripped her soul as though Haley had latched onto it and tried to pull it out through the wounds. Her veins felt like barbed wire was dragged through them, ripping them apart. She heard herself screaming but couldn't stop as she struggled to get away. The warmth from a reservoir of magic inside her empowered her. Even though the fear of what Haley could do to her burned in her mind, the sear of the magic lit her veins. She wanted him dead for violating her. Power built within her. She couldn't move her hands to blast him, but she had learned if she pictured it hard enough, she could conjure the same effect. Jasmine pictured the green energy flowing through her veins. She was not his dinner. She poured her intention into the thought. Every drop would be lethal. The cries she heard were no longer her own. Haley clutched his throat. His mouth opened to say something. He dropped to his knees as red stains formed on his shirt. Her blood melted his insides.

He gasped as his throat dissolved. Haley tore at his shirt, revealing the place where his heart should have been. He reached out to Dorothy. She dashed over to him and tried to pull him into her arms, but he liquefied. Jasmine struggled to get free of her bonds. The heat within her hadn't died. When she glanced at the rest of the occupants, Leon slipped the shackles and bolted. He wouldn't abandon her. Her gaze fell on Micha. He was alert and watching them.

"I guess he didn't have a heart after all," Micha chuckled as he gestured to Haley with his chin.

Dorothy got up slowly. Whatever remained of Haley clung to her black dress. Jasmine caught the evil look on her face. Dorothy twirled her wrist and lobbed a purple ball of energy at Micha. It penetrated his stomach. He convulsed and slumped down. A few stalks of straw fell out of his wound. His flesh took on a brown appearance. When Micha lifted his head, one large black button and one blue eye stared at her from a skull that was half human and half fabric. The human he'd become was disintegrating. It broke her heart to see him that way. Dorothy hit him with another ball of energy until he shrieked.

"Have no heart? You never knew him. His heart

was bigger than anyone's. He loved me even though I was this." A small flame grew in the center of her palm. "It's time you were undone, Scarecrow. If I remember correctly, you've always been afraid of fire." Dorothy shoved her palm into one of his wounds. Although, the straw didn't catch because it was wet with his blood, Micha howled in pain.

"Stop it!" Jasmine screamed.

Dorothy turned to her. Gone was any semblance of humanity within the girl's eyes. Her warped outside reflected the thing she had become on the inside. "Would you take his place?"

"Jasmine, no," Micha whimpered.

"I'll do whatever you want as long as you leave him alone," Jasmine pleaded with her. She didn't know if Dorothy had noticed Leon's absence, but she wasn't going to mention it. "I can't let her hurt you anymore," she told Micha.

"Very well." Dorothy threw the fire at Jasmine. It grazed her cheek. The intense pain made her hiss. The smell of burnt hair made her sneeze. "No more stalling. You're going to open the portal. I will be gone from this accursed place and --" She glanced at what remained of the Tinman and shook her head. "-- Find someone else to rule with." Dorothy waved her hand. The chains released Jasmine from the wall. Dorothy took hold of them and tugged.

Jasmine didn't dare go over to Micha in case the psycho decided to harm him again. She stumbled after Dorothy who dragged Jasmine through the dark and twisted halls of the castle. Jasmine tripped over large ropes scattered across the corridor. The ropes climbed the walls and were embedded into the stones of the castle each branching off into different sections of the fortress. Jasmine caught the soft luminosity of a light source as they passed several rooms. Large crystals nestled in the rooms inside a bed of vines. She focused on one and felt the tingle of energy trapped within. *I bet that's where she's storing the magic she's stolen.* Before she could think about it anymore, she was pulled onto the roof.

Wind whipped around them and pushed the hair into her face. In the center of the platform was a large crystal the size of a Volkswagen with black tendrils growing from it pushing into the bricks of the castle. Other vines twined over the stones and back through the windows to feed the other crystals. The countless tentacles looked almost like the plantapus that attacked them when they first landed in Oz. Gertrude stood on the other side of the crystal. An opaque pink opening fluctuated in the heavy breeze. On the other side were black ribbons that could have been paved streets. Metal objects flashed in the sunlight. Jasmine figured they were cars. The roots thrummed with power and made her teeth her ache. The side of her face hurt where the fireball had scorched her.

"You okay, Dot?" Gertrude asked.

"Haley's dead."

Her gaze flicked to Jasmine. "What happened?"

"Her blood poisoned him."

Gert hugged Dot, but Dorothy pulled away and wiped her eyes. Her expression grew cold once more. "He served his purpose. He would've been a burden for me in the end. How is the portal?"

"It's good. You'll be able to leave through the gateway once Jasmine's activated it," Gertrude told her.

"You're not going with her?" Jasmine asked.

"Of course not. I've been in your world long enough. I prefer this one much better. Besides, Dorothy will need someone to keep the candle burning, so to speak, if she needs to get back here. All the energy stored here will need to be replenished. I hadn't quite figured out how to remotely connect to the stored crystals. That will come in time."

"That's enough chitchat, Gert. Don't need to be giving away all our evil plans. Didn't you learn something from planning that villains' convention of yours? At least we sussed out Helena," Dot replied to her.

"Yeah. Helena's finally dead, but we couldn't get the Erlqueen. She flew out of our grasp."

"Stupid bitch was trying to get in on what I have going on here." Dorothy tugged on Jasmine's chain.

Jasmine snickered. "I don't think so. She, Hess, and the Wicked Witch wanted to take you down. They know you've been draining magic from this world and encroaching on their domains. They weren't going to stand for it. I'm not going to let you go to Earth and poach its magic either." She rubbed her hands together from the cold to warm her numb fingers. Her own magic sparked. Her palms warmed, but she couldn't make it do anything.

"It won't work. Those cuffs are ensorcelled against any type of magic. You can concentrate until you're blue in the face, but those shackles won't let you get the magic into your hands. Your trick in there with Haley was ingenious, but you'll pay for it in the end." Dot smiled and showed her off yellowed and crooked teeth.

"Be careful, Dot. Your inner hag is showing," Jasmine jabbed at her.

Dorothy threw a bolt of energy that struck Jasmine's shoulder. She grunted and stumbled backward over one of the roots, landing on her ass. The tendril broke where she tripped, and light exploded out of it. The illumination seared her skin with raw power. Jasmine held the shackles over the flux of energy. The metal heated up. As the cuffs glowed red, they burned her wrists. The immense pain nearly made her black out, but she held her hands over it until the chain melted. She pulled them apart and tried to regain her footing. Once the chain was broken, she felt the power rise within her.

"I don't think so." Gertrude waved her hand. One of the tentacles wrapped around Jasmine's legs.

"Enough fucking around," Dot spat. She reached into her cloak and pulled out a small golden dagger. "Gert, are the pen and axe in place?"

"The pen is ready, but I don't have the axe. I thought you did."

"Where the hell is it?" Dorothy asked Jasmine.

"Right here." Leon threw the axe. The blade struck Gertrude in the center of the chest.

She looked down with a startled expression and tried to pull it out. Her fingers disintegrated before she could touch the handle. Her body collapsed in on itself and the breeze scattered her remains to the four corners of Oz. Dorothy ran at him with curved hands to claw him, but she also stumbled on the roots of the large crystal. Jasmine scrambled over the vines and grabbed the axe. Its power zinged through her arms. The manacles glowed from the power and broke. The pain from the burns receded. Dot charged Leon, but he had transformed back into the lion. Hs swatted at her with his massive paw. Jasmine brought the axe down on top of the large crystal. A blast of energy rolled off the main battery. It flared through the vines connecting the others to it. Dorothy spun around, and her lips twisted into a scream.

"No. No. What did you do?"

Jasmine tried to pull the blade from the large stone, but the metal from the axe had melted over the crystal's grooves from the force of the magic stored in the main crystal. The portal collapsed without the energy to sustain it. Leon rushed over to her, but Dorothy waved her hand. The roots dragged themselves from the stone and wrapped around him. He struggled to get out of the vine cage as they tightened around him.

"You shut down my only way of getting out of this place and yours. Oz is a prison you can't escape from. The East and West sisters could never return home."

"But you found a way," said Jasmine.

"Gertrude was my way. She had the ability to open small slits between dimensions. It's how I kept track of her and her progress on finding Helena's descendants."

"So, you could send your minions through."

"Had to keep Micha motivated somehow. Now all the monkeys are dead. I sucked the magic out of them, too."

"You're done. The magic will go back to where it came from."

Dorothy cackled. All she needed was the pointed hat and she would fit the stereotypical witch. "Magic won't resurrect the dead. I'm going to take it from you. Then I can repair the damage." She pulled out a red crystal from around her neck. "I should've done this in the first place. Although, I'd hoped you might want to join us since you have Helena's blood in you. She was rotten to the core." Dot cupped her hands around the crystal and whispered a few words into it.

Jasmine slipped by her and tried to remove the

roots that cocooned Leon. They writhed on top of him like long black eels. They tightened when she touched them. The air grew heavier with the magic like it would trigger a storm. It just needed a spark to ignite. Power raged within her. As she was about to pull on her magic, something stung her. Jasmine saw a red leech fasten onto the glow of her power working its suckers deeper, aiming for the core. Once it did, she was a goner. Jasmine thought about how she would generate a storm and she had no idea what the consequences would be.

Jasmine thought back to the magic panel at the villains' convention. There were different types of magic, but sometimes magic went on frequency, sounds, or the feelings. Pain started in her chest. She could see the leech latched onto her power working deeper.

"You can't fight it. I've already gotten a hold of you. You're strong even without Helena's power."

Jasmine ignored her and stayed focused on the energy around her. The magic escaping from the crystal dissipated. Her arms grew numb. She felt hollow, as though she was being sucked out from the inside. Something clicked as she pulled the last of the energy she could muster. A word slipped from her mouth. As it came out, the power left her in a rush. Darkness threatened her. Dorothy screamed. Magic combusted in blue and purple flames that danced after Dorothy. The flames engulfed her in a quick burst. The heatwave knocked Jasmine over and she hit her head.

Chapter Seven

Something thumped her cheek. Jasmine opened her eyes and found herself looking into Leon's gold ones. Elation rolled through her knowing he had survived the blast. She wrapped her arms around his neck and buried her face into his shoulder. He hugged her harder.

"It's okay. It's all over. Dorothy's dead."

"Ding dong, the witch is dead," Jasmine muttered.

The crystal was nothing but smoking bits and pieces scattered around the rooftop. The magic siphoning roots had shriveled from the heat. A pile of overdone clothes was all that remained of Dorothy. Jasmine poked them with her foot and hit something. Leon grabbed her hand before she could touch it.

"Whoa, we don't know what that is, and I need to make sure you're okay." He tilted her face up to his and kissed her. She could taste the magic on his lips and the animal on his breath. The smell of the lion mingled with the musk of a man. She stared at her hands and all the burns had healed. Her whole body felt different.

"I'm okay. What about you?"

He traced his fingers over her cheeks. "We need to get Micha. I tried before, but I wasn't able to break his shackles."

"Let's go get him." They went back inside the castle and she glimpsed the other crystals. All the crystals had exploded save one. The tendrils died around it, but there was still life in this one. Something within it called to Jasmine, but she couldn't focus on the whispering she heard coming from the crystal. They found Micha slumped in the chains that bound him. He appeared more scarecrow than human. His wounds hadn't stopped bleeding. Crimson-stained straw stuck out from the gashes. The color of his flesh was ashen. Some of it was burlap blended into the flesh of his face and across his chest.

Leon touched his arm. Micha opened his one human eye as the black button one looked brittle.

"You're alive," he wheezed.

Leon struggled with the shackles until they snapped. Jasmine touched the side of Micha's face that was human. "Don't touch me. I --"

"No... shh." She pressed her lips to his, feeling the softness of his mouth and the itchy burlap, but also the tang of the blood and dirt.

"You're free, love. We have to get you to Glenda. He'll know what to do." Leon lifted him from the chains.

"It's too late for me. Half of my stuffing is gone. I can barely feel my limbs. Dot did a number on me. Is she dead?" Micha asked. "I want to see for myself. Help me out there so I can see her remains as my dying wish."

Leon looked at her with a pained expression. "We have to get him back to Glen-da. I -- I can't lose him."

Jasmine nodded, trying to think of a way. "Where did you get the axe from?"

"It was in the other room with the intact crystal."

"Was my bag there?"

Leon nodded.

"Good. Take him outside. I'll meet you there in a minute."

Micha cried out when Leon picked him up to help him walk. They went out slowly and turned toward the landing. Jasmine felt the call of the crystal and found the room with her bag among other artifacts. One of them was a mirror. She touched the surface and a face appeared.

"How may I serve, my queen?" the voice boomed.

"Shit. Umm… not a queen."

"Then how may I serve you, not a queen?"

"Can you go anywhere?" Jasmine asked, not really believing she was talking to the real magic mirror.

"Anywhere there is a mirror if madam wishes it. On one condition."

"What is that?"

"Take me with you. I don't wish to rot in this hellhole for the rest of my eternal life."

She glanced at the mirror as it leaned against the wall. The full-length mirror wasn't something she could carry around. "How? I can't lift you."

The face in the mirror smiled. "Watch."

The mirror glowed and shrank down to the size of a compact. The face remained in the mirror. "Now you may transport me anywhere you wish. What is it you want of me?"

Jasmine shook her head. "I need you to go to the Emerald City and deliver a message to Glen-da. Tell him, 'Dot is dust and Micha's dying. We need you to be ready for us.' Can you do that?"

"As you wish, with your word that you'll take me with you."

"You have it." She snapped the mirror shut when the face disappeared.

Among the other spoils, she found her bag. Jasmine stuck the mirror inside her beaten up backpack and found the feathered cloak from the Erlqueen. She slung her pack on her shoulder and stopped at the crystal. Jasmine slid her fingers over the top of it, feeling the rough surface. Pink energy flowed from the crystal and into her. As it filled her, some part of her felt complete once more. Her magic had been returned to her. Maybe the rest of the magic could be returned to where Dorothy stole it from. The light within the crystal burned out and the stone cracked. She glanced at the other treasures in the room. A set of glass slippers rested against a large golden egg. The head of a silver stag guarded over the treasures along the wall. Heaps of gold in one corner appeared to be smoking. She moved closer and the pile moved as a head lifted up from under the gold. Jasmine stopped not sure what she was looking at was real. The creature's blue eye blinked at her.

"Are you going to keep me as a trophy as the others who have won this castle before or will you free me?" The deep voice wound though the hall.

"What are you?" Jasmine asked.

"I'm a dragon, silly witch."

"Do you eat people?"

"Only when I'm hungry."

"If I free you, will you swear not to eat anyone?"

"As you have won me, I am bound to do as you ask," the dragon replied, but didn't seem happy about it.

Jasmine wasn't sure what she was getting herself into, but it sounded like this creature had been kept a prisoner by the Wicked Witch of the West and Dorothy. She couldn't let it stay cooped up. "Okay. Go to Glen-da in the Emerald City. I'm sure he can make a deal with you on providing you some livestock to eat instead of people. If you can do that, then you are free to go."

The dragon shivered. It grabbed something in its

mouth and dropped it at her feet. A bag overflowing with gold coins and jewels. "I will do as you ask. My gift to you for freeing me. Treasure beyond what you can see."

"Thanks, I guess." Jasmine grabbed the heavy bag and put it into her backpack. She didn't have the time to look through the prize. She had to get back to Micha and Leon. More coins slid from the pile as the dragon moved. Jasmine left him to free himself from the room.

Jasmine rushed out to the men and found Micha in Leon's arms, holding a large black book. Micha was nothing more than a sack of straw. Even his human eye had turned back into a button.

"He's dying. We have to get him to Glen-da," Leon told her. His eyes glistened.

Tears stung her eyes as she looked at her two lovers. Emotion clogged her throat. She wasn't about to let him die. If he did, then a part of her would also die. She pulled out the cloak. "I don't know how this works, but the Erlqueen said it would get us where we needed to go." Jasmine pressed herself to Leon and flung the cloak around them. "Emerald City," she told the cloak. Her feet floated off the ground. The cloak tightened around them until it felt like a second skin. She could still feel Leon and Micha next to her. Her body grew light. They lifted from the roof and the castle grew smaller. Jasmine caught a glimpse of the gold dragon flying in the opposite direction. She hoped she did the right thing by freeing him. Her feet touched air and Leon held onto her tighter. The world whizzed by and yet they didn't fall out of the cloak's grasp. When she looked at the ground, the shadow they cast was that of a large bird.

The aerial view of Emerald City showed battered

walls. Crumbling emerald spires were darkened from attacks. The land around the city was barren and the hills blackened. A dry riverbed wound close to the city. The sun reflected off a rainbow bubble over part of the city, but as they got closer, small holes could be seen where things had punched through. The cloak took them lower. Glen-da waved at them as they approached. Seeing him gave her hope. They landed in a courtyard. Once their feet touched solid ground, the cloak burst into hundreds of birds and flew away. Glen-da gestured for Leon to give him Micha.

"You have to save him. He's fading fast," Leon told him.

Micha's chest still went up and down as he breathed. "Come on." Glen-da ushered them into the castle.

Jasmine and Leon followed Glen-da to an untouched part of the city. They entered a room where the sun hit the dome that covered the room and cast a green glow over the chamber. A long altar stood in the middle of the room. The energy in the place hummed. Glen-da laid him on the surface. Micha moaned. Leon knelt next to him and put the black book down. Jasmine stood behind him. Her fingers trailed over his shoulder to give him a little bit of comfort. She couldn't lose Micha any more than Leon could.

"Can you help him?" Jasmine asked.

"He's really far gone. I'm not sure even I have the magic to do it. But --" Glen-da tapped his pink lacquered nail to his chin. "But you could help me. Both you and Leon, because you love Micha."

"I'm not magical in anyway," Leon whispered.

"It doesn't matter. You love him and that's a magic in itself. You three have shared experiences and are bound by laws even I can't break. This is the most sacred place in all Oz. It's where the magic of this land originates. Dorothy couldn't tap into the very heart of it. It's what helped me keep the Emerald City. It can aid in his restoration, but you need to keep in mind how you want to build the magic around him. You can either have him as the man he was or the scarecrow."

"I just want him alive. I'll do anything you want," Leon replied.

"Place your hands over his heart and take one of his hands," Glen-da instructed him.

"What about me?" Jasmine asked.

Glen-da led her away from the altar. "You've changed from being in Oz."

She shrugged. "I guess. I don't care about me. We need to save Micha."

"Do you love Micha? I know you've been together, but he brought you here. Micha's different. I saw what happened in Dracula's realm. You helped him deal with it, but I need to hear it from you. Do you love him?"

"I don't want him to die. I didn't think I'd love him when I first met him, but yes, I do."

"Good. I was concerned at first. It's why I locked you in the room with him when you first came here, so you could grow on one another."

"I'm glad you did. What can I do to help him? "

"Your power bubbles under your flesh. I'm exhausted to the max. This place is the only thing that's kept me going. I tap into it when I need to. Then you came along and freed us. I'll need your help."

Jasmine glanced back at Leon and saw him whispering to Micha and his tears flowing freely. Micha's chest rose and fell hardly at all. "I'll do whatever I can."

"That's all I can ask for."

They went back to Micha. Glen-da placed Jasmine's hand over Micha's heart so her fingers touched Leon's. The energy passed between them. Leon looked into her eyes and she could see his hope. Micha's chest lifted underneath their combined hands, but she didn't feel his heart beating. Glen-da stood at Micha's head which was now just a sack with lackluster black button eyes with heavy thread stitched into a badly formed mouth. Jasmine's eyes burned with tears and so did her heart. When she looked back at Leon, there was nothing but love in the lion shifter's eyes for the bag of straw. Glen-da said some words that Jasmine didn't recognize. The light in the chamber focused on the table. Glen-da dropped his arms.

"Something's missing."

"What?" Leon growled.

"No one has used this temple in ages. Besides, the last time we did, it opened a rift and brought Dorothy through," Glen-da told them.

"What do you need?" Jasmine asked.

"A large emerald that resembles the city. It went missing around the time the Wizard was killed."

"Shit. I think I know where that is." Jasmine dug into her bag and pulled out the emerald Gert had given her. "Is this it? Gertrude gave it to me."

"That minx. Yes. It focuses power. It must've been what linked her to Oz. Smart cookie."

"Glen -- please!" Leon urged him to stop talking and focus.

"Right. Sorry." Glen-da placed the crystal in a small divot by the top of Micha's head.

When the sun's rays hit the gemstone, they refracted around the room and struck a central crystal above them that bathed the space in emerald light. A rush of power flew up Jasmine's spine and made her giddy. Glen-da said the words again. Leon held onto her hand as their fingers entwined over Micha's heart. The rush left Jasmine with a near orgasmic feeling and yet she felt it settle in the center of her being. The magic sparked around the dome like they were in the center of a lightning storm.

Glen-da touched their hands. "Bring him back from death. Let your love for him rebuild what he was."

Jasmine remembered him in her mind, reimagining him as a man. His attitude and loving gaze and how much he adored Leon. The way he touched her while making love. Even with him being an ass. A bolt of energy hit her. It worked deep within her soul and she could feel the lock on her own magic unravel. The rush of energy needed to go somewhere, so she concentrated on Micha. The roughness of burlap morphed beneath her fingers until it became smooth flesh. Magic continued to fill her. It needed to go somewhere.

She unwound from Leon and stepped away from the table. A green glow engulfed Micha, resurrecting him as a human. She didn't know if this reawakening banished the dark taint of the vampire from his soul or not, but it had brought him back to her. Jasmine didn't know what to do with all the power. It turned her into a lightning rod. She groaned as it expanded her and brought her to her knees. The core of Oz below her still contained magic, but everywhere else cried out for it. She brought her hands down and touched the parched earth. The land sucked up the energy greedily as Jasmine gave back the magic so it could spread throughout the realm. Forests and fields needed the power to thrive once more. Evil creatures still lingered in the shadows. Dorothy had done a number on the place. Jasmine wanted to restore it. This was the first step. The magic ebbed and left her feeling wrung out. Jasmine collapsed as the power left her. Glen-da helped her up and over to the slab where Leon hugged Micha to him.

"You okay?" Glen-da asked.

"I don't know. Feel kinda small. I guess."

He nodded. "Magic will make you do that the more you stretch it. You went to the edges of this land. You did the right thing by putting the magic back. You could've used it for yourself."

Jasmine shook her head. "No one person should be able to control that much power. I can see why Dorothy became as twisted as she did."

Glen-da patted her shoulder. "Good girl. I'm proud of you."

"Will Oz recover?"

"Yes, but it'll take time. I can divert the magic to where it needs to go from here. Right now, be sure all is well with your two men. I'll prepare some quarters for you guys. I'm sure you want to get some rest after all you've been through."

Jasmine smiled. "Sleep would be good. And food. I guess. Nothing that's poisoned."

Glen-da smiled and put his hand on his hip. "Do I look like that old crone from Snow White? Bitch, please! She wouldn't be able to pull off this outfit." He gestured to the full-length black ball gown topped with a pink corset.

"I guess not," she chuckled.

"This calls for a celebration. I'm going to put the word out. Have fun recovering with your fellas." He swished out of the room.

Jasmine walked over to her mates. Micha separated from Leon when she got close. "You're all better."

"Thanks to you. I was a straw away from being dust." Micha lifted her hand and kissed her palm. "You saved my life. Thank you."

A rush of warmth flashed across her cheeks. "I think we're about even now on saving one another. I'm just glad you're better. Don't forget that Leon helped."

"Jasmine, I owe you more than thanks. I also owe you an apology for how I acted when we first met. I brought you here against your will. I was a dick because… well, I didn't know."

"You did it at first to save me from Dot's monkeys. How many girls get to tell their friends they've been in their own fairy tale and killed Dorothy Gale?"

He chuckled. "True. But you did and now Oz can start on its road to recovery."

"You're not mad that you're not a scarecrow anymore, are you? I couldn't see you as cloth and straw as the magic was healing you. Did we erase the vampire in you, too?"

"No, I don't mind. Being this way lets me be with you, but I'm not sure about the vampire. We'll have to see." Micha kissed her with a passion that caught her off guard.

"Actually, we're a package deal." Leon turned her away from Micha and kissed her in a slow burn that made her lips ache. Micha slipped behind her sandwiching her in-between the two of them and nipped her throat.

"What do you say? I think we're a little overdue for some celebrating."

"I think you're about right," Jasmine answered as she relaxed knowing they were all going to be okay.

"Follow me," Leon led them from the temple,

through the city back to his room. Jasmine remembered it from when she first came to Oz. It was surprisingly warm even with the large fireplace not lit. In the center of the room was a lion sculpture on top of a large round table that almost looked it was ready to pounce. Micha walked over to it and ran his fingers over the wooden carving.

"I forgot you did this," he said.

"I've done others, but this was always my favorite. Can you light the fire, Micha? It does get a bit chilly in here." Leon asked.

Micha said something and flicked his hand. This was the first time Jasmine had seen him do magic without using the magic pen. He turned and flashed her a knowing smile. "I still do have a few tricks you don't know about."

Jasmine burst into laughter. It felt so good to joke and not have more life-threatening moves hanging over her head. All she had to do was exist and not worry about getting chased, eaten, or killed. She could be with the two men she loved. Leon grabbed her around the waist and pulled her into him. He pushed the hair away from her neck and kissed her throat. A loud purr tickled her ear.

"You were remarkable today the way you handled everything." He dragged his hands over her sides and up over her breasts. His sharpened nails ran furrows in her shirt. Leon nipped her flesh. "I need you."

"What about me?" Micha asked. "Don't I get a say?"

Leon glared at him and held Jasmine closer. "Mine." A low growl came from behind her. He picked her up and tossed her over his shoulder.

"Leon, put me down," she said to him, but he

tightened his grip on her and went into his bedroom. Another fire burned in the fireplace. Jasmine poked him in the back, but he didn't stop. Instead he deposited her onto the bed. She sank into the soft mattress. He stripped off his clothes as he came over to the bed until he was naked. His eyes glowed golden. Jasmine caught Micha standing in the doorway, watching their interaction with a smug smile on his face. "Enjoying this?"

He nodded and licked his lips.

Jasmine rolled her eyes, but Leon tugged at her shoes and threw them across the room. He struggled with her jeans as he tugged one leg off. She grabbed his hands. He grumbled in frustration and tried to break away from her. "Let me do it." She leaned up and kissed the back of his hand. That seemed to appease the beast within him. Leon released her hands. She took off her jeans and panties. His eyes burned with his satisfaction as her hands moved over her still-clothed breasts, then took her shirt off and worked on opening her bra. He licked his lips when she was naked before him. Then he pounced. He pushed her back onto the bed and buried his face between her breasts. His rough tongue swiped over one nipple and then the other. His hands roved over her hips, and then he cupped her pussy.

He bit down on her nipple. Jasmine cried out as his thumb found her clit. "Leon, God."

He looked up and smiled at her. "You're already wet for me."

Jasmine trailed her fingers over his face feeling the light velvet of fur instead of flesh. His cheekbones were more angular. His eyes were more spaced out and rounder as the lion meshed with him. "I'm already yours, my mate."

He growled contentedly and claimed her lips. Before she could pull away, he opened her legs with his knee and pushed his cock into her. Jasmine rose up to meet him and groaned as he entered her. He pushed his tongue into her mouth. His hands went underneath her and lifted her up. Jasmine wrapped her arms around his neck and held on while they moved together. He bit her bottom lip. She wrapped her legs around his waist and glanced over his shoulder to see Micha, naked, stroking his cock as he watched. Leon pushed inside of her and rubbed along her clit at the same time. She groaned and kissed Leon's throat. He didn't stop and brought her higher into the orgasm as it grew closer. He increased their tempo and she could barely onto her sanity. She raked her nails down his back feeling the magic within her sparking. It raced within her until it tingled on her fingertips and engulfed the both of them. Once it hit her, Jasmine bit down on his shoulder. Leon roared as she came. The magic left her in a rush and the fire flared out of the hearth. Leon held her tighter as he moved inside her until she stopped shivering. Jasmine tasted a bit of blood on her lips and licked the place on Leon's shoulder.

"Oh, my beautiful mate!" He shuddered and moaned. "You do know how to please me."

"Biting you gets you off?" Jasmine asked.

"It reinforces you chose me as your mate. It pleases me very much."

"I'm glad. Do you think we should invite Micha to join us now?" Jasmine asked.

"It's only fair he watches since you tormented me." Micha sauntered over to them. His dick pointed at them.

"He has a point," Jasmine joked to Leon.

Leon rolled his eyes and shimmied off her. Jasmine sat up as Micha came forward to join her on the bed. She put a hand on his stomach and traced the defined lines of his lean muscles. He flashed her a questioning look. She gave him a small smile and took his cock into her hand. The power flared along her hand as she called it into her palm. Jasmine made a conscious effort to control the magic in her hand. She touched his length and he grabbed her shoulder and rocked on his feet.

"What the hell is that?"

"Guess I have a few tricks up my sleeve." She trailed her finger along the outline of his shaft.

"Great trick, but I'm not sure I can hold on."

Jasmine clutched his balls. Micha quivered once more. "Maybe I can make you." She took his cock into her mouth and swirled her tongue over it. The tingling of her magic stayed in her palm as she kept holding Micha. She concentrated on not tipping him over the edge. The energy stayed in her hand as her mouth went lower, taking him in until he hit the back of her throat. Leon purred next to her. His hand traced her inner thigh. Jasmine tried to ignore his soft caress. She dragged her teeth over the smooth skin of Micha's dick. Her scarecrow slid his fingers through her hair as she drew him in and out, taking as much of his length as she could. His breathing intensified. Micha thrust his hips forward and moaned, but he didn't come. His fingers dug into her shoulders.

"You need to… I -- I can't…" Micha stammered.

Leon's finger found her clit one more time and rubbed her. Jasmine couldn't hold onto her magic. Instead she took Micha into her mouth one last time. Leon kissed her shoulder and massaged her clit. Jasmine drank in Micha's seed as he came. She released his cock and quivered from the pleasure that seared her. Leon rubbed her once more and she cried out.

"I love it when you scream," he purred.

"Me or her?" Micha asked as he collapsed onto the bed next to Leon.

"Both," Leon said to them.

Jasmine rolled her eyes and lay back on the bed.

Micha traced her breast. "You want to go another round?"

"I think we could." Leon kissed her shoulder.

"You two are devils," Jasmine replied.

Chapter Eight

Jasmine dragged her fingers over the emerald altar. The tips tingled from the remaining magic embedded in the room. It lingered in the very air leaving a light copper taste on her tongue when she breathed. Something niggled on the edge of her newly awakened magical power. She couldn't put her finger on it. In the past couple of days, she was strongly pulled back to the crystal room where the magic waited for someone to use it. Micha and Leon were spending some time alone together. She needed some breathing room from both men. Glen-da was in party planning mode. The holes in the dome around Emerald City were healing. Her foot hit something. She cleared away the debris and found a black leather book the size of a large hardcover. The magic embedded in the leather ran over her fingers. Her stomach turned at the feeling of the power. This wasn't anything good. The design on the cover was an embossed face, but it kept shifting its expression.

The echo of heels sounded in the room. Jasmine glanced behind her to find Glen-da walking in.

"Those two too much for you to handle?" Glen-da giggled.

"No. Just giving them some alone time."

"And you came here?" He twirled a string of long pink pearls in his hand.

"Let me take that from you."

Jasmine handed him the black leather book. Glen-da tapped his fingers on the outside of the book and then pulled them away quickly. "Bitchy little thing. Guess Dorothy didn't like being turned into a book. Serves her right after all the shit she pulled. If anyone gets their hands on Dot, then she could do a lot of damage. I can keep her here."

"What makes you say that?"

"That's why you were drawn here, wasn't it? The portal that's opened in the corner. I told you last time anyone used this place it opened up a gateway. Lord knows what else came through, but the entryway remains open. I wonder if you might be holding it open." Glen-da ran the pearls over his lips.

"Is that even possible? I still don't even know really what I'm doing or how to control the magic."

"Anything is possible with magic. You have some idea how to bend it to your will. If not, Micha wouldn't be restored, and you wouldn't have been able to push the magic back into Oz."

She shrugged. "I guess, but it's not like what you read about in books. I expected there to be a set of rules and magical language I'd have to learn."

"Of course, it's different. It's not all fairy godmothers or wizards hiding behind curtains. There are rules and theory, some of which I can teach you if you stay. If you leave, then I'm not sure what your powers will do. They could grow or go dormant if you decide to return home. Your realm does have an enormous amount of untapped magical energy."

Jasmine rubbed her arms over her shoulders as the words sank in. Going home loomed at the edge of her mind. Getting back to Earth had been her original goal when she got to Oz, not falling in love with two storybook characters. "I didn't think about it, really."

"You *are* the reason the portal is staying open, then."

"How am I doing that?"

Glen-da squeezed her shoulders. "Because part of you wants to go home."

"Sure, part of me does want to go home. But --"

"What about your two boy toys? What about the magical potential you have? Do you go back to the boring day job you've had all these years? Or do you say fuck it, stay here, and figure out how unpredictable your life has become?"

"Sounds about right. You read my mind?" Jasmine shifted away from him.

"Not exactly. It's flashing across your face. Darlin', it's not easy being here and trying to figure out the rest of your life."

"Can't just click the heels of my slippers together and make it all easy." She laughed.

"Do you know how much of a bitch it was to melt those suckers down into the pen and that stupid axe?" Glen-da kissed both of her cheeks.

Jasmine looked at him as a strange smile spread over his features. "Gert told me that the Wizard melted those down and Dorothy killed him."

Glen-da winked. "Maybe she did. Maybe she didn't. Stories are funny that way. They can change depending on who tells them. Sometimes other people are behind the curtain, too. Take some time to think about what you want to do. Celebrations start tonight at sundown. Speaking of celebrations, I had a visit from a most interesting sight. One I thought had been extinguished from Oz -- a golden drake. He said he was freed by a powerful witch who won the Wicked Dorothy's castle. Instead of claiming him as a prize, she released him with the promise to come to me about arranging his feeding habits. Know anything about that?"

Her cheeks burned. "Sorry, I forgot to mention. Yeah, he said he ate people. I figured you might know of a place where he could hunt deer or something."

"I've already directed him to a location. I think

you made a friend of Vein."

"He gave me a bag of gold and jewels. I haven't dug it out yet."

"He saw you had a good soul by letting him go. The idea of power and wealth didn't trap you as it did the others who trapped him before. Good choice sending him my way."

"Thanks."

"No worries, love. Now, I've chosen a dress for you. See you at the celebration." He waved his hand as he walked out of the room.

She slid down next to the altar with the black book. Jasmine set the book on her knees and opened it. The first page was blank. She turned to another page and dark ink appeared.

Hello, Jasmine. Do you like what you've done with me?

"Dorothy, Glen-da said it was you, but I wasn't sure."

In the flesh. Or, well, in the pages. Dorothy's words appeared on the page.

"I didn't do this."

Of course, you did. You wanted to punish me for everything I did to you.

She didn't disagree with that. "What now? You're going to learn how to rewrite the future of the lives around you."

Heh! I'd love to write you out of existence, but I don't have that kind of juice. Although, I did figure out something that rubbed off from Gert. Looks, like I have a knack for opening slits in other universes or telling stories. Writing scribbled onto the page as Dot shared her new abilities.

"You're the one keeping the portal open to Earth."

Ding. Dong. Looks like the little witch is smart after

all.

"You don't need to be a bitch about it."

Why not? I'm a fucking book thanks to you. Why don't you go home -- back to the life you're really meant to be living? The boys don't love you.

"That's not true. They love me."

Really?

"You're just being a cunt because you're a book."

Once upon a time lived an ordinary girl who lived a humdrum life, avoiding papercuts until one day a hunky man kidnapped her and threw her into a book. Little did she know, she would end up traveling from Oz to Dracula's realm and meet the Tinman, the Scarecrow, and the Cowardly Lion. Nothing was what it seemed. The evil witch wasn't actually dead. The girl is a means to an end for the Scarecrow to finally reunite with his true love and kill the Tinman and save Oz from the conniving Dorothy. Even though the ordinary girl had grown to love the Scarecrow and the lion, deep down she knows she's nothing to them.

Jasmine nearly threw the book across the room. Tears burned her eyes at reading the words, but she knew Micha and Leon loved her. Her lion marked her for his mate, and Micha's vampire side was only aroused by those he loved as they discovered after they brought him back from death. She couldn't let Dorothy get into her head.

"Say what you want, but I know the truth. They love me or we wouldn't have been able to restore Micha. You can take your twisted tales and shove them."

Maybe you do love them, but you've had a taste of magic. You want more. Once it has a hold of you, you'll forsake everything and everyone in order to drink in the power. Bathe in it until it consumes you. One day, you'll be as twisted as I was. Dorothy seemed to be laughing at her.

"It'll never happen." Jasmine threw the book across the room until it slid into a pile of old dried leaves. Dorothy's words made her take in a slow breath. The worlds rang true. The magic within her called to her to use it. *I won't become like her. I'll be a good witch.*

* * *

Jasmine sat on the bed as she stared out of the window. Fireworks boomed above. Rainbow displays changed shapes and colors as they exploded in the night sky, illuminating the city itself. When she'd looked down off the balcony earlier, people gathered inside the city and camped outside the walls. More were coming. Glen-da sent out a call for celebration now Dorothy was dead. He didn't want to announce Dorothy had been turned into a book. It was easier for the regular folk to believe she'd been killed. Micha and Leon were helping him out, leaving Jasmine to roam the castle. Dot's statements stung her mind about her magic.

"Jasmine, are you in there?" Leon's voice came from the other side of the door.

She thought about staying silent, but she hadn't seen them all day. Instead, she opened the door and put her best smile on, brushing away Dot's words. "Hey."

His brow lined with worry. "What's the matter?"

"Nothing. Is everything okay?"

Leon hugged her. Jasmine buried her head in his shoulder. The tears she'd been holding back came out in a flood. He rubbed her back and murmured to her until she calmed down. Jasmine stepped away from him embarrassed she had lost it. "Sorry."

"What's the matter, love? You can tell me and

Micha anything."

"I don't want to become like Dorothy. I don't want to be the Wicked Witch of the West. I want to be a good witch. With all this magic, how is it going to affect me? I don't want to hurt either of you."

"Where is this coming from?" Leon asked.

"Where is what coming from?" Micha came in and slid his hand around Leon's waist.

Jasmine noticed the gesture. It only drove home the point of what Dorothy had said that Micha and Leon used her. "That all this new magic is going to corrupt her, and she's going to end up like Dorothy."

"That's ridiculous, Jasmine. Did she put this in your head?" Micha took her hand and kissed the back of it. "The power might whisper to you, but it works on what's already in you. She was a bad egg to begin with. You're nothing like her."

She wanted to believe them. "Are you sure? It scares me, Micha, because I can hear it whispering to me. It wants me to use it."

He touched her face. "It whispers to me, too, but you get used to it. Soon you'll be able to turn the volume down like I do -- the way Glen-da does -- until it's second nature. We can help you do that." Micha kissed her. "We love you and won't let anything happen to you. It's also a reason why we came to find you. I know we've been busy helping Glen-da, leaving you to wander the city."

Leon took her hand and led her over to the balcony, so she was sandwiched between him and Micha. "Glen-da told us about the open portal. He said it could take you home if you wanted. But -- we want you to stay with us. Or if you decide you want to go home, we're coming with you." Leon pushed the hair from her face. Another firework exploded in the background that made her jump.

"Come on. You need to see something. This will prove what I'm saying about your magic." Micha grabbed her hand and pulled her after him. They walked through the castle until they came to a large door. "Leon, do you still have access?"

"I do." He pushed on the door and it opened, revealing rows of bookshelves.

"What is this place?" Jasmine asked.

"It's the greatest treasure Oz has. Dorothy was never able to crack it. I think it's the way Gert figured out how to jump into different stories. She spent a lot of time in here."

"What are we looking for?" Jasmine glanced around as Micha led her farther into the library. They stopped at one row and went in about five shelves. Leon plucked a book off the bookcase. He sat down on a sofa and patted the cushion. Jasmine settled down between them. Leon placed the book on her lap. The cover was silver with golden text that kept morphing so she couldn't read it. The volume felt familiar.

"What is this?"

"It's your story." Micha ran his fingers over hers.

"How is this possible?" Jasmine asked. "Are all these lives of different people?" She almost didn't want to open the book and see what was within the pages.

"Only special books get shelved. This library is kinda between places. If you happen to be special enough, then one appears. It doesn't lie, and it shows you what happens next. Do you want to see?" Leon asked.

She held her breath and opened the book. Words blurred on the pages as she looked at them, but the title page stood out.

The Accidental Fairy Tale

Jasmine chuckled. It was some sort of odd fairy tale she had found herself in. She flipped through the volume and found the words were readable in the middle of the book. They said she wasn't going to turn into a monster. They believed in her. She wasn't sure she believed in herself.

You don't need some evil villainess turned into a book to get into your head. Stop doing that. Live your life. Remember what the Erlqueen said, Open your heart. Deep down you already know you won't turn into the evil queen.

"If this is my story, how can the book be talking to me?" Jasmine asked.

"Books are funny things. They like to tell stories. Who says whoever is writing them can't interject once and a while?" Glen-da's voice came from behind them. "Sorry to interrupt, but I came in here to make sure this gets locked away safely." He held up the black book that was Dorothy.

"Is that a good idea?" Leon asked. "She could hatch another evil plan."

Glen-da held up the package. "She's wrapped up and spelled so she can't break out. I have a secure place in the back where nothing will get to her. She'll be safe. Finish what you were reading and come meet me on the Great Balcony. All Oz wants to see the heroes who saved us from the Wicked Dorothy." He blew kisses at them and left the library.

Leon tapped the page to draw her attention back to Jasmine's life story. "Do you believe the book?"

Jasmine looked into his eyes and saw his love. Micha squeezed her shoulder. Her fears had been abated. She didn't need to listen to Dorothy. They believed in her. She had to believe in herself. She sighed and closed the book. "I don't need a book to tell me how to live my life." She put it back on the shelf. "I make my own destiny with the help of the men I love."

Micha nuzzled her neck. He trailed his fingers over her arms and the energy crackled between them. His power and hers mingled. Leon kissed her. In their arms she felt complete. "Then we're glad to be along for the ride. How about we get ready for whatever Glen-da has in store for us? I'm sure he'll have us dancing the night away."

"Sounds good to me." Jasmine kissed Leon and then turned to kiss Micha. Together they walked her back to her to her room. She slipped on the dress that Glen-da left for her. The material was almost black or purple. She couldn't tell from the light. When she looked in the mirror, Jasmine didn't see the woman who'd gone on the disastrous camping trip. She was someone completely different, and she was okay with that. An idea popped into her head and she grabbed the compact from her bag she had brought from Dorothy's castle.

"Mirror, mirror in my hand, who is the fairest in the land?"

A face appeared in the reflection and rolled its eyes. "Don't tell me you're going to be one of those? I'll tell you right now I'm not doing the fairest of them all gig anymore."

Jasmine laughed. "Sorry. I couldn't help it."

"Very funny. What can I do for my lady?"

"Can you keep an eye on things in other realms to see if trouble is lurking?"

The corner of his mouth turned up in a smirk. "You want me to be your watchdog? I don't do woof woof."

"Look, I'm not asking you to sit and stay. I just have... a feeling I don't know. If you see something off that might be coming this way, can you let me know?

It's not like I can throw you a treat."

"We can work on that, but for now I shall obey."

"Thanks." She snapped the compact shut. "Damn, fairy-tale objects have attitude!"

When the men knocked on her door again, she didn't stop them. They were both dressed in suits that took her breath away. They went into the main hall as a group and found Glen-da dressed in his finest gown and a pink cape with a high collar.

"Come on, my lovelies. They whole of Oz is waiting."

"You ready to do this?" Micha asked her.

"Think so."

"You'll be awesome," Leon reassured her.

She interlaced her fingers with theirs and they stepped out onto the balcony together. A crowd of thousands cheered them on as fireworks exploded above them all. Glen-da raised his hands and the crowd silenced immediately.

"These are the magic ones who delivered us from the dark cloud that's been hanging over Oz for all these years. My friends."

The crowd applauded.

Jasmine looked at the men she loved. A line she had read before went through her mind:

Once upon a time, there lived an ordinary girl…

Well, she wasn't so ordinary anymore.

Crymsyn Hart

Crymsyn Hart is a national bestselling author of over eighty paranormal romance and horror novels. Her experiences as a psychic and ghostly encounters have given her a lot of material to use in her books. Vampires, grim reapers, shifters, and other paranormal creatures tend to end up in her books no matter how hard she tries to keep them away.

She currently resides in Charlotte, NC with her hubby and her three dogs. If she's not writing, she's curled up with the dogs watching a good horror movie or off with friends.

Crymsyn at Changeling: changelingpress.com/ crymsyn-hart-a-188

Changeling Press E-Books

More Sci-Fi, Fantasy, Paranormal, and BDSM adventures available in e-book format for immediate download at ChangelingPress.com -- Werewolves, Vampires, Dragons, Shapeshifters and more -- Erotic Tales from the edge of your imagination.

What are E-Books?

E-books, or electronic books, are books designed to be read in digital format -- on your desktop or laptop computer, notebook, tablet, Smart Phone, or any electronic e-book reader.

Where can I get Changeling Press E-Books?

Changeling Press e-books are available at ChangelingPress.com, Amazon, Apple Books, Barnes & Noble, and Kobo/Walmart.

ChangelingPress.com-